Flying Hero
Class

Flying Hero Class

THOMAS KENEALLY

Hodder & Stoughton

LONDON SYDNEY AUCKLAND TORONTO

ACKNOWLEDGEMENT

In the making of this fiction went some experience and a certain diffuse reading. Four works in particular provided valuable intelligence, and the author would like to express his debt to them, and *their* authors:

Dreamings by Dr Peter Sutton;
The Jigalong Mob: Aboriginal Victors of the Desert Crusade by Robert Tonkinson;
Bible & Sword by Barbara W. Tuchman;
Dispossessed: The Ordeal of the Palestinians by David Gilmour.

The last work provided the basis for the fictive backgrounds of Hasni and his colleagues, as relayed to McCloud.

British Library Cataloguing in Publication Data

Keneally, Thomas 1935–
  Flying hero class.
  I. Title
  823[F]

ISBN 0-340-53147-9

Published by Hodder and Stoughton, a division of Hodder and Stoughton Ltd, Mill Road, Dunton Green, Sevenoaks, Kent TN13 2YA. Editorial Office: 47 Bedford Square, London WC1B 3DP.

Photoset by Rowland Phototypesetting Ltd, Bury St Edmunds, Suffolk

Printed in Great Britain by BPCC Hazell Books Ltd, Member of BPCC Ltd, Aylesbury, Bucks.

To my daughter Margaret,
for her splendid research into the minds
of hijackers.

CONTENTS

A question heard amongst Western Australian desert
Aboriginal tribes:

"Who dreamed you,
Carried you,
Set you down?"

Prologue

THE remote Australian tribe called the Barramatjara had two early brushes with Christianity, one so different from the other as to make the tribespeople question whether Christianity was one entity or a series of intrusions from remote space.

For some reason Benedictine monks from Spain had, in the last years of the nineteenth century, conceived an ambition to bring the Barramatjara to Catholicism. The Benedictines travelled with camels on the tracks of the first European explorers, four-square British travellers who had not intended to blaze a trail for Papism, who were good members of the Established church or of rugged non-conformism.

But on the Western Australian coast, the Benedictine monks had already found an echo of Spain and – as had been the case with Spanish missionaries in California and New Mexico – it grew to be a matter of urgency for them in the name of Catholic Spain to find the furthest place and the furthest people. They were not frightened off by the prospect of either thirst or the spear. Their Saviour and their template had already died of thirst and the spear upon the cross.

The Benedictines brought lay brothers who were carpenters and who built the remotest boys' and girls' dormitories in the world out of sawn planks, transported from the coast by camel. The dormitories were meant to separate the Barramatjara young from the calls and rituals of night, of marsupial rat and banded possum, of euro and wallaby, of blue-tongued lizard and crow, of numbat and desert eagle.

A century later, Frank McCloud, manager of the renowned Barramatjara Dance Troupe, imagined Dom Estevez, the abbot of the

Barramatjara, patrolling the dormitories on horseback by night, a carbine on his shoulder to prevent the kidnapping of his students and their bearing away for instruction in the older initiations.

Dom Estevez – it needed to be said – also had the humane intention of saving young girls from marriage to the older men to whom they'd been promised in childhood.

Reading briefly into the history of the Benedictine Order in Australia, McCloud was informed that by abandoning the coastline to the heavy-handed Irish priests, the Benedictines would lose their sway over the nation as a whole. But it was as if they were conscious of the sacrifice and were still content, if it came to a choice, to hold its Barramatjara core.

In the early years of the twentieth century they ordained eight of the Barramatjara Dance Troupe's great-grandfathers and -uncles priests. Vestments and chalices were shipped from Catalonia and carried across the wilderness by camel train to be employed in the ordination of the Barramatjara priests. As Pizarro strangled the King of the Incas, the Spanish friars now sealed up the lips of the Barramatjara with the sacraments of Christ.

The priesthood didn't take with the Barramatjara however. Dom Estevez, riding around the thirsty borders of the Gibson Desert to visit his parishes and priests, found chalices tossed under bushes, dispensed with as no good for holding water. He would discover sets of vestments – the red of Martyrs, the white of Virgins and of the Requiems of Children, the black of Easter Week and of the death of adults, the purple of Lent – all these gifts of devout Spaniards to the remote Barramatjara priests – cut up and distributed amongst various elders. Estevez records his shock at finding a Barramatjara man out hunting and dressed in a cutaway green Sundays-after-Pentecost chasuble. The priests themselves had taken wives from the neighbouring people, the Arritjula, whom the Benedictines had not yet instructed in the mysteries of faith.

Estevez was not a narrow man, although his grief now was heroic in scale and put him in the way of his own death. He wrote in his notebook: "They are not guilty, because they are the most complacent race on earth. When they were under my training, they did everything they could to please me and to believe courteously what I believed. What I took to be an understanding of Catholic dogma may have simply been politeness. And likely they were polite to any old man in the wilderness who asked them for their Lenten vestments, and to any woman who offered herself."

*   *   *

After the failed ordinations, Estevez stayed on in Baruda a further three years, Vicar-General for the Barramatjara. But he had lost credit with his superiors. Some of the lay brothers were withdrawn by their superiors in Spain, and donations were sporadic. Even in Barcelona the faithful could sense the unsuccess of the mission to the Barramatjara. The Barramatjara were no longer interesting or hopeful pulpit-news.

In the end Estevez himself, with his one remaining aged lay brother, was ordered back to the coast. As he went into his dotage on the shore of the Indian Ocean north of Perth, the dormitories built to separate Barramatjara children from the mysteries became prey to sandstorms and termites and Barramatjara people looking for wood for their campfires.

For the next twenty years many of the Barramatjara lived on in Baruda, addicted to rations of tea and sugar, flour and tobacco doled out by the Protector of Aborigines, a government official.

Baruda, after all, lay at the meeting place of two dry creek beds, and there was always water there, if not on the surface then in deep waterholes. So what the Barramatjara called "big ceremonies" could be performed there, when people from all over the region, united by some common ancestors – by the Two Brothers, for example, who had pierced each other's nasal septum with a bone just two miles out on the Easter Creek road; or by Malu the Kangaroo Man – could collect in large numbers.

The burden of European presence was next taken up by cattlemen. Many of the younger Barramatjara scattered to cattle stations at the eastern end of the desert country and earned their rations rounding up cattle. The Barramatjara worked with the cattle for eighty years. Few of them listened to their Arritjula relatives from further north, who had found work in bauxite mines and who believed *that* to be the best way to absorb the impact of the newcomers, to work them out, to find a way of living with them. The horse- and cattle-mustering was the way the Barramatjara chose. The way of cattle had been ordained for them by the dreams some of their elders had. The way of mining had not been ordained by any of their dreams.

In the early 1920s, German Lutherans appeared at Baruda. Using trucks, they had crossed the arid stretch from Alice Springs in the east. To get through sand bogs, they used matting which they laid under the wheels of their vehicles. Like Estevez, they were men of powerful character. Like him too, they built dormitories for the young men and women.

They would stay there for fifty years.

All the Barramatjara remembered Pastor Freiniemer who protected them from massacre in the '20s and '30s, who made himself unpopular with cattlemen by demanding better terms for those of them who worked as stockmen further east. They considered him one of those mystifying whitefeller Christians, so different from the whitefeller miners and cattlemen, since he frowned on booze and fornication, the preferred activities of the others. Less mystifyingly, he frowned on brutality as well, more than he did on their mysteries. He was moderately loved by them for it.

It had been in Freiniemer's dormitories that most of the Barramatjara Dance Troupe took their first instruction as Christians. McCloud the troupe manager could imagine them accepting it all in the same spirit their grandfathers had accepted ordination from Estevez. Attending services with their native politeness. Absenting themselves in the bush however for three months at a time for the big ceremonies of initiation.

Even early in the tour, before he was further enlightened on the matter, McCloud liked to think that the Barramatjara were now on their own mission to those who lay in that outer dark which went by the name of Europe and America.

1

BEFORE THE TAKE-OFF

IT always surprised the troupe manager, Frank McCloud, how calmly they sat. In their big first-class seats, all of them, even tormented Bluey Kannata, looked as self-contained as rich children. They had conquered New York, and it was hard to know what that meant to them. Now they were going – composedly – to Frankfurt. There the full-colour programmes had already been printed up in a language Whitey Wappitji and the others had no familiarity with.

The troupe were calm about that venue too. Here, at the start of their flight, they were suffering no pre-performance trembles for the sake of Frankfurt. They never seemed to hold any narrow post-mortems that McCloud could see, or blame each other for mistakes on stage. They didn't worry about the perversity or mental blinkers of critics.

It was clear to McCloud now, at the close of their New York adventure, that they suffered from dreads and obsessions of their own; Whitey and the Christian Phil and the movie actor Bluey. But they lacked the sort of self-absorption artists were supposed to have. *Their* show business was in some ways more light, more casual than show business itself. It was something they did without fear. It was as familiar as buttoning a shirt.

McCloud noticed too this night of the take-off from New York how Whitey Wappitji, the man of authority and – if there was such a thing in this troupe – tacitly recognised leader, sat in his large aisle seat, hemming in high-living Bluey Kannata from the good things which would soon be rolling up the aisle on the cocktail trolley.

In a jazz bar in the Village, just ten days back, Bluey – a man famous quite apart from his dancing – had asked McCloud, "You reckon I could get any work as a gigolo round here?"

"Here? In New York?"

McCloud was sure he was joking. Bluey was – as he'd frequently proved – the jetsetter of the troupe. Still, you couldn't help but wonder what knowledge of dream trails in the deserts could lead Bluey, the only Barramatjara gigolo in New York, along those complicated streets down there, in SoHo and Tribeca? Or up the island, for that matter, where the streets were all on a grid and dubbed with numbers but were just as treacherous?

Bluey had been born in the centre of an old and apparently barren continent, on a dry river four hundred miles from Alice Springs. He was made from the blood of people who could paint and dance well before anyone else could. The oldest painters then, the oldest dancers.

But here he'd been in the jazz bar in Greenwich Village, weaving to the industrial-strength music and saying *gigolo*!

McCloud had asked him, "Have you ever been one before?"

"In Melbourne," Bluey asserted. "After the picture finished."

For Bluey had been a star in a number of films, but "the picture" was the first one, the one which made his name, the one which film societies gave special screenings of wherever the dancers turned up. In fact in New York, a city which had taken to the Barramatjara Dance Troupe with passion, the film had been revived and shown on one of the networks. No doubt a print of it, dubbed in German or sub-titled, was waiting for their arrival in Frankfurt and would appear on local television during the dance company's run.

Bluey could tell McCloud was sceptical.

"I was a gigolo bloke six months," he confessed – with that brittle levity which was his style. "Got in the shit with the old blokes back home." He said that a lot, that he was regularly in trouble with the Barramatjara elders back in the desert. And the other members of the dance troupe made veiled remarks of the same kind about him.

"I was at it six months," said Bluey. "And listen, don't get the wrong impression, mate. I met nice ladies. They were just fed up with hanging round with yobbos, that's all."

And so – Bluey Kannata: negligent tribesman, sublime dancer, movie star, believer in curses, gigolo bloke! Hemmed in now aboard this flight and for his own health by Wappitji. Because Bluey could take on an edge of bitterness, give off a hot breath of anger, or even see phantoms whenever he was allowed too much bourbon.

*   *   *

14

Behind Wappitji and Kannata, also strictly composed and already wrapped in a blanket, sat the musician Paul Mungina, who had managed to bring his *didjeridoo* on board with him. The *didj*, as Paul familiarly called it, was a tube of wood, carved and painted with totemic designs. From it Paul could evince a sound audiences of all stripes thought of as straight from the earth's most antique lungs. If the mountains talked, you would believe, those ground-down Barramatjara mounds of ochre forty times older than the Alps or Rockies, they would have spoken through Mungina's *didjeridoo*.

Curiously, the *didj* came from the tropic north, not the deserts the dancers considered their home. White settlement had mixed peoples up. But whatever evils it had visited on Mungina, it had alerted him to the existence of the *didj* of the northern tribes, in which instrument he had become an easy master, a sort of joking James Galway of the holy tube of eucalyptus wood.

Paul's *didj* was not at his side at the moment but had been stowed in the closet up the back with all the businessmen's coats!

Beside Paul Mungina sat the sober Philip Puduma, who was both a tribal elder and a devout Christian. He hadn't attended jazz clubs or seemed to be much tempted at all by terrible New York. Sometimes he had complained in a small voice about how bitter the city's autumn was.

Then, third row from the nose cone, McCloud had the aisle, and the fifth troupe member, a renowned horserider and stock drover in the Barramatjara country, a man named Tom Gullagara, nicknamed Cowboy, was already asleep, sitting formally straight in the window seat. A quiet, measured drinker, a man who waited in the corner for women with the wit to find him, Cowboy Tom had lived high in New York, but without making the sort of noise about it Bluey couldn't help himself making.

McCloud himself had for his various reasons stayed up late in New York, even by the standards of performing groups. His vision was now ochred and speckled from whisky excess, and he thought he might even have a minor tremble. He had needed throughout the tour to keep an eye on the fragile Bluey, and to be with the troupe in the small hours when they were looking for somewhere to go. Apart from Phil Puduma, who'd suspected the city's Satanic openness, they loved New York for its business-at-all-hours air.

McCloud's own guilty sense now was that his wife Pauline had assumed the role of, or been manoeuvred into being one who kept office hours and rose early to talk to bus companies or make airline reservations – all this even though she was not on the tour payroll. She didn't always go out with them on those late-night adventures. Her professional sense told her that someone had to be at the base in the hotel, ready to take to the streets if necessary to explain to policemen Bluey's volatile blend of innocence and worldliness. Someone had to explain in emergencies what they would never themselves explain, that they were not *brothers* in the New York sense. They were not party to either the wisdoms or the griefs of the black underclass. They were Barramatjara tribesmen, and their history was sad, yes, but – even by the standards of this city – fantastical.

Not that there were problems worth mentioning during their New York nights. Yet too often McCloud arrived at Pauline's bedside in a brittle condition to find her sleeping lightly, and with a frown, as if like a doctor on call, prepared for interruptions.

McCloud's experience of New York, the city which was now an unregarded wet blur outside Tom Gullagara's window, hadn't earned him tranquil sleep, and he knew that all night over the Atlantic and Ireland and Western Europe he would be hollow and tremulous and remorseful.

To start with, Pauline was at the back of the plane. He'd hoped that seat vacancies up here would leave him a chance to approach one of the stewards. "My wife's back there – you see, my ticket's paid for by other parties. Whereas she's travelling at her own expense. I wanted her to switch seats but she's determined. I don't suppose she could . . ."

The naïve impulses of McCloud's imagination could too readily envision her in a large seat, appeased by the superior booze and food of this end of things. The informed regions, however, projected the exact frown she would wear above the luxury items, wishing she had the proper amplitude of love in which to relish them.

In wanting Pauline up here, at the front of the plane, McCloud couldn't help favouring his simplest suspicions. They were his only source of guidance, and had failed him so consistently in the past that he was addicted to them, sealed to them by habitual pain.

All around the troupe, square-jawed and tired-eyed businessmen were disposing their fancy briefcases in lockers, or slinging wads of computer printout negligently onto their seats, data to be devoured during the flight, indices to their coming success in West Germany. The most notable figure, however, was a handsome Japanese woman of about thirty or perhaps even thirty-five years.

She was ridding herself of her coat, putting it into the hands of a steward.

She was a chatterer, and the tendency seemed to have been wound to a high pitch by – perhaps – the exhilaration of this journey. She talked a lot in a cowboy drawl which marked her as an American Japanese. What did they call them – Nisei, Issei? She couldn't have been in business like the eaters of data. For she was dressed exactly the wrong way for flying on business – in an undulant green dress suitable only for a cocktail party.

"Why thanks, honey," she told the steward who had taken her coat.

Even in the chastened condition his New York experience had put him in, McCloud felt an aesthetic duty to savour the wonderful contrast between her cowboy voice and her broad Asian face.

From the seat in front, however, he heard Paul Mungina murmur, "Bloody Nip!"

For Paul was an old-fashioned patriot and xenophobe. As an instance, he believed in the Queen of England and Australia and wouldn't hear a fashionable, republican word against her. And he believed too in the idea that the Japanese had once, during World War II, done frightful things to innocent Australian boys. The fact that supposedly innocent Australian boys had done terrible things to Mungina's tribe – including a massacre of some twenty-seven Barramatjara souls around a desert waterhole on the Northern Territory border as late as 1929 – had done nothing to diminish Paul's respect for Australian institutions and myths. The triumphs and the martyrdoms of Australia's army belonged to Mungina, were part of his story of the world, more than they were for McCloud himself, the white manager of dance troupes, worldling and novelist-by-intent.

McCloud heard the Japanese cowgirl say, "My, my!" as she accepted a fluted glass from a stewardess. "This Californian, honey?"

"It's French," said the stewardess, showing the label.

"My God," said the woman. "You folks certainly live on the whole hog up here at the front of the plane!"

It seemed that she had been luckily bounced upwards, as the dance troupe had been themselves in view of their New York success. He with them. He wondered what booking accident had got her here, and wished it had befallen Pauline.

*　　*　　*

There was only one seat left – and that in the smoking section. The last passenger now shuffled in. He was dressed far less carefully than the businessmen who had already arrived. He had an old-fashioned, scuffed briefcase of the kind he had probably brought out of boyhood with him. His shabbiness marked him infallibly (McCloud thought) as British rather than American. He wore a yachting jacket which was not intended to fool anyone, and it was flecked either with ash or dead skin, the fallout of a whiskified middle life.

"Do you have spirits?" he asked the girl who was offering him a drink. She explained that there was no whisky until they were certain thousands of feet above the earth.

"Then I'll wait," he said. "If you don't mind, love."

To McCloud, this man looked all at once ill beyond bearing, hungover at least to the same limit as McCloud himself, and barely consoled by sleep. From his unfashionable briefcase he took a book printed in German, slung it on his seat. Then he disposed of his case, flopped, and lit a cigarette.

So that was it. Every damn seat was done for now.

In the front row, Wappitji ordered a 7-Up, as if to teach Bluey moderation. But Bluey insisted on champagne. "*Champers*," he intoned, as if he were an English rake.

McCloud noticed the scuffed Englishman watching Wappitji and Bluey from across the aisle. With frank interest he studied first them, then the dancer and the musician in the next row, and then McCloud himself and Tom Gullagara. He rose and approached McCloud, a cigarette in his hand in spite of the No Smoking sign.

"You're with that dance troupe?" he asked McCloud. "The famous Abo one?"

"Yes," said McCloud. He took the hand the man offered, and said who he was: McCloud; troupe manager.

The Englishman shook his hand. "I should tell you, everyone was talking about them in Manhattan. Absolutely everyone!"

"Yes," McCloud laughed. The idea of the troupe's glory produced in him a sort of pride and a wry joy. "I know all about it."

But as always when the troupe casually attracted frenzies of approval, McCloud thought one way or another of the novel he had taken the opportunity during the tour to leave with six New York publishers. No one was talking about *it*. Everyone was talking about the Barramatjara Dance Troupe, and *they* didn't even relish fame. Fame was an irrelevance to them. Only for their manager was it a raging and unrequited need.

"But tell me," said the Englishman, dropping his voice, "they don't have any sense of high culture, do they? Isn't it a case of *they dance because they dance because they dance*? Isn't that so? They don't dance for the same reason the kids at the Juilliard or Covent Garden do, that's for sure." The voice dropped theatrically further. He was not so much a man being wary of his opinions. He was playing at it though. "So, given that, isn't there something artificial to their appearing in dance theatres?"

McCloud didn't want to discuss this question. He had already earnestly faced it from a dozen ageing and wrinkled Manhattan smartalecs at receptions for the troupe; while the Barramatjaras cut their sundry swathes through cocktail receptions in New York, he'd been stuck with the sour enquiries.

He knew it was based on some knowledge of what people annoyed him by calling *primitivism*. But it was so clever an idea that it missed everything, it disqualified the questioners from the Barramatjara joy.

For he had learned that the troupe had their cogent reasons for dancing.

"In one sense, you're right," he said. He didn't like talking about the dancers like this, in the third person, in the anthropologist mode. But Tom Gullagara was comatose for the moment, and the others could not hear. "People come to see them for that very reason. That they don't care. And believe me, they *don't* care. Not in that artistic sense. And that's why they succeed."

"Sure," said the Englishman, mocking McCloud as a sentimentalist.

"Don't worry. They've got a powerful motive to dance."

"And what's that?" asked the Englishman.

"They want to civilise us."

"No," said the Englishman, turning away with lenient little guffaws. "No. Sorry. I'm sure they're dynamite. But I just don't go for *that*."

They're civilising *you*, McCloud considered saying, but he'd said too much anyhow, that idea of the Barramatjara on a humanising mission: something Bluey had confessed in anger one morning, something not meant to be repeated or used against any stray Englishman.

So McCloud switched back to mere questions of art. He was surprised to notice that although he wanted to rout the man, he wasn't as angry with him as he expected. The fellow had a crooked charm of some sort.

"As for the other kind of stuff," McCloud continued, "you

know, the dance and the art. I just wish we *could* all stop ourselves trying too damn hard. Because *they* can, and people love it."

The Englishman seemed to have had his fun out of the argument and now he dropped it. He stubbed out a cigarette and said his name was Victor Cale, and that he worked for the *Daily Telegraph*.

He now did an awkward knee bend until he was on a level with Tom Gullagara's window. He squinted out through the Perspex and the rain at slurred, meaningless lights. "I hope we're not too much delayed. This French lollywater they're handing out is no use to me. Scotch is more or less heart, blood and gender to me. Wouldn't say so in front of the wife. You wouldn't happen to have any duty free, would you?"

McCloud said he hadn't. The Englishman off-handedly cursed himself for not having gone to the trouble of fetching some.

"But I didn't have time, you see. I had to interview the Secretary of State at the Helmsley Palace, and the bastard was late!"

The Englishman glanced around then, looked dolefully at the happy woman in the green dress and, like a genuine dipsomaniac, did not seem to see her, except perhaps as a debased being satisfied with French fizz.

Meanwhile Pauline McCloud was back there, amongst the seats in the tail. Her elbows tucked in in the narrow limits of one of the middle seats, she faced a night journey which refused to begin and which she doubted the wisdom of making in any case. In that crowded tail McCloud wouldn't even be able to sit beside her and try appeasement. They could perhaps have a muffled, elliptical talk outside the bank of lavatories, while polite fraus – returning from visiting their war-bride sisters in New Jersey – came and went, excusing themselves.

The Englishman wandered off without warning. McCloud could hear him – genially imperious – urging a steward to release some whisky to him. The steward invoked a new federal regulation. The bar, at least as regards spirits and cocktails, was to remain sealed until the plane achieved international airspace.

"Come on, man," Cale could be heard saying, slipping ironically into the New York idiom in a way which should have made the steward want to hit him. "The Grand Republic lies behind us, sonny Jim. Either we crash at take-off, son, in which case my blood alcohol will be burned off, wouldn't you say? Or else we're as good as in God's own sky right now."

Glancing over his shoulder, McCloud saw the steward pressing some whisky miniatures and a glass with ice into Cale's hand.

"You're a Christian, man," said Cale satirically.

Bluey Kannata had risen from his seat, climbed over Wappitji's legs and come sauntering down the aisle. He nodded sagely at Mungina the *didj* player, and had just about passed McCloud when he bent like a bird swooping, an appropriately balletic movement which startled McCloud just the same.

"Hey mate," he whispered. "They give the Pommy bastard whisky, mate. Why don't they give us whisky?"

"He had to be rude to them to get it," McCloud told Bluey.

McCloud could feel Bluey's impishness like a minor electric crackle in the air. "I reckon it might be some more of that race discrimination, mate? What do you say?"

But he was smiling in his crooked way. All the curses he had so recently believed to have descended on him were forgotten.

"No. Listen, Bluey, just go to the toilet like a dancer on tour and leave it till we take off. The Englishman had to admit he was an alcoholic out loud."

"Well," said Bluey, "a little more working on it, and you and I could fit that ticket. Eh, mate?"

But then with one quick, sombre wink, he had straightened and gone.

It was believed that men of Whitey Wappitji's or even Bluey Kannata's level of knowledge could render themselves invisible. Could insert themselves through an aperture in time and inhabit for a moment a parallel but not apparent world or scheme, but one from which they could intrude and act on the seen and the known. Critics had even said Wappitji and the others danced like that, always on the edge of disappearing, a remarkable but habitual achievement. Not art so much as shadow play.

Sometimes, as now with Bluey, they even walked like it.

In following Bluey's hypnotic passage aft, McCloud's eyes met those of the Japanese-American woman, the Nisei or Issei in the green dress.

"Hello," said McCloud.

"Hello to you," she replied. "Daisy Nakamura."

She had surrendered her name innocently and without caution. In the same spirit, McCloud surrendered his.

The captain had just announced that they were waiting for a

wheelchair passenger. There was so much demand on airport wheelchairs tonight, he'd told them in that rural, easy way favoured by airline pilots; the voice of the common man exalted to technological management of this prodigious machine.

"If it weren't for the big winds off the Great Lakes," the Nisei or Issei woman told McCloud, her face succulently earnest, "we'd be hours late into Frankfurt. When I flew out of Flagstaff at dawn, there was I swear a fresh three feet of snow on the ground and it was drifting. You couldn't see the San Francisco Peaks. I had those winds on my tail all the way flying here, couldn't drink a cup of coffee it was so rocky. But the weather's a little milder now. We should get what's called positive assistance over the Atlantic, but it won't spill our drinks."

McCloud took in the fine, broad features leaning towards him across the aisle, her sublimely-sculpted features. He could imagine some airline official assuring her at the check-in counter, *Oh no, ma'am, no more weather problems. From now on only positive assistance.*

McCloud kept watch over any reflex desires though. He wanted to achieve a worthiness, a greater mana perhaps, against the time he would get a chance to speak to Pauline.

"Where are you from, Mrs Nakamura?" he asked. He risked the *Mrs* since there was something connubial about her which denied the evidence of her single-girl green cocktail dress.

"Oh, I'm from a place named Budapest. Northern Arizona. Navajos and Mormons and cowboys called Kelly and Campbell! And then truckers – there's always scads of truckers! And Colorado River rafting guides and back-country mule-wranglers. That's about the sum-total of the Budapest traffic. This is just about my first time out of Arizona, though I did go to Salt Lake once to see the Temple up there, the one with the golden angel on the spire. It's certain it's my first time out of the US." She dropped her voice. "Why, I bought no more than a small coach ticket, and here they just upped me to first class as if I knew the Board of Directors. See, what happened, they gave my pre-selected seat to a fairly antsy asthmatic gentleman who always takes a particular bulkhead nonsmoker. That meant there was just one other place they could put me. The luck of the Irish!"

She could laugh very ripely, like a woman who had not yet learned to be careful. McCloud felt sure Pauline wasn't laughing like that, back there in her straitened seat.

"Your friends?" said Daisy Nakamura, gesturing towards the dance troupe. "They're African gentlemen or something?"

He told her who they were.

"Wild!" she said. "You don't mean it! You say they paint the set they're going to dance on?"

"Yes. And not just with any designs. With designs they own, that they're entitled to use. People come at noon, bring a hamper with smoked turkey and champagne and watch them work all afternoon, getting the dance cloth ready, painting the designs. And then in the evening, without rehearsal, they dance around what they have painted. Well, almost without rehearsal. They need what are called lighting and technical rehearsals . . ."

"I'll be switched," Daisy Nakamura breathed. "Out our way, we got the Navajo like I said. Very mysterious people too." She waved her hand, as if resisting a burning sensation. "*Very* mysterious, sir, let me tell you. And some Hopi too, working on a water project. Mysterious-er still. Heavy dudes! Mean drinkers, the ones that're drinkers. Real mean drinkers. Though there's no meaner a drinker than a Mormon breaking the rules of a lifetime!"

In the end McCloud could not in the course of talk help asking why she was going to Frankfurt?

She volunteered the information that she had a sister who was married to an American officer in West Germany, at an airfield not far from Munich. She hadn't seen the sister for six years. "Now I'm a widow," she said improbably, since her sumptuous green dress seemed to have little to do with widowhood. "I want to be close to family, you know how it is. When I was married to Mr Nakamura, Ronnie . . . my life was so full I just didn't have the urge to go visiting. And we were so busy with the roadhouse. We have this roadhouse called the Polka Barn. Ronnie bought it from a Polish gentleman who wanted to move to San Diego. You can only work those long hours with someone you have a special thing with, like Ronnie and me. We had a special thing."

Pitiable remembrance had entered her face.

"I'm sorry," she continued. "I suppose I'm lucky, with a chance to visit my sister. The leisure to go all the way over there to Frankfurt."

With a lustrous sensuality still shining in her face, even in bereavement, how the gentlemen of Budapest, Arizona, must have longed to offer her fraternal comfort!

She said, as if in fact she read the thought, "Oh, I had lots of friends. Ronnie never was strict. And he was a good quarter century older than me. What they call an Issei. Him and his parents were in the detainment camps out there in the wilderness during the big war, and my parents were too, though the two sets didn't really know each other well. Ronnie himself was a kid in the camps, and his brother fought in the American Issei battalions in Italy and was killed. When the war ended, my folks were scared of going back to California, so they stayed on in Arizona, market gardening near Flagstaff. Arizona people aren't too bad. Very short on college professors, a place like Budapest. Very short on great minds of the Western world and table manners. Kind of limited, like I suppose I am. But not bad people. If you stick with them."

She hooded her eyes and let her mind run on the clientele of the Polka Barn and the populace of Budapest.

"And I had lots of these friends, guys who were casual with me, and Ronnie was kind of lenient. But when Ronnie went, all those friends, men and women, didn't mean anything at all, sir. All I wanted to do was draw close to my own blood, to my sister and the others. Why, I went all the way out to Los Angeles, to the Japanese fishing fleet, for the Shinto funeral of an uncle I'd only met when I was a kid, and never once since. I really liked that – that was a *real* funeral. The Shinto priest chanting in a beautiful black robe, and the fishing boats bobbing around out there behind his head on the Los Angeles River. Oh my, I even grew a little sad that Ronnie and I were Methodists. But you can't be Shinto in a town like Budapest. It's a town with some goodwill and nice people. But their range don't extend to Shinto."

A sudden shriek of engines told Mrs Nakamura that she couldn't pursue any further for the moment the question of ancestral religion versus Methodism in Arizona. One of those plane-tug machines had torn them away from their inertia and was harrying them out into the dark, towards what McCloud thought of as the unlikely duty of taking wing.

There was always this excitement for McCloud to anticipate: by the end of a long flight, the aircraft seemed an entirely different vehicle than it had seemed at the start, as if while it sliced through the time zones it left some of its old nature behind and grew new matter, a new atmosphere, appropriate to the fresh hours it was screaming towards. Not even smoke fug nor the stale recycled air ever convinced him it was otherwise.

2

TAKING OFF AND TAKING OVER

FROM the trolley he ordered white wine – he would have
enjoyed Scotch, the drink of the man from the *Telegraph*,
Cale. But then Whitey Wappitji, on his way to the toilets,
might see and give that little ironic flinch of the forehead and eyes,
the one which implied that as a troupe they, McCloud maybe in
particular, weren't setting Bluey Kannata much of an example.

Waiting for the wine, McCloud stood up and explained to a
steward dispiritedly, without any hope of favours, that he was
going back to visit his wife. The plane banked briefly and he had
a glimpse of Long Island suburbs below, and the Atlantic blackness
beyond. Probably even down there, a long way north-east of the
magic city, they had seen Whitey, Bluey, Paul Mungina the *didj*
man on their televisions. They had seen Cowboy Tom Gullagara
and Philip the Christian. The more modest fame he himself had
come to New York for had evaded him, and despite his professional
joy at the Barramatjaras' unrivalled success, those moist lights
below struck him now with a deadly wistfulness.

He was pleased when the plane levelled back so that he could
see nothing but the soothing darkness. Reaching up from the
windows to the limits of space's infinite parabola.

He'd brought with him to New York – a justifiable mix of business
with business – his short stories in a paperback edition with a
terrible cover, and his unpublished novel. The novel had consumed
three years – he'd gone freelance to finish the thing, becoming a
part-time tour administrator rather than the full-time one he had
been, getting more work that way than he would have liked to but
still not enough to add up to an economic existence of his own.

Pauline was therefore his true patron. She went on working all throughout. She founded her own small company and became what he, by writing his book, forfeited becoming – a serious, known-in-the-trade tour administrator. She was wonderful at it. She could fly a youth orchestra and its instruments from Melbourne to Leningrad, she could ensure they all got through customs and onto the bus and into their beds at the hotel, and determine that coffee and pastries awaited them off-stage during rehearsal breaks. She was impeccable at that sort of thing and in heavy demand. The truth was that this tour of the Barramatjara Dance Troupe was seen as too small in scope to waste her time with, and so her dilettante husband had been approached to manage it.

Her dilettante husband had then proposed to her that the Barramatjara tour would be painless, a journey she could come on to spend time with her spouse away from the complications which beset the big tours she handled.

The idea behind his being a dilettante arts administrator was that his sacrifice of career and time would be returned to the McClouds by the end of the American tour, when publishers would compete to reward him for his great antipodean tale.

In the writing, he had used – looting and consecrating at the one time – their childhoods, his and Pauline's, and the pattern of their parents' marriages as the material of the story. This was the most serious ancestor-worship he had ever committed himself to. He had spent a larger part of the three years in a state of exaltation over the book, the peculiar permanence it would give to his memories and his parents and even – by extension – to the brisk, reliable, pretty woman he had married.

While the extraordinary Barramatjara Dance Troupe were being photographed by *Vogue* or *Harper's Bazaar*, he had been in the office of an agent far downtown whose name had been given to him. The agent was intelligent to the point of scaring him, but her cramped little office in Hudson Street had a "little-magazine" atmosphere to it, as if she represented many of the worthy, a few of the famous, and none of the rich.

She had received a copy of his novel weeks before, and McCloud had hoped that the gimcrack bookshelves, the yellowing stacks of *New York Review of Books*, the old-fashioned desk, the battered steel door with its obsolescent steel bar – the sort of out-of-date security device which stated most directly and most brutally that this office sat, and this woman breathed, in a besieged city – that

26

all *that* would be transmuted to a sort of glamour by her literary enthusiasm for his book.

She had certainly *approved* of his book. But no one abandons a career, strains forth and weighs sentences for three years for the sake of approval. Instead of declaring it unique, she mentioned a dozen obscure American books of which it reminded her. She implied that it was already treading water in a flooded market. But that she might be able to find a place for it.

She had sent copies to nine publishers, she said; three of whom had, while Wappitji and Bluey exercised their casual dominance over the American media, rejected it. The agent did not say *reject*. She used the term *passed on it*. An imprint, as they called it, a section of a large publisher but with its own line of books, generally worthy ones, had made an offer – $10,000, which the agent thought she could up to $12,000.

"Four thousand dollars per year, that means," said McCloud. "Because it took three years to write."

"It's rotten," the agent agreed. "It's normal. But God knows, there *are* possibilities. Books *do* get found and taken up. They attract paperback and movie deals . . ."

But he didn't really want wealth, he tried to explain. It was that he wanted to be taken seriously as an artist, and some instinct of his told him that in this commercial republic publishers took writers seriously with money.

He hadn't had the nervous strength yet to confront Pauline with this offer conveyed to him, without promises of certain acclaim, by the agent. Just the same he knew Pauline would take it better than he had. She might actually be proud of him for finding a New York publisher; it wasn't in any case the major question of her life. She would forgive all too easily a failed literary husband. If he wanted it, she would make all-too-generous room for him in her company.

He didn't know what to do in this matter of the imprint's offer. As the agent had said, it was very likely better to cast your bread upon the waters.

Making his way aft, he was half-hoping that the aisles would be full of cocktail trolleys so that he could have a pensive few minutes dawdling behind them. But the way to the back of the plane was totally clear. All the passengers wore a locked-in, dazed look under the needlessly severe lighting.

He stopped by her seat. She was jammed in between a plump man determinedly taking up space to one flank. To the other was a freckled and raw-boned young mother holding a sleeping baby, and a scholarly-looking young Pakistani or Arab reading *U.S. News and World Report*. She should not try to haul herself over the fat man, he indicated by gesture. She should essay the mother and child and the Pakistani/Arab and meet him at the back.

This was not easily performed without crushing and waking the baby. But the young student of international affairs made things easy by standing in the aisle. Pauline thanked him with a nice, sad-eyed smile.

Before meeting the Hudson Street agent, McCloud had of course envisioned a time when they would both fly ceaselessly together, gusted across oceans by weatherfronts of literary applause.

When Pauline and McCloud reached the toilets at the back, he poured two cups of water and handed one to her. She didn't refuse to take it – thank God, she didn't play such heavy-handed symbolic games. But she *did* refuse to take it without question.

"What's this for?"

"To stop our brains from drying out. At this altitude, I mean." He drank his in front of her, as if he was displaying to a child the lack of tartness in a given medicine. She began to sip hers.

She was brown-haired and had fine features. A small woman who cocked her head. She carried on each hip a small rich wedge of flesh. In fifteen years' time, of course, she might consider such congenital baggage a curse. At the moment it made her a symmetric little woman, and McCloud wished that both for the sake of the disorder between them and the joy it would be, they could sit for a time spaciously with each other and even try a few caresses. The deregulation of the aircraft industry had so cramped the interior of planes, however, that no broad gestures were possible.

Pauline said, "I've been thinking. I have work backing up in the office. Deborah's trying to handle the Kirov tour of Australia and New Zealand on her own, and I don't know if she can really do that. I should go home early from Frankfurt."

"No," he said. "We all need you. The boys and I."

"Oh, I'm aware I'm handy. I know how to order a limo or charter a bus. But to be handy isn't enough. I'm an unpaid supernumerary, and it's infallible in this business that that's the person who always ruins things. Especially if she's a wife or a girlfriend."

He took her hand and said something plain about her being more than handy to him.

But she went on talking – not like the harridans of old, for whom he had been trained by his father's generation and by received male folk-wisdom – but levelly, a modern woman, if you like; a woman afloat in her own water. She said, "You certainly needed time away from me. After the book, and all that dependence. My God, you needed a break. And that's okay by me. You know I don't go for the deathless-love idea, or perpetual joy-in-each-other's-company.

"But what's offensive about you, Frank, is that no sooner do you decide it would be really good to be away from your old woman than you get guilty, and you go to her and say, *Please, please, come on the American and European tour. I'll feel ashamed of myself if you don't come.* And so I spend some thousands of dollars of my own money so that you won't feel uncomfortable about leaving me behind. I can't believe I did it! I'd like to think I'm not as stupid as that. I could have spent two weeks reading and diving on the Great Barrier Reef. Instead I'm unpaid labour and fifth wheel."

He tried to make the standard reassurances but she held her hand up.

"And then there's the other side of the equation, mate!" she told him. "Because you've gone to the trouble of talking the old girl into coming along, even against your own profoundest desires, you all at once feel worthy enough to unload some of your tasks on me. You become entertainment-and-booze officer for your dancers, for example, and leave the hard-edged stuff to me. And you feel entitled too to charge down on other women in my presence. If I weren't here you'd be too busy, too professional, for any of that. But you know that with me here you can be a fool and neglect things and I'll tidy up after you. Because, after all, I do entire dramatic and dance companies. While everyone knows you're a novelist, and no one distracts you with more than a chamber orchestra or a dance ensemble."

The termagants he had somehow been raised to expect left their men with moral room to manoeuvre. They overstated the treachery and foulness of their target. Each declared her man the worst who ever breathed, and on good evidence he knew he probably wasn't; was too lacking in strength of purpose and in pathology to be the worst bastard alive! Pauline went in for accuracy, though, and left you with nothing, no grounds, no headroom for balancing and weighing with yourself, no saving and absolving rage.

Instead of a gracious anger therefore, McCloud felt melancholy and the genuine weight of his pitiable wrongdoings.

"And the other thing I did which was utter stupidity," said

29

Pauline, "was to go looking for you and that Slavic blonde. You're downstairs at the reception and the speeches are still going on. And she says in your ear that there are some paintings on the second floor she wants to show you – the best acrylics are up there, little Miss Hotblood says. Barely three years out of Lodz and she knows about the best American-Indian paintings. A fast learner, this little Miss Poland!"

"The speeches had ended," McCloud found himself gently insisting.

"Oh, good! Had the applause? You surely aren't telling me the best thing to do as soon as the speeches have ended is to run upstairs to a remote corner of a gallery? If so, it's a convention no one else in the gallery last night followed."

There *was* an explanation for both mysteries, the mystery of insisting Pauline travel with him, the mystery of the Polish aficionado. And Pauline – he knew – would accept the explanation in both cases and be reconciled. But the sad thing was he could not utter it. First, of course, the story of his literary failure, or a success so meagre as to be worse than failure. Perhaps it had made him susceptible to the attentions of a Pole, to that heroic, that solemn, that spacious accent, to the furthest East of Europe pronouncing so piquantly on the furthest West of America.

And then there was jealousy. Pauline had mentioned the Kirov. Who was bringing the Kirov to eastern Australia, to the plush, balletomaniac cities of Sydney and Melbourne? An impresario named Peter Drury, who had been divorced at forty and had since grazed sensitively and with a sense of *droit de seigneur* amongst the handsome women of Sydney; who kept on telling feature writers that mere girls, popsies, sheilas, mere heartiness and animal generosity weren't enough for him and never would be; who drank like a sailor and looked like an athlete; and who kept sending work to Pauline's company and would tell powerful people at cocktail parties that she was the best there was.

Sometimes, after much booze and even in the bed he shared with Pauline, he dreamed of Drury and Pauline together – the dreams arose like revelations – and it all caused him a curious and unique pain and brought an unspeakable sense of nullity.

The nullity had been assuaged by the Slav's attentions.

If he therefore confessed something as ancient and unfashionable as jealousy, he would be forgiven. He *knew* it was a coherent explanation too, but he could not humble himself to make it.

So he fell back on impotent and conventional pleadings.

*   *   *

"I think you have to make allowances for honest impulse," he said. "The girl is an acknowledged expert in Navajo acrylics. I think that what you saw up there ... We stumbled into each other." In fact, he could have told Pauline, he was so drunk with Californian wine and with spirits that, admiring one of the Navajo sand paintings, he had toppled into the girl and she had held him and then, with greater grace, opened her moist mouth. And he had thought how ignorant this woman was of his literary paltriness, and how attractive that made her. Whereas Pauline would in the end sniff it all infallibly on his breath.

Beyond everything, the fantasy which attaches to women who do not know you, cannot read you, attached to this Solidarity refugee who had an interest in Navajo acrylics!

"But you're right, of course," he hurried to say; since Pauline *was* right and nothing could come from a merciless reiteration of his New York behaviour. "I was totally pissed. I behaved like an adolescent . . ."

That, at least, was an easy version to pronounce.

Now he had to make way for a solid woman with a beatific face who wanted to get into one of the toilets. Both the McClouds waited, trying miserably to make all this look like normal discourse. Until the woman was inside and they heard her shoot the lock.

"Don't misunderstand me," said Pauline then. "I don't mind that the blonde from Lodz fancied you – or that if I hadn't been trapped into following you the worst might have happened. A lot of girls who kiss quick don't always come good in the end. I'm just asking for consistency. Either you *don't* want to travel with your wife, and in that case you are free to go upstairs with any Navajo art expert as soon as the speeches are done, incurring nothing but mild disapproval from your peers. Or else you *do* travel with your wife and disqualify yourself from clearing out up the stairs before the applause for the welcoming of the Barramatjara Dance Troupe has ended. It isn't glands I'm complaining about, McCloud. It's mere fucking manners! And it's professional standards too. I wonder, for example, what Whitey *really* thinks about you as a manager!"

McCloud was angry for a second. "Come on. Leave me some pride. Whitey and I are fine."

"Whitey," she said, "is very polite. And very forgiving."

He poured himself more water. He was ready to undertake the water therapy. He hated the idea that at some time in the future his name might be mentioned to Whitey by some official of Australian Aboriginal or Foreign Affairs, and Whitey's eyes might politely waver.

"I understand," McCloud admitted to Pauline. He drained the cup. It disappeared into the ill ease, the hollow dryness. "I admit I've learned bad habits. But please don't go home from Frankfurt, Pauline. I'll behave differently in Frankfurt. And we'll have fun . . ."

Perhaps, it occurred to him, they'd have it when he broke the news that $12,000 seemed to be the best he could get. She might even be happy at that. It would either put him back under her high-earning patronage or send him back to regular hours of work. And in some nice little *gasthaus* in Frankfurt the disarming Pauline, so rigorous on herself and others, so strenuous on manners, who had seen in her father – the Dentist as everyone still called him – the berserk shifts which can derive from a lack of rigour, might admit to him her ultimate contentment. Or else her easy forgiveness for his literary failure. And they would make love then and be reconciled.

He went on talking about Frankfurt, and how they would hire a van and all ride together into Italy. And he would keep Bluey Kannata out of bars, and she could keep him, McCloud, out of bars too.

"Oh no," she said. "I'm not a mother superior. You'll have to do it yourself."

Of course, he said. Of course. He understood that. It would be wonderful though, he said, because in Milan they were *really* waiting for the dance troupe! No one took this sort of event more seriously than the Northern Italian press. They wrote as if every day's paper was an instalment in an encyclopaedia. Beside them, the *New York Times* was a callow rag.

During this council with Pauline he had been able to see, around a corner of the partition which screened them, the stewards and – as the airline industry still chose to call them, long after poetesses had become poets – the stewardesses begin to move forward up the length of the plane. They wore no more than their usual pained frown at the mass of passengers who had to be fed and watered.

The captain's voice was heard. It seemed to rise up from some blithe rural place far back behind the American coast the aircraft was still skirting, a voice unmarred by ambiguous America, by the Village and Alphabet City, by Georgetown and Washington downtown, by all America's cheek-by-jowl glories and threats. The voice mentioned some improbable altitude they were supposed to have reached. It nominated another even less credible number as their aimed-for cruising altitude. It made the darkness – taller than Everest beyond this little flask of human light – sound homely and convivial.

"That weather front which caused such havoc in the mid-West earlier today has moderated and should be of positive assistance to us," the captain advised the passengers in his country accent. "Given that we arrive in Europe in the morning and have to put in a full day, I suggest you get as much rest as you can find."

To McCloud, the idea of finding sleep, as if it were something hidden behind a tree trunk in a forest, seemed appealing.

The polite young Pakistani/Arab, Pauline's travelling companion, appeared in the gap between the bank of lavatories and the partition. He held something which looked as if it had been made of fibre glass. McCloud woodenly remembered that the thing he held was called a machine pistol. Pauline, with her back to the boy, had not yet seen this shocking, rarely glimpsed yet somehow familiar possession in his hands.

"Is that an Uzi?" McCloud asked the boy. It was a name he'd read in the New York papers. Adolescent drug dealers were said to tote them in the Bronx. This boy seemed hardly more than adolescent.

Pauline turned and took one step backwards then, until she was exactly and tightly slotted against the dip of McCloud's shoulder.

The polite Pakistani, who was possibly an Arab after all, said, "It's a Polish WZ–63. Would you return to your seats?"

"Why?" asked McCloud. "You aren't going to tell me this is . . .?"

"Be calm about it, sir," said the boy. His voice had an overlaying American accent, as if he were a foreign student at some American campus. And he had that appeasing tone which foreigners who get their English in America pick up from the natives. "My brothers and I have taken the plane over. Back to your seats, please."

"Your *brothers*?" asked McCloud. The boy had been seated on his own beside Pauline. McCloud had not noticed any potential brothers of this boy's during his journey down from first class.

The boy did not answer. He'd noticed the locked toilet door which the German woman had entered. He began knocking on it. He was insistent but he didn't pound away. The woman emerged, bleared and shocked, as if she'd been asleep in there. He ordered her to her seat.

"And you," he told the McClouds yet again. "Please. Quick. This is a serious matter. To your seats."

To McCloud, he looked vaguely disappointed, as if he had expected a Polish WZ–63 to work better than this in exacting obedience from ordinary people.

McCloud, Pauline and the German woman turned into the aisle and saw something both as accustomed and as very strange as the firearm they'd already beheld in the boy's hands. All the stewards and stewardesses had been mustered by an exit forward. Here they were under guard by a man older than Pauline's polite young reader of *U.S. News and World Report*.

In one upraised hand so that everyone in the plane could see it, this man, short but broad-shouldered, displayed a grenade which he had taken from a collection he wore on his belt. None of this seemed aberrant to McCloud. Yet the temptation not to believe in these phenomena was strong. For the man with the grenade was always there, and not there at the same time, in any aircraft you boarded. He stood just beyond the precise reach of your imagination. Here, on this New York–Frankfurt flight, he had simply taken on a little more flesh.

He kept a calm demeanour too, this stocky operative by the door. He had an ordinary, grizzled, balding look. He didn't seem rabid or frantic like the fellow you'd projected to yourself. He possessed an air of easy practice and efficiency.

McCloud felt the shock of having the unthinkable made flesh in front of his eyes. A mute alarm arose in him. Yet with it came the strange suspicion that to work up too much of a head of distress at the moment would be a waste, a gesture of disorder akin to other disorderly gestures he'd already made in New York. So he moved on, absorbing everything.

The boy told Pauline, who had halted in the aisle, "Go to your seat, madam."

Pauline raised her eyebrows, let her hand have fleeting contact with McCloud's forearm, and before McCloud could gauge whether his kiss would be welcome, struggled in past the freckled girl with the baby. The young mother did not seem more wan than she had before. No one had stood up and protested. They had not achieved belief in these events yet. People frowned slightly, as if all this was a minor hold-up in cocktail service.

"Where is your seat, sir?" the young man asked McCloud.

"I am up the front. But I'd like to stay with my wife. If I can't stay here, can't she come up there with me?"

Crazily, he suspected for a moment there might be a separate system of politics up there beyond the curtain, and he might talk the steward into admitting Pauline into it.

But then of course he understood the madness of the idea. "I'll stay here," he announced. He knew he would be happier here anyhow. He did not want to deal with these people on his own, in a separate seat. At the moment he felt profoundly married in a way he rarely felt in daily life. Separation would require surgery or death. He had not felt like that when the intense Polish woman promised him a sight of the best Navajo acrylics on the second floor.

"Go to your seat, sir," said the boy, nudging him with the Polish thing.

Pauline, nodding, consigning him forward, called from her place in the middle of the row. "You'd better go. The dancers mightn't know what in the hell is happening."

It was for sentiments like that that Peter Drury thought her the best in her business.

"Who are you people?" McCloud asked the young man.

"An announcement will be made on the public address system," the boy told him, in the style of a sentence learned by rote.

With the armed boy following, McCloud began to walk forward. He felt that people were watching him disapprovingly. Even then he thought that perhaps they'd transferred the blame for the inconvenience from the men with the machine pistols to him. Reaching the older and tougher man who faced the pale cabin crew, the young reader of U.S. News and World Report bent to a bag at the man's feet. He took from it a grenade belt like the one the small man already wore, and a little press-button radio of neatest design. The two of them didn't look like brothers. And then it struck McCloud: the boy had been talking of brothers in the tribal sense; in the sense of ideology and mission!

Through the first-class curtain, still drawn, the hijackers feeling bound for the moment to recognise the airline's policy as regards division of the classes, he found – forward by the book and magazine racks – a young man armed just like Pauline's boy and hardly any older. Tom Gullagara had of course awoken or been awakened in his place by the window, and contemplated the boy levelly.

That loaded and perhaps ambiguous word, terrorist, had not yet entered the mental vocabulary McCloud was applying to this evening's occurrences. But it struck him now. It came up from the back of his brain like unexpected data. *Terrorist*, he thought. *These are what are known as terrorists.* But it wasn't a very useful thought. It gave him less purchase, not more. In the mouths of politicians and editors it meant something. By not being a useful tool for this hour, however, it disappointed him.

From her seat Daisy Nakamura raised her eyebrows towards him. She could have been saying, "Nothing surprises me." And indeed she seemed to shine with a sort of assertive air of unsurprise.

His drink had arrived. The new masters of the aircraft had not interfered with that. A number of these people up here were sipping wine or spirits or mineral water. Across the aisle, Cale held an envelope briefly towards McCloud. Written on its back, the side the young man by the magazine racks could not see, were printed the words, "For Christ's sake, I am *not* a journalist!" The message was aimed at McCloud for a second, before Cale crumpled and hid it in his pocket.

The intercom came on. It whistled and thudded like the wake of some other, safer jet above tonight's Atlantic.

"My friends," said the captain's cosily breathy voice, "I recently introduced myself to you as your captain, but I have to tell you I've been deprived of control of this aircraft. There are folks here who want to speak to you, and I have no option but to permit them to. I recommend you do what they ask and remain calm, and we'll all soon have an end to this thing." But there was a sigh. He didn't seem happy now with his own promises. "May God see us all through this night!"

McCloud wondered with a kind of envy how the man could so naturally invoke God at this enormous and improper height. Miles of blackness below and above kept them packed tight in the hostage condition. How could you mention God when the distances, the height of intentions, defied Him?

The male voice which then took up the message was no more manic and barely more stressed than the captain's.

It announced in slightly accented *English* English, rather than American English, that the plane had been seized by the Arab Youth Popular Socialist Front. Those who had not been guilty of war crimes against the Palestinian people, it said, would be very, *very* safe and should look to strict obedience as their hope. Everyone sitting by a window was to lean forward now and draw the shutters down, and to keep them closed until ordered.

"You must understand," the voice explained, "that with the difficult negotiations still to come, my party of brothers may become exhausted, and we are therefore determined from the start to be consistently harsh on anyone who is disobedient."

There was a hiatus, though the choppy sound of the intercom, the static of a happy world parallel to this one, continued.

McCloud heard Cale murmur arrantly across the aisle, "No one needs your fucking difficult negotiations. No one asked you to take the fucking jet!"

Very amiable, leaning forward in his front seat, Bluey Kannata called to the young man with the Polish gun. "Hey mate! Tell me. This some sort of hijack?"

So the word had been uttered at last, by that naïve cosmopolitan Bluey Kannata. McCloud felt a surge of gratitude towards him.

"You will get to know us more in hours to come," said the *English* English voice from the flight deck. "But for the moment, you may understand that my name is Taliq. My brother Yusuf has control of the front cabin. Razir, an old comrade of mine, will manage the middle section, while my brother Hasni controls the rear of the plane. The section upstairs is managed by my brother Musa. These are chosen revolutionary names, and though they might be unfamiliar to some of you, everyone should try to remember them for any conversations between passengers and the revolutionary brothers."

"Pig's arse," declared Cale across the aisle.

This boy up here, Yusuf, with his deadly Polish implement, seemed very tolerant of whispering in the classroom, McCloud thought. He hoped that Pauline's Hasni, in the rear, would be equally lenient, though – from appearances – he might turn out to be more straight-laced.

The intercom remained on, still wheezing of the safe night and all the safe planes beyond this particular tube of aluminium. Then, with a profound breath, a new phase of Taliq's message began. "While we are flying, or even on the ground, one of us will be in the cockpit here holding a grenade from which the pin has been withdrawn. Our men are equipped also with appropriate radio devices on which there are letter and numeral keys. Each of my brothers knows a short codeword which, if punched out on our radio receivers, will ignite a wad of *plastique* secreted in a suitcase in the baggage area. If any of us is attacked, I – or whoever stands in my place on the flight deck – will punch the code into our radios.

"We are not supermen. But we are trained and of one mind and

37

ready to die! Are you ready to die? Even if your section is left for a time without one of my brothers, do not doubt for a second that any wild gesture will cause the destruction of the plane and of all your individual hopes."

At this, McCloud heard a long release of breath from Daisy Nakamura across the aisle. But Tom Gullagara, at his side, seemed to listen to the voice from the flight deck as if it were some routine though complicated message about luggage collection.

The voice said, "Stewards will now take trays and collect everyone's passport. I must thank you on behalf of our revolution. Thank you. You will hear further from me. But later."

The intercom noise ceased. Yusuf – full-moustached and with a more sensual and less scholarly face than Hasni's, the not unpleasant face of a Levantine coffee-drinker and doer of fast business – pointed to the two stewards, a middle-aged man and a girl with a stricken face, who now began to work the compartment, each of them with a silver tray.

McCloud murmured, in the hope it could be heard by the dancers, "Passports, that's all. They just want our passports."

Yusuf did not make any objection to this noise. He glanced briefly and placidly at the stewards with the trays and made little gestures of the head to show they should start at the front.

"I'm sorry, sir," you could hear the stewards tell passengers. "Our Chief Purser refused to co-operate at first but was threatened . . ."

Bluey Kannata was a world traveller and did not need McCloud's extra advice on what was required. The others had not travelled much outside the continent at whose core lay their millennial home, the Barramatjara country and the settlement called Baruda. They were not as accustomed as Bluey to the European rituals and meanings of the passport.

For that very reason perhaps, because they couldn't see passports as having any intimate connection with themselves, all the members of the dance troupe gave them up without wavering, without feeling as orphaned and naked in the world as McCloud did when he let his drop on the anodised silver of the tray.

One of the American businessmen on the other side of the cabin, a well-ordered and athletic-looking man, threw *his* American passport down on the tray and then covered his eyes with his hand, as if he had suddenly been deprived of the power to see. But no one argued with the stewards. Everyone, McCloud was sure, had in his head an image of the suitcase down in the hold which, if caressed with the right word, would blow this little planet, the Frankfurt flight, to pieces, scattering passengers out into the untold darkness.

Across the aisle, Daisy Nakamura was yielding up her US passport by its patent leather cover, the kind of thing friends give to those who are making the first big journey of their lives. A bald eagle was embossed upon Daisy's leather. McCloud wondered, did she know that that emphatic eagle might be enough to stamp her as guilty in the present company? He looked at her, but she merely seemed engrossed in the procedure, as the dance troupe were. As if she too were studying an alien ceremony.

In fact her expression, McCloud noticed with some fascination, resembled that of Gullagara at his side. Tall Tom Gullagara was sitting up straight now, peering over the tops of the seats. He observed the collection for its educative value.

McCloud remembered the night – it could only have been a few nights past in fact – when Gullagara stood outside an Italian restaurant in Greenwich Village watching him stuff coins into a parking meter. The van Pauline had organised for transporting the troupe on their little jaunts around the city stood by the kerb. As he assessed McCloud's actions an amusement had entered Gullagara's face. He never looked like that, squinting over a tolerant smile, unless he'd had a few evening drinks. And similarly, he rarely asked questions during the day; he had an easy air of omniscience and might have been loth to risk losing it. Anyhow, he was at his ease that night in the Village – or rather at a different sort of ease than he seemed to be at during the day.

"Why do you blokes do that?" he'd asked McCloud.

"Pay for parking?"

"Yeah. Where do those coins go?"

"Into the parking meter," said McCloud.

"I know that. A man's not a fool, Frank. Just the same, where do those bloody coins go in the end?"

McCloud could tell he must try hard to pick up the tenor of the question, for Gullagara was aware of exactly the distance he was exposing himself by asking this question. He was beginning to frown too and to adjust the great leather belt around his slight beer gut. He seemed to be aware he was risking his dignity, asking for information that every five-year-old city child might have knowledge of. Here, outside the Italian place, he wondered if he had done the right thing to ask an intimate, cultural question like this; just as a European might wonder after asking a question about something so basic to the Barramatjara cosmos that no one ever thought of explaining it.

In the deserts of Australia, men of influence like Gullagara and Whitey Wappitji were sometimes engaged in rituals involving the stroking and advising of certain rocks, stones associated with this animal or that. They spoke to, charmed, persuaded the stone. And the species was increased in number, or at least maintained in its levels.

In the street in New York, it had been McCloud's guess that Gullagara saw the parking meter as a white model of this rite of rock-persuasion. Pour coins into the meter's narrow little mouth, and the metropolis with all its strange and ambiguous species was sustained! So the ceremony of parking brought a sort of immunity, Tom Gullagara might have thought, and an indefinable richness.

What Tom did not know was how thoroughly the city had expunged all myth.

So McCloud rushed to reassure him. There were no serious rites here. The meter had a little gut in which the money sat, and men with meter keys came round and took the money to cover the city's expenses. It was not the physics of magic. It was the physics of urban economics.

So Gullagara, like Daisy Nakamura, was staring at the hijacker in the cabin and at the backs of the two stewards collecting the passports as if he were trying to work out whether this too was just business or a powerful ceremony.

McCloud chose a light tone. "They want to look at people's passports so they can see whether any of their enemies are on board," he whispered. "I don't think you're likely to be one of their enemies, Tom."

He was not as successful a whisperer as Cale, however. Yusuf the hijacker called, "That gentleman down there should shut up." His voice, like Hasni's, was quaintly accented with American. Or perhaps Canadian, or some other brand of English which spelled opportunity to a young Palestinian.

As if to prove the normality of whatever demands they might make, of whatever acts they might perform, Taliq and his men permitted a meal to be served. McCloud had no appetite. He felt that he was tasting ashes. Yusuf watched the serving and eating but made no ideological comment on the food that was presented up here. Even the Sevruga caviare and the Stolichnaya vodka were permitted to be offered. The only requirement was that the diners should not speak to each other, nor listen in on headphones to the plane's broadcast system.

Occasionally McCloud would raise his glass to Tom Gullagara, who would in return toss his head in a way that said, *The things that can happen to a man when he goes on a dance tour!*

Palpable fragments of hijacking accounts McCloud had read in newspapers recurred to him. The half-remembered details stifled him. Wasn't there one hijack where Egyptian commandos were ordered to liberate the plane, yet destroyed in their efforts ten times as many hostages as hijackers? Was there another where the cabin blew up? And others where some mistake or wayward surge of electricity set off the *plastique* in the hold and carried all the exalted ambitions of the hijackers, all the pedestrian hopes of travellers screaming together down to earth?

There were more serious questions than these honestly horrifying ones. He was not American or Israeli. But how could he watch Americans and Israelis beaten and bloodied and remain silent? The experts said that for some people it became all too easy. He could not imagine it becoming all too easy for him, though, but everyone said you never knew these things ahead of time. Under terror, would he get into a frame of mind where he'd start believing that a single American carried a lethal portion of blame for American policy? And if – as he hoped – he refused to believe that, if he did not remain silent, how prepared was he for punishment?

The event was rumoured to make the man. This event held no promise of making him. It was as if his lack of literary, managerial and marital credit fitted him badly for this moment.

He wondered too if Pauline would have any trouble from her seating neighbour Hasni? He suspected she might be safer relying on Hasni's apparent good manners than on any fighting return by him, by McCloud, to the rear of the plane – even if it were possible. For if he appeared, he thought, she might be unsettled into a sort of recklessness, the recklessness of a mother or spouse. Or else the recklessness – if any were left in her – of the lover.

Then the Barramatjaras. Surely they were safe? Surely they were the oppressed of the earth, bearing no blame for anyone's policy?

Victims of policy in fact. And dispossessed of their land? Well, against the wishes of many whites, in recent years they'd been given it back freehold by an embarrassed government. But dispossessed in the past, and potentially dispossessed in the present! And surely – according to these men with the Polish automatic weapons – daily and spiritually dispossessed by capitalism?

The first-class passengers had coffee in front of them: Cale and – McCloud suspected, though he couldn't see directly – Bluey Kannata a cognac apiece as well, and Daisy Nakamura a port. Cale was smoking, hungrily and with energy.

A beeper on Yusuf's belt began to bleat. Yusuf, his eyes darting around from the face of one of his well-fed passengers to that of another, pulled his small radio from his back pocket and spoke softly into it. He inclined his head then and listened to the words which emerged in return. He nodded and then seemed to prepare himself for a visit from someone.

Within seconds McCloud saw a tall, clean-shaven man, a solid being in his late thirties, wearing a close imitation of army fatigues, pass down the aisle and stand by Yusuf. He turned and faced the passengers. His features were large and not unpleasant. There was already a faint bluishness of fatigue or disenchantment under his eyes.

He pulled cigarettes from his breast pocket. "Since some of you are smoking," he said, "I shall join you." He lit the cigarette with one of those transparent lighters you can see the fluid in and looked reflectively at his prisoners.

"I suppose you think you know what to expect," he said in a well-modulated Anglo-Arab voice; the same voice which earlier had come from the flight deck. "You have all seen this on the movies, haven't you? The chief hijacker standing before you? He is a fanatic, isn't he? He is rabid. He is not a man born of woman. He speaks in jargon. Oh yes, my friends and my enemies, we shall hear jargon. There *will* be what you might call *classes. This* will be for some of you a short, sharp seminar. Some things will seem familiar to you, some things beyond your imaginings.

"For the moment, I ask you to consider one idea: that the alienation, the – if you like – *trauma* you are suffering at the moment is but an echo of the trauma suffered by my people for the past fifty years. Imagine this, as an instance! A Sunni Muslim woman in the village of Saf in October 1948. An enemy soldier rapes and then executes her. Trauma, you see. My grandmother,

42

as it happens. I know you have heard such stories before. Now you may listen to them with a little more immediacy of spirit . . . For the moment, I wanted you to see me, and I wanted to see you."

Examining them, he took one quick, energetic gulp from his cigarette.

"My name is Taliq. *T–a–l–i–q*. I hope you all ate well, since these matters are likely to become more erratic as we go."

He nodded to Yusuf and walked down the aisle again. McCloud looked over his shoulder and saw him ascending the stairwell to the upper deck. Returning to the cockpit, the threatened core of this small hostage planet.

Tom Gullagara leaned towards McCloud. "What's that he says about his grandmother?" he asked.

"She was raped," murmured McCloud, trying not to move his lips. He saw Tom Gullagara close one eye and consider this news. From across the aisle he could hear distinctly the journalist Cale's words. "I was in Palestine in '48 when the Mandate ran out. The Arabs couldn't have organised a farting contest! Now it's everyone's fault but theirs that they were beaten."

"Shut up, fatso," called Yusuf. Yet casually, as if he hadn't heard nor cared about the content of what Cale said.

Cale is mad and dangerous, McCloud decided. Wanting to keep his profession a secret but making sure Yusuf notices him. Seeking anonymity but crying, "I was in Palestine in '48 . . ."

One of the American businessmen asked now if he could use the lavatory. Yusuf searched him, feeling for weapon bumps on the man's body. Cale – forcing the issue again – rose in his place at once, as if he intended to go step-by-step with the American. But Yusuf seemed bent on ignoring Cale as a problem-figure in the cabin. He muttered to him in passing that it was to be one at a time.

McCloud watched the American go past. He walked slowly. He was the one McCloud had seen close his eyes as he yielded up his passport: one of those well-made, middle-aged men who wear a tan in autumnal New York, as if they spend every second weekend in the Bahamas.

Through all this – the serving of meals, the speech by Taliq – the Barramatjara Dance Troupe seemed to McCloud to sustain their normal calm. Bluey Kannata, star and troubled soul, remained penned in the window seat by Whitey Wappitji. McCloud had seen

43

his head following events in the cabin, darting in that birdlike way
he reproduced when dancing the emu or the brush turkey.

Across the aisle, Daisy Nakamura in her emerald dress had
actually fallen serenely asleep. McCloud was astonished by *her*
calmness, as distinct from the calmness of the Barramatjara Dance
Troupe, by now well-canvassed by the press and commented on
in feature articles.

When the businessman returned, Yusuf searched Cale, who stepped
forward up the cabin as if to accommodate the hijacker. The search
over, the Englishman turned and, brushing against McCloud's seat,
murmured, "You come next. First toilet on your left."

McCloud considered not putting his hand up. But then he
wondered why Cale had specified the cabinet on the left? Did he
plan to leave something there? And if McCloud did not pick it
up, wasn't Yusuf sure to find it in the end? McCloud therefore
flinchingly raised his hand like a child in the classroom. He feared
the Englishman was somehow going to give him an extra care, on
top of his care for the troupe and for Pauline. It struck him now
that he very likely had more responsibilities than anyone on the
plane other than the captain and, of course, the handsome Taliq,
who also had – after his own strange fashion – responsibilities of
a dual nature.

Yusuf, searching McCloud now, gave off a musk of mint and fresh,
moderate sweat. A boy with a pleasant savour.

"*Made in Singapore by Vincent Fong Tailors, Orchard Road,*"
Yusuf read from a label on the inside of McCloud's jacket. He
did not seem to be adducing the label as evidence of imperialist
decadence. He seemed interested in an old-fashioned way in cloth
and stitching. His features, McCloud thought, were little different
from those of Lebanese immigrants who ran menswear stores in
Australian country towns.

"I was in Singapore with a chamber orchestra last year,"
McCloud said, an excuse if it was needed. He chose not to say it
was a twenty-four-hour jacket – "I don't wear suits," he'd told
the incredulous and natty Mr Fong. McCloud felt guilty enough
ordering the thing, since he knew that however good the cloth, no
one could make a twenty-four-hour jacket without sweated labour.
He'd imagined a Singapore Chinese machinist working a treadle
sewer by dim light while two of her small children coughed and
were restive on a mattress in the corner. Such were the dreams of
an uneasy foreign devil ordering clothes in Singapore.

"My father was a tailor," murmured Yusuf, continuing the search. "Even at home we used to see this Asian stitching. It stinks, you know."

"I know," said McCloud, displaying a section where the lining had come adrift. *You have grievances? This is my grievance!*

When he entered the cabinet and locked the door, he could not see any evident signs, unless you considered the sodden towel Cale had left in the basin a sign. He pulled open the small tray where aftershave and skin lotion were kept and found a note.

"Flush this!" it said. *"In view of the passport thing, my name is not Cale. My name on the passport I handed in is Bennett. Be careful with this Taliq, old son. My early judgement is: a complicated and well-trained fellow of some psychological resources. Again, flush this."* And then below that, C for Cale.

The onus is not so great then. A drunk named Cale had become a drunk named Bennett. I needn't call him anything at all, since no one need know the two of us have talked.

Finished urinating, a gush of startled yellow, he watched Cale's slip of paper disappear in a swirl of blue water as he obeyed the man and flushed.

Instead of moving back to his seat, he decided to risk getting a sight of Pauline, maybe even speaking brief words with her. For it seemed the hijackers were in unchallenged command now, as they weren't when Hasni first ordered him forward. He wanted to share this observation with his wife, to give comfort and be comforted.

McCloud turned right towards the rear of the plane and came through a curtain. A stocky man in a sports shirt and jeans and a sort of cricketing sweater blocked his path. This must be, McCloud concluded from the automatic weapon the young man held in his hands, one of the *brothers* – Musa, temporarily down from upstairs. "Back, back," Musa yelled.

"I want to visit my wife," he said. McCloud felt tears prick his eyelids. "Please. My wife is back there. I want to tell her everything will be all right. Have some compassion."

"You've had a chance to start the compassion. All you damn fools up there. You've had a chance to set the tone," said stocky Musa. He spoke with a Midlands British accent and smiled ironically but without too much enmity. "You should let her travel with you. I thought only the unwashed Arabs did such things to their wives."

"It was a mix-up," McCloud began to explain.

45

"Don't worry," said the young man. "I'm a Christian just like you. Orthodox. We treat our women like shit too. Back, back, or I'll shoot you. What do I care for your sodding little marriage?"

A small yelp escaped a middle-aged couple in the window seats who were listening to this exchange. He saw in their faces an unfeigned shock at the idea that there were people who could so brutally deny an appeal to do with marriage.

Musa pushed him from behind with the metal handle of the weapon. Such hard edges! From the door of the first-class compartment Musa yelled in Arabic at Yusuf, abusing him – apparently – for being too relaxed.

Yusuf seemed to reply good-naturedly. Then he spoke in English to the passengers. "My brother Musa is ready to shoot dead anyone who tries to go out." He gave a shrug, again a sporting man's, a skirt-chaser's shrug. "That's the way it is." He walked down the aisle towards McCloud. "Sir, from now on you will need to piss and shit in a corner, in full view. Your lavatory rights are cancelled."

But Yusuf sounded so friendly about it, McCloud was left with a basis for hoping this was as severe as they'd be on him.

The lights were dimmed. Taliq announced from the flight deck that passengers should take some rest while he and his brothers of the Arab Youth Popular Socialist Front examined their passports. There was actually, McCloud thought, a quotient of paternal care in his voice.

McCloud noticed that Tom Gullagara did not settle to sleep. He sat upright, as if to have a solid think. Occasionally he rolled a thin cigarette and smoked it. Tobacco, which the Barramatjara had encountered as a gift from cattlemen and governments, which had kept them captive in their reservation and soothed them and served as their wages when they worked livestock on the great stations! Now Tom smoked the first skinny stockman's cigarette, the first bush durry, of his life as a hostage.

3

SEARCHING OUT THE GUILTY

F EW seemed to sleep, McCloud noticed, but all – even Cale/
Bennett – seemed passive in the cabin. McCloud knew that
in the version of this plane which they carried in their heads,
there was a grenade on the flight deck above and *plastique* in the
hold below. People were sandwiched by these threats, and Yusuf
strolled the aisle with an air of easy knowledge of how most of
them breathed shallowly for fear of acting as a trigger.

Secretly watching him around the edge of his seat, McCloud saw
the young hijacker, as if impishly, knowing how utter was his
control, disappear through the curtain towards the back of the
plane.

Almost at once, passengers became aware that they were for the
moment without supervision. A few of them began to whisper to
each other in the near-darkness Taliq intended them to use for
sleep.

"These are those PLO fellers, eh?" Tom Gullagara asked
McCloud all at once.

"Something like that, Tom." He remembered Arafat on television, with apparent good faith renouncing terror. He regretted
he had not paid more attention to the maps and tables of Palestinian
organisation, of the fragments of Palestinian alienation and fervour, which sometimes appeared in the press. "Maybe just what
they call a splinter group," he said.

Gullagara nodded. He may have been unfamiliar with parking
meters but was something of a practical politician himself and
understood splinter groups. Tom and all the Barramatjara had a
different view of the white world, of what should be taken from

47

it and given, than their cousins the Arritjula, who made what some might call a more *developed-world* living in the bauxite mines to the north-west of Baruda. With Whitey, Tom flew off in light aircraft to Perth and Darwin to discuss matters of housing and health with the appropriate ministers of state, who needed to be told that what the Arritjula wanted was not always what the Barramatjara wanted. Splinter groups, if you liked!

As well as that, news of the world, of the *Intifada* and Shamir and Yasir Arafat, came into Tom's settlement at Baruda by way of a large white dish installed the year before.

McCloud had in fact overheard Tom Gullagara discussing the Middle East with a girl at a party in New York. It had been the big news of the world that winter, and everyone's attention had not quite yet been seized by the first indices of great change in Eastern Europe.

"Do your people have contacts with the liberation fronts?" the girl had asked.

Tom had not at first been sure what she meant.

"The PLO for example?" she suggested.

"No," said Tom, reflectively sipping beer. "We never met any of them. Not those fellers."

He must have known that some city Aborigines, of tribes far from his, terrified suburban Australia by trying to talk with Arafat or Gaddafi. But the Barramatjara, who could speak some of the idioms of Christianity, had not yet been introduced to what you could call liberation-front idiom, to revolutionary jargon.

Until now, anyhow. Taliq had already indicated there might soon be seminars here in the plane.

The girl Tom had been speaking to at the time had been New York and Jewish and liberal. She had seemed to McCloud to stand enchanted within Tom's circle of tranquillity. She had told Tom energetically that the Palestinians should have a homeland.

"Yes," said Tom with an authoritative shyness, a lack of assertiveness which had proved itself strangely adequate to settle most arguments during the Barramatjara Dance Troupe's tour of the United States. "What I've seen, they get pushed around."

And although he could justly have impressed and horrified her with the history of the pushing round of the Barramatjara, of missionary follies and the treachery of cattle barons, of the arrogance of miners and the deceits of governments, he'd said nothing, keeping the Barramatjara chronicles deeply to himself, concealed in his own blood, where they meant something more than graphic tales for the cocktail hour.

In the continuing absence of Yusuf, full-blown conversations began to break out.

Daisy Nakamura addressed McCloud from across the aisle. "Can you beat it? My one and only international flight. My one and only first-class seat. And now my one and only hijack." She laughed musically. "I remember my father. He had a little shrine. Before ever he took off in his pick-up to sell vegetables along the road, he'd offer up some rice and saki. Maybe I should have done the same thing before I left Phoenix. Because – let me be the one to tell you! – he always came home okay."

McCloud saw her delicately-made shoulders trembling with laughter in the green dress. Old Ronnie Nakamura had known the score, putting her behind a bar to chatter and twinkle for lonely cowboys and truckers.

The handsome American man who had been the first to the lavatories now stood up in the aisle and turned to face his fellow-passengers. He held out his hands in a conciliatory gesture in front of him. Even in the dim light there was a gloss on his blue-black hair, hair soft and well-tended beyond the dreams of his emigrant ancestors. Perhaps, as was likely in such a perfected and deliberately ageless man, surgically implanted hair, so much more impeccable than the vegetable uncertainties of nature!

"Excuse me, ladies and gentlemen, while our hosts are out of the room. My name is Stone. I'm not unfamiliar with this sort of event. My corporation's done some studies on these matters. Enough to know the best hope we have here is solidarity with one another. Jew with Gentile, black with white."

Cale made a satiric face across the aisle at McCloud. "No shit, pardner," he said. He called then, "And how is this solidarity achieved, comrade?"

Stone would not be baited. "I can tell you with some degree of certainty that the first thing they will do is to subject some of us to special punishment on the basis of our backgrounds. Those who are not so selected will feel a distance developing between themselves and the punished. Believe me, this is the way it works. It's an age-old technique but it's been studied constructively only in this century. You understand what I mean, ladies and gentlemen. The ones *not* selected for treatment will feel reassured. They'll begin to tell themselves things. Such as: there's some way in which the ones being punished are different, are more guilty, more foolish. That's the trick we mustn't fall for. My friends, I urge you not to be duped . . ."

The man surveyed them with his blue, Eastern European and Manhattan eyes, and sat down.

Why are they permitting us to stand unsupervised and make speeches? McCloud wondered. Was it negligence, or itself a strategy?

In any case the American's speech had been given in a hushed and wary voice, suitable for the situation. Whereas Cale seemed to want something like an open debate. He began grumbling from his seat, loudly enough for most people in the compartment to hear, "You're right, my good friend. And it is some help to be forewarned, but – may I suggest? – very bloody little help. Because what's stronger, Mr Stone? Fraternity or – say – the resentment of America which many Europeans on board feel? What about the anti-Semitism which lies deep in all of us? Anti-Semitism which works so well, Mr Stone, that even in the deeps of his soul the Jew cries slogans against himself?"

A number of passengers hissed, not because they agreed or disagreed with Cale but because they could tell he was a boat-rocker, feverish, turbulent, indelicate.

The American businessman had turned round in his seat. "You speak like you're Jewish yourself."

For though Cale didn't look Jewish, he certainly looked like the man he had been describing: a man who detested and punished himself, who fed himself badly, who went in for systematic poisoning of his system, who clothed himself as negligently as any enemy would.

"I'm just your ugly *goy*, my friend," Cale cried out, laughing, "commenting on a great mystery."

"Rumour is we're civilised people," said the American. "Don't you believe a little solidarity is possible?"

Cale did not answer at first but gave a shrug the man, given the awkwardness of his backward-looking posture, couldn't see. "It depends how each of us looks them in the eye," he said then. "That's where salvation lies. For instance, how do we know that they've got a lode of *plastique* in the hold, as this Taliq chap claims? Do they really want to be consumed in a great blast? Maybe they do, maybe they don't. I can't guess. But I intend to show the buggers, in my demeanour, that I know it's a bluff, that I could call it at any second."

"For Christ's sake, don't take any risks," said one of the business-men. "You aren't out skiing, you know. You can't endanger yourself without endangering the lot of us."

Cale seemed to ignore this. "And by the way, how did they get these arms and the *plastique* aboard? Did they appeal to the solidarity of baggage handlers and luggage clerks? You bet your balls they did! They won them politically or they bought them or they most likely did both. I knew this would be one of the results of cracking down on the handlers! Putting television cameras in the baggage holds, stopping the lads creaming off a little jewellery here, a custom-made suspender belt there. It set them up as easy meat for boys like this."

"It doesn't matter," Stone asserted, "how they got their arms and the *plastique* aboard. We're stuck with the fact they did."

"In that case," said Cale, expanding the discussion, his chin raised like a schoolboy debater's, "we should remember that most of these people who've taken over here are mere infants. They will have spent time in the West, waiting for this Taliq and his superiors to call on them. They'll know Westerners of their own age. This means that they could go to a lot of trouble to assert their revol-utionary stance, to show that they haven't been softened up and seduced . . ."

The limpid-eyed Daisy Nakamura stared at him as he rose and put his hands in front of him professorially. Cale grinned, warming to the business of informing such a sublime hostage as Daisy. "They want to show us their fibre. They want to show whomsoever it is who paid to send them to the West – the Iraqi secret police, the Syrians, I don't know. But above all they want to show themselves."

Stone tried to resume what he had been saying earlier, but the unspeakable Cale drove over the top of him. "So, they're asking themselves can they manage to shoot one or more of us? And they're steeling themselves. And this makes them dangerous. But, you see, it makes them susceptible too."

The well-made businessman, Mr Stone, laughed. "So you know these guys, eh? Met their kind before?"

"I've spent time on their turf," admitted Cale. "In that sense I suppose I know them. What I'm saying is: watch the little buggers. You'll learn more that way than by depending on some sort of brotherhood with your fellow passengers."

McCloud was still frowning over the question of Cale/Bennett, and why a man who wanted to keep a secret should talk loudly and unnecessarily like that, when Bluey Kannata stood up in his place.

"Listen, I'm not patient enough for this sort of stuff. All this stuff about sticking together or looking them in the eye. I'm willing to rush them if you blokes are. Sod it!"

It seemed that some nihilism in Cale had infected Bluey. McCloud was pleased to see Wappitji trying to sit Bluey down as other passengers groaned.

Cale had begun laughing. "You chaps, you dancers! You can afford to sit tight. You're going to have privileged status on this flight. Believe me. They'll love you."

"Love us?" said Bluey. "Why would they love us?"

"Because they believe you've been cheated. Like them. Because they think you'd be likely to love them."

"I don't love those buggers," said Bluey. "And listen. I'm no-body's victim, nobody's favourite bloody exhibit. In the first place, I'm a paid-up member of Actors' Equity."

He'd said it with a jaunty, teasing smile. He often told people that. It was part of his professional vanity that like any man of gifts he didn't perform for nothing. "Some of them Africans," he'd told McCloud once, "go dancing round the world just for their keep and tucker. Supposed to be happy they're getting a trip to America! Bugger that for a joke. If you're good enough to perform in front of a paying crowd, you're good enough to earn a living like any other dancer!"

Acting in movies under the aegis of Actors' Equity had taught Bluey such propositions.

"Please, please, gentlemen," Stone was saying. "I'm just trying to prepare people. This wasn't meant to be a seminar."

Cale growled. "It's very kind of you to enlighten us, mate. Except the methods these people use – the people who have us – are more psychologically effective than any little corporate study can tell you."

McCloud could tell that Stone would have liked to stop talking, but Cale's wilful disinformation had to be answered. "That doesn't happen to be the truth. My corporation has advised governments in this very area . . ."

"All the more reason to keep your counsel, Mr Stone."

Cale, who had wanted to stay so obscure he'd put the weight of his alias on McCloud, moved forward now towards Stone, who in his ardour to advise the people of the cabin had himself begun to advance into the aisle.

"The size of the egos!" Daisy Nakamura remarked to McCloud.

"Okay, comrade," Cale/Bennett cried. "You say you want unity and you advise us against division. But we're already divided. We have here, on the other side of the aisle, representatives of an ancient race who have no reason to show solidarity with you and me. We aren't like a township, old chap. We have no ties of shared experience or blood or memory. In a plane, nobody knows his neighbour. No one belongs to the same Rotary Club or garden society as the person across the aisle. We're just a slice of the history of the world, grievances and all. My old son, this *solidarity* you urge is purest bloody fantasy in these circumstances. I wish to God you'd stop pushing that particular barrow."

Like everyone else, McCloud was beginning to feel anger towards both men. "Do you think they left us alone by accident?" he asked. "They left us alone to ensure we'd have an argument just like this."

There was a clatter of feet on the stairs leading from the upper deck. The dozen or so passengers who had been seated up there appeared briefly and were herded aft by the wiry young man in the cricket sweater whom Taliq had identified earlier as Musa. Yet the last time McCloud saw Musa he had been downstairs blocking the way to the rear of the plane. So Taliq's men were all moving, changing places, vanishing and appearing.

The clearing of the upper deck was an obvious arrangement for anyone taking illicit control of a plane to make, yet the sight of the mute transit of these passengers down the spiral staircase seemed to chasten everyone.

All the comforts the plane had to offer now seemed to McCloud used up, sucked dry. The air flowing from vents above his head turned at once more sour. It was at that time, with the jailhouse-like procession of the upstairs people, that the plane declared itself – without any ambiguity – a prison.

Our children, thought McCloud then. He and Pauline called them "the Boy" and "the Girl". The argot of the kitchen. It had all begun when they were so small that talking about them in the third person was normal, and then became habitual. They were prisoners too. Their breath and their education would be in suspension once this news got out, and it would reach them, since they were a little too old – eight and ten years – for people to hide newspaper headlines from them or switch channels when the news came on.

"Oh, my children," he murmured aloud. He'd always believed they would never have to carry any clan baggage, that they would not grow up to be the sort of men and women who were pointed out at parties. "Did you ever hear what happened to *their* parents?"

He had marked them by catching a hijacked plane. How could he make this up to them?

On the edge of sleep, McCloud suffered one of those sharply defined memories which occur at such times. On their first morning in New York, Bluey had invited him to go on a visit to an address a long way down the island, in what New Yorkers called "the Lower East". It was credible to McCloud that Bluey, who had been for a time a common figure on daytime television in New York, should have contacts all over the city.

The building he and McCloud came to that morning, however, was not some elegant condominium. It was one of those 1890s cast-iron structures, its façade tarnished by a subsequent, dirty century. Opposite its stoop and entryway stood a precinct house of the New York Police Department. Squad cars full of hefty Celts and tall Hispanics were double-parked in the street.

McCloud was astonished therefore when Bluey knocked at the first door on the left inside the building, paid over a $100 bill to a fat man who answered the knock, and received from him a clear plastic packet of white powder. Bluey placed the sachet casually in the pocket of his jacket. The fat man vanished into the dimness without a word.

McCloud took Bluey by the elbow and held him back from going out of the hallway onto the street. "Bluey, you might have noticed. There's a police station opposite this bloody place!"

"It's okay," the worldling Bluey reassured him. "I reckon if they're as close as that, Frank, they probably know something about it. Must be part of their retirement fund, eh?"

"But this is hopeless, Bluey," McCloud complained. "I don't mind so much that you're compromising me. You're compromising the troupe and the tour."

Bluey looked at him and the familiar, oblique smile came crookedly back. "Don't be a bloody old maid, Frank. It isn't your tour, mate. It's *our* tour. It's called the Barramatjara Dance Troupe, eh? Not the Frank McCloud bloody dance troupe."

"I never said it was mine. It's the others I feel sorry for." Because they were not members of Actors' Equity. They did not distinguish between the professional from Actors' Equity and the wanderer upon whom the hero ancestors breathed. They had never been to New York before or ingested powders so far up in the Caucasian scales of infamy as the powder in Bluey's sachet.

"Yeah." Bluey winked. "What'll the white racist bastards at home say about a junkie dancer, eh?"

"Look, if you don't think there's a chance of arrest . . . Well, I have to tell you there is one, that's all. I want you to hand me the powder, Bluey."

Bluey made a number of unbelieving noises. He produced the sachet and held it before McCloud's face. "I don't know if I ought to give you this, Frank. You white blokes have no self-control. Look what you're like with booze."

McCloud grabbed the sachet, rushed to a bank of letter boxes and pushed it inside the one nearest to hand. He expected Bluey's rage but was not prepared for the stuttering grief, the gasp of pain. Though it soon enough resolved itself into a kind of mockery. "Fuck you, McCloud. I know a dozen places I can get more."

All the way up Broadway that day, as far as the 20s, keeping by Bluey's side, McCloud had felt hunted and had listened for a siren, the one meant for him as distinct from the general cacophony of sirens in that city. Whereas Bluey could have been, *had the presence of* a city-wise American black who knew how the law advantaged him.

Then, as they waited together at a traffic light, Bluey turned to McCloud. "D'you know why this started, Frank? All the painting? All this dancing stuff? The souvenir programme says it all started when a schoolteacher called David Ransome put the idea to us. No one questions that, Frank. Every white fat-arse in the audience reads that and thinks, yes, it had to be something like that. And we're too polite to say otherwise."

"It's not the truth?"

"Not exactly, Frank."

The light changed to *Walk*, and at Bluey's side, McCloud made a troubled crossing of 21st Street. Bluey went to walk on, but McCloud took him by the lower arm.

"So. What should the programme notes say?"

"Whitey had a dream. It was full of important old men. More important than the old men at Baruda. And the old men said, *You've hung back, you've hung back, you haven't let the white blokes see us. If you gave them more, if you let them see more, it would change them.* That's when it started, all this. David Ransome could have saved his breath if it hadn't been for Whitey's dream. And the old men in Baruda are saying, *Don't dance this in front of the white feller, don't paint that.* But Whitey had the authority to dance and paint more than ever before. Not from some white artist but from his dream. Authority to civilise you poor people.

55

So that's what this tour's about, cobber. We're civilising you bastards. You know what Tom says? We're making you relatives! That's what Gullagara says."

This business of making the audience relatives had always fascinated McCloud, though he was not sure he understood it fully. To see the designs which belonged to a particular person's dreaming or mystery, you needed to be a relative. Did Tom Gullagara's statement mean that Whitey and the others were admitting people to designs and dances only relatives usually saw? The size of a gesture like this shook and shamed McCloud.

For he too had swallowed the schoolteacher story, grabbing for the European-style cause even in a world where causes were never so mechanical. He had swallowed the Ransome story with the same readiness as any amateur ethnographer or stockbroker dance-fiend in the stalls. He had not had even a suspicion that things might be different.

"Do you think we're submissive like that?" Bluey mocked him. "A schoolteacher tells us it's a good idea and shows us a pot of acrylic, and we call out, *Yes, no worries, sir. We've got the paintings you need! Yes, boss. No worries, Bwana. Sure thing, sir!*"

"It's so obvious, Bluey," McCloud admitted in a daze. "When you put it like that."

Before his eyes then, that day in New York, Bluey grew forgiving and laughed. It was that old-fashioned thing they used to call glee. "I could have told Whitey. I could have told him, *Give 'em whatever you like. But they won't see what it is. They'll make out of it what they want to see.* But, see, you can't argue with a bloke's dreams. He's got a lot of authority, Whitey."

"Maybe he's right. Maybe people are getting the message. The reviews have been superb!"

"Well, you know reviewers, Frank. They don't review things outside themselves. They review the insides of their own heads. If they find space in there for you, then the reviews *are* what you call *superb*." He imitated McCloud's city accent, so different from his own, since his had been laid down by the Spanish and the Lutherans, the cattlemen and the miners of a rough era. "Listen, McCloud, I'm going to find some bastard who's dealing, and you're not coming with me. Because you're bloody expensive, mate."

"No," McCloud begged him. "Don't buy any of that stuff."

Bluey tossed his head and jogged away, inserting himself deftly into the narrow spaces between pedestrians. It was useless to follow. He had disappeared with ease.

The memory of that day, of the wrong information in the programme notes, disturbed McCloud on the edge of sleep. If he had so misread the Barramatjara, who had no malice towards him, how could he read Taliq and the boys?

He fretted at that question, and then spent a further phase of torment over the Girl and the Boy, before being taken suddenly and in the midst of anguished insomnia by sleep.

He was awakened, as many aboard the plane must have been, by light. All the lights in the cabin had been turned on, and there was a blush of dawn coming up from the south and showing under the merest crack of window blind. Either in defiance or by accident, Tom Gullagara had not closed the shade the whole way. All around people were stirring and stretching, and beautiful Daisy Nakamura rubbed her ivory jawline, reviving herself.

Taliq led the good-looking Yusuf, son of a tailor, up the aisle to the front of the cabin. They both halted by the seat of Stone, the businessman who had counselled everyone towards solidarity.

"You have two passports!" Taliq told the man. "You must have a diplomatic one you haven't shown us."

"I don't understand what you're saying," the American told Taliq calmly.

Taliq turned to Yusuf. "Shoot the man next to him. Shoot him dead in his seat."

McCloud couldn't see the man who sat next to the businessman, could see only a balding head there.

"No," said Stone. "You're right. I have another passport, but it's in my luggage. I don't have it here."

"Shoot the man next to him," Taliq told Yusuf again. McCloud heard the automatic weapon click as Yusuf did something with it – set it to single shot, perhaps, for fear of puncturing the plane's skin. There seemed no hesitation in Yusuf. To McCloud, all this appeared both astounding and normal. The tailor's son about to shoot dead a neighbour whose features had barely been seen or remembered by the rest of the passengers.

"It's in my briefcase," said the handsome American businessman in the aisle seat. "Please. Allow me to get it?"

He stood up and fetched a briefcase out of a knee locker which lay on the far side of the threatened man with the bald head. He stood, put the briefcase on his seat, produced a passport from it and handed it to Taliq.

"Earlier, I said *all passports*," Taliq told him reasonably.

"I'm sorry," said the businessman. "I don't make use of that one very much."

"Especially not in Arab nations," said Taliq nearly indulgently. He looked fresh, as if he might have had some sleep himself. He began to leaf the American's second passport like any average immigration officer. "And certainly not in this situation. You use this one to travel to Israel, and various countries friendly to her. When the Daniel Stone of your normal passport becomes the Ivrim Steinberg of this special passport of yours. I take it you work for someone influential. Without being too melodramatic about it, for your government or for the Israelis or for someone's Department of Defence . . . "

"My company has some electronic contracts with a number of governments, that's all. We all need to make a living, Mr Taliq."

"Some of us do, it seems."

"I have a doctorate from Caltech in cybernetics. Surely you don't expect me to earn my keep selling vacuum cleaners? I have considerable respect for your people."

"Your respect will grow, Mr Stone. Please undress to your underwear. Take off your shoes and your watch and kneel in the aisle."

"You're not serious!"

Taliq turned to Yusuf. "Shoot the Zionist bastard now," he told the boy.

McCloud inspected Yusuf again and saw that he was pale but intent, his spirit coiled up for the act. McCloud thought it seemed very early in the enterprise to be making death threats. According to his reading, all that was supposed to begin after the issuing of some ultimatum to officials safe on the ground?

"Please, I'll do it," said Daniel Stone.

He took off his tie and his handmade shirt – McCloud could see a D.S. monogrammed on the striped pocket as it fell to the floor. He folded his trousers on the seat, picked up the shirt and folded it on top of them, and took off his shoes. He was as lean, sinewy, and broad-shouldered out of his suit as in it. Americans called it *working out*. This Stone fellow worked out. Though he himself might have been as much as ten years younger than Stone, McCloud knew he could not have stripped with the same credit.

Taliq next told the American to kneel. Stone obeyed. His thighs and calves were tanned and seemed to have a healthy residue of oil as if, just before leaving for the airport, Mr Stone had had a rubdown. Disrobing, instead of undermining the man's dignity, had somehow confirmed it.

"I reckon I'd let him play in my football team," Tom Gullagara murmured with approval.

Taliq and Yusuf left Stone kneeling and progressed down the aisle, and for a second McCloud feared they were coming to punish Tom for his whimsical observation. But they stopped at Cale. Or Bennett, as McCloud now had to remember to call him. Cale was smoking a cigarette with his accustomed avidity.

"Mr Bennett," said Taliq. He lit a cigarette of his own as he spoke and drew on it. "I want your other passport please."

Cale burrowed his shoulders into his seat and answered drowsily. "I simply don't have another passport, old son."

"I give you credit for being professional, Mr Bennett," Taliq reasoned. "Give me some credit in return. This plane is equipped with five radios. Two of them long distance. We have read your passport number to our associates on the ground and they tell us that you have a second passport. And they are of sufficient eminence and influence to know these things."

"That's nonsense, sonny," said Cale. "Do I look to you like a man important enough to bother with a second passport?"

Taliq turned to Yusuf, at the same time pointing to Daisy Nakamura who sat behind Cale/Bennett. "This woman is an American citizen. We'll lose no credit in our world for shooting her."

McCloud thought that a curious term. *Lose no credit.*

Yusuf's eyes turned quite predatorily to Daisy Nakamura. It was frightening to see the distance the young man contemptuous of Asian stitching had moved, yet his present willingness to consider shooting Daisy did not seem a break from his earlier, conversational, flirtatious self. It was just another face of that exaltation of fright, that revolutionary intent, that fixity of will which mad Cale had earlier described.

McCloud heard someone say, "That's ridiculous." He didn't know that it was himself until Taliq turned to him. And now he must say more or be left to drift with those two banal words for buoyancy.

"She's American, yes, but Japanese-American," he explained.

"If you're concerned with the dispossessed, then her people fit your description. Don't you know your bloody history?"

He let a heady anger swell that question. He was determined not to be cowed. Maybe this was like the brave fury which moved mad Cale. He wondered where this bravery and folly came from. But he felt a duty to embrace it and to finish his argument. "Or is it only one section of history you're interested in?"

"Well said, old fellow," said Cale/Bennett.

Taliq turned his attention to Daisy Nakamura and studied her for some time under her new status as specimen of history. McCloud too watched her. If Taliq adjudged her a victim, then she and McCloud were both saved. Under Taliq's gaze, Daisy looked levelly ahead, neither hanging her head nor taking on Taliq's gaze. McCloud noticed that she swallowed, and her throat was appallingly white.

"What does the woman herself say?" Taliq asked the cabin at large. "Is she an American or isn't she?"

"Mr Taliq," Daisy announced, "I'm a registered Barry Goldwater Republican, and an American, and newly widowed. I don't appreciate this. You'll get no trouble from me, but you won't get me to say I'm someone I'm not. Aside from that, I haven't even owned *one* passport until August last."

Taliq nodded. He flexed the fingers of his right hand in front of him. McCloud noticed scarring on the knuckles and the back of the hand, and it seemed the gesture was meant to get the muscles working. Or else it was hesitation. He brought the hand down and laid it briefly over Daisy's on the armrest of her seat. He exerted an emphatic pressure for a few seconds. It looked to McCloud like reassurance and even a sort of claim.

Producing a pistol then, he turned and pushed its muzzle beneath Cale's left eye.

"From the Crusades onwards, the English have been the instigators of all our grief. *That's* history I do know. Find me your passport, please."

McCloud was alarmed to sense in himself the magnetic drag of Cale's nihilism. Cale – you could tell – sat there considering whether after all this mightn't be the appropriate time to perish.

Twenty seconds afterwards McCloud, trembling, found it fascinating to consider what it must have been which turned the balance. The thought of a girlfriend in London? An unfinished manuscript? A sick wife? Or a concern that once the hijackers made one execution, they would become habituated to it, and active terror would supplant the present passive version.

In any case, Cale got his briefcase from beneath the seat in front of him, opened it, unzipped an inner compartment and produced a second passport. Taliq considered it, leafing its pages. When he spoke, it was to demand the same of Cale as he had of the American businessman.

The condition of Cale's clothes as they came off and of his body as it was revealed was not edifying to watch. McCloud noticed that Daisy Nakamura averted her eyes until, groaning and flinching like an arthritic, Cale knelt.

In the aisle Taliq walked to middle ground between the two kneelers. He considered for a while the now obvious scar tissue on the back of his hand and the cigarette which emerged from the mess of healed skin and knuckle. Then he raised his head and addressed the passengers again.

"These two are our enemies," he said wearily. The weight of turpitude the earth and even the air held seemed to oppress him. "Mr Stone is a Zionist and does business with Mossad. Mr Cale, who tried to pass himself off as Mr Bennett, is a notorious Zionist of the London right-wing press."

From his kneeling position, Cale said, "I am not a Zionist. Not in your sense. Look at me, for Christ's sake. What sort of fucking threat am I to you, comrade?"

Taliq spoke quietly to his acolyte. "He had his chance to be brave. If he speaks again, execute this man."

And Taliq put his ruined, cigarette-holding hand on McCloud's wrist, and was so close for a moment that McCloud could smell his musk again, the aftershave and the gamey redolence of his strength of purpose.

Cale did not speak and Taliq lifted his hand, which had held both Daisy's wrist and McCloud's, and left the compartment. In his wake, McCloud watched Cale scratching his armpit. He felt intimately connected to the man. Cale wore a most unmuscular undergarment, what the English called a vest and the Australians a singlet. His underpants were linen and voluminous, not athletic at all but unexpectedly pristine. Kneeling, he looked like a fat boy under punishment in a boarding-school. But not a vulnerable fat boy. A dangerous one who dreamed up humiliations for the staff.

Terrified at the risks he had already taken, McCloud felt tears prick his eyes for his potentially orphaned children – the Boy and the Girl. Waking to be told the news, or being called out of class to receive it.

He'd thought earlier of himself in the mass of passengers, and – though they had primacy amongst all other children – of them as sharing somehow in the communal anxieties of the mass of passengers' children. But he had deliberately brought himself to Taliq's attention. He had been for a time and in a sense Taliq's pre-eminent passenger and so Taliq's pre-eminent candidate for a bullet. Again, he knew well, having written about it for the past three years, how oddities of event altered a child. He and Pauline had both been children of sudden and yet not outrageous or particularly memorable oddities of direction. How much more would his children be marred if they became hijack orphans!

Was it possible too, McCloud asked himself, that Pauline was taking risks with Hasni at the rear of the plane?

The lights remained on after Taliq had gone. An unacknowledged day prevailed beyond the windows. McCloud exchanged a tight smile with Daisy Nakamura the Arizonan. Yusuf seemed to notice it. For he walked down the aisle and stood above Daisy. Some minutes before he had been ready to execute her, so there was a certain unreality, McCloud thought, about his sudden air of Levantine charmer.

"Do you have a boyfriend?" he asked her pleasantly.

"I'm a widow, son," she said. "And you wouldn't believe it, but I'm old enough to be your mother."

"You are a very beautiful woman," said Yusuf, shy and assertive at the same time. His hips trembled. If she'd been at a café table he would have done a little seducer's dance around it.

"Son, let me say . . . I don't turn on for men with automatic weapons," said Daisy Nakamura, unyielding.

In Yusuf's eyes there appeared something between anger and regret. Closer to regret, however, than to the other.

"Like any soldier in a total war," he said, "I am under orders. Does this mean I have no finer feelings? Ma'am, all of us, my brothers and I . . . we are all men of sensitive emotions and educational ambitions. We would all be richer if we forgot our people and became doctors and engineers and lived in San Diego, and sent an occasional sentimental donation to those who are fighting the battle. Right? And then we would not have had to take jetplanes over. Right? And wave automatic weapons at beautiful women."

Daisy shook her head, but with an expression of lenient reproof even McCloud in his anxiety found charming. It was as if she were lumping Yusuf's behaviour in with all the other male mysteries, all the cowboy perversities of Budapest, all the crassness, drinking, whoring and telling of lies.

Yusuf of course could sense at once he might be partially forgiven, though Daisy said nothing.

"It's sad the world does not let me take the normal course, ma'am. I would rather drink brandy with you than meet you like this. But my family is a family without a home and a nation. We once had a home, in Jaffa, where my grandfather is buried. What sort of man would I be if I forgot that? I would be untrue to his memory if I did not carry arms."

"Oh, Jesus!" Cale said from his position on the floor, though Yusuf did not seem to hear him.

"My grandfather's buried in an internment camp in the Rockies," said Daisy Nakamura with a small shake of her shoulders. How exquisitely adamant she was. "You don't find me threatening to shoot people aboard aircraft."

Before the force of her continuing contempt, Yusuf smiled behind his seducer's moustache. McCloud felt a sudden improper pity for him. If the *plastique* was not detonated, he, Yusuf, more than anyone else on the plane apart from his *brothers*, had such a strong statistical chance of becoming a casualty. For it was established, he'd read somewhere, that the deathrate amongst the inflictors of terror was – in relation to those they imposed terror on – very high. And like Hasni in the rear of the aircraft, Yusuf was just a child, overarmed, overinformed of the past, instilled with awesome motives, and yet ecstatic at any attention at all from a woman of Daisy Nakamura's compelling presence.

"You know how to make me walk," said Yusuf. "But you won't make Taliq walk. Let me tell you, women are hypnotised by that guy Taliq."

"I can't wait, sonny," said Daisy. "Meanwhile, why not let these gentlemen kneeling here sit in their seats? They're not going anywhere."

Yusuf did not answer, but smiled. A lustful boy content to leave the conquests to an older man. A *brother*, as Hasni put it.

Hasni, the polite reader of news magazines, appeared in the compartment. He spoke to Yusuf in Arabic. Yusuf went to the front of the compartment and ordered Whitey Wappitji, principal dancer, to stand up and move down the aisle.

McCloud, his hams trembling, stood up as a manager should and blocked Whitey's passage.

"Where are you taking my friend Mr Wappitji?" he asked Yusuf.

"It's okay," said Whitey with that long-browed, lean-featured authority which was his forte – a Barramatjara characteristic, in fact, of which he and Tom Gullagara were the main exponents amongst the dancers. "It's cool, Frank."

He'd picked up that *cool* from lighting and other technicians at the Mark Taper in Los Angeles, at the Kennedy Center in Washington, at the Lincoln Center in New York. It wasn't his usual idiom. He gave a slow, solemn wink, but it was more than the normal insider's rictus. It was a command.

"You just look after yourself, Frank," he advised McCloud. "See, I think *we*'re all jake with this mob . . ." He nodded towards Yusuf. "I'm not so sure everyone else is."

Look after yourself, mate . . . we're all jake. The oddments of Australian English Whitey had picked up working on cattle stations in his youth. No doubt a flash horseman, a real gun, as all the tribespeople of the central and western deserts of Australia had a reputation for being.

Having barely seen a horse before 1900, the Barramatjara had at first considered the horseman and the beast the one animal. In the spirit of that first sighting – which was after all within living memory – when they rode they became in turn the one, rhythmic animal. *Flash horseman*, they said. *Gun rider.* The sublimest praise.

But what was the texture of the Barramatjara tongue itself? McCloud knew only occasional words. He had heard of Malu the Kangaroo Ancestor. He knew from Bluey that *badunjari* were journeys undertaken in sleep or in trance, and that Bluey was plagued by a form of *badunjari* as others might be by migraine. He knew from casual conversation that *djimari* was a knife, and that *redjabu* was their name for Baruda, the central Barramatjara settlement.

But these were oddments, and he could only guess how much better the Barramatjara language, after such a long residence in the desert, fitted the Barramatjara earth than the most plenteous and rich of English might. For English, Portuguese or French or any other come-lately tongue, McCloud surmised, must be a very loose tool to apply to the Australian deserts.

If only Wappitji had that subtle option to talk to Taliq in, instead of the few tokens, the few loose spanners and wrenches of English which were spoken in remotest Australia! How would *jake with this mob* come up in Barramatjara, if you had the gift to see Barramatjara from the inside? That was something on which they'd never given McCloud any intimation. Nor, though they were members of a waning language group, had they ever expressed aloud to him a sense of loss or a reproach.

Wappitji and Yusuf passed McCloud and went upstairs. Hasni was left. His eyes met McCloud's. They were as young as Yusuf's but lacking in Yusuf's sensual ambition. Hasni was in a way beautiful – he had the sort of translucent, spiritual and epicene Arab beauty which, according to the latest word on the matter, had excited T. E. Lawrence.

He said, "Your wife is well and tells you not to worry."

After all the threats of the past quarter hour, and even with Cale kneeling half-naked and flaccid in the aisle, McCloud became suffused with a dangerous gratitude towards this clear-faced young man. He chose to fight it just the same.

"Thank you. Would you let her join me here?"

Hasni smiled painfully. You could see in the smile that he was wound up tightly like Yusuf. Yet at the same time he seemed to cherish the vanity of being thought the considerate hijacker.

"Well, if not that," said McCloud, "tell her to take care of herself and sit still and wait. You *can't* disapprove of that advice."

"No, that is our advice to everyone. Except for those who must kneel."

"Is that necessary. Surely they can sit . . .?"

"No, they can't. And you know why?" Hasni was shaking his head didactically. "They're kneeling to show they're separate from the rest of you. Okay? You understand that?"

"We understand it all right," said McCloud. He took the chance of saying, "It's exactly what some of us guessed would happen."

Hasni did not like that. He had a young zealot's sudden onset of lack of humour. "Make shrewd guesses all you want, Mr McCloud. You won't keep up with us. You won't keep up with Taliq anyhow."

The radio at his hip began to chirp amongst his leather-pouched grenades; sufficient there for mayhem or a violent siege.

Hasni lifted the instrument and punched a button. McCloud couldn't stop himself flinching, on the chance that some electrical quirk set off the *plastique* in the hold. Hasni listened to the thing with a frown, made an answer and returned the radio to his belt. He went to the front seat and ordered Bluey Kannata to stand up, then Mungina the *didj* player and Philip Puduma, the balding Christian dancer. Next he leaned across McCloud's lap and gestured that Tom Gullagara should stand up too.

"Excuse me, mate," said Tom Gullagara, rising and passing into the aisle. He looked wary, and McCloud could see he was being brave. Tom didn't know what any of this separating out meant. He was sure though that *they* had the power to do it.

McCloud half stood in his seat. "We are a dance troupe. I'm the manager appointed at the request of the dancers." That was very nearly the truth. "Where they go, I have to go too."

"No," said Hasni. Even in refusal, he showed some of that American college-boy courtliness. "You are not to come, sir. They have been under your management too long."

"They haven't been *under my management*, as you put it. But they are prodigiously talented people and I'm responsible for their convenience and well-being."

Except of course when Pauline took all that over and he, McCloud, became merely a counsellor and boozing companion.

Hasni held up a hand. "No. You have no responsibility. Not any more. Didn't you ever question whether they are capable of being responsible for themselves?"

"They *are* responsible. But someone has to order transportation from the airport to the hotel to the venue. Do you want them to have to do all that and dance as well?"

Bluey Kannata drew level with McCloud. "You're not coming too, Frank?"

"They say not."

"Jesus, mate. Who'll pour the beer?"

And Bluey, movie star and dancer, laughed in his uproarious, brittle way. He was no more afraid than he might usually be. No more bewildered than when he won Best Actor at the Toronto Film Festival, or when his film won the Gold Palm at Cannes. No more in trepidation than when he was plagued with *badunjari* dream journeys, or believed that his uncle had been fatally cursed.

As McCloud watched the Barramatjara Dance Troupe ascending towards Taliq, he believed that for the moment they were in danger from nothing but rhetoric. Though Gullagara and Wappitji might regularly shake hands and make deals with politicians, though their profound gaze might compel and alter the crassest parliamentarian, they were not used to fitting their daily arguments to the language

66

of twentieth-century revolutions. They were going upstairs, therefore, to be given these new implements of discourse, this lexicon
of insurrection. Taliq would imbue them with the jargon, and
although God knew they had grounds to be revolutionaries, it
would all be unfamiliar terminology to them. They would sit
mutely and politely while the words were cast like dice – *the
international proletariat, the Zionist conspirators, the imperialist
cartel.* As they had mutely sat while the cattlemen dealt them terms
like *flash, guns, cleanskin* cattle, and taught them to expect that
everything would be *jake.*

There was a chance, surely, that one or two of the dancers might
find in the terminology of Taliq's revolution a weapon or a device
by which to unleash the fury they *should* – McCloud assured
himself he would be the first to acknowledge it! – feel.

Yet it didn't seem credible of these laughing cowboys and stars
of the dance. The greater danger was probably that Taliq would
take their silent and customary politeness as a rejection and an
insult.

In the absence of the dancers, McCloud hungered even more to see
Pauline who was – in her own sense – dispossessed. Though her
birthright had not been stolen by any nation, by anyone who owned
a jet, her parents had none the less been forced forth from their
accustomed track. She too had been a marked child and a child of
exile. Maybe not, however, sufficient for her to be taken upstairs –
to Taliq's zone of kindness and instruction – with the dancers!

And then handsome Taliq returned. As he stood over Daisy Nakamura, he held a colour magazine in his hand, one of the glossy
American weeklies.

"Madam," he said, "you must forgive what happened earlier.
Events move very quickly and often in a confused manner." Again,
he put a hand gently, stylishly over Daisy's wrist. It was an older
man's performance of the same gesture Yusuf had tried on her
earlier. "We are living at a terrible pace," he sighed.

"Yes," said Daisy, giving nothing. "I'd guess, about five hundred
miles an hour."

"Come, come," said the chief hijacker in his old-fashioned
British style. "You know what I mean."

He increased the minor pressure. His hand was large and at the
same time militant and subtle.

"Oh dearie, Mr Taliq," said Daisy. She was frowning. "How
did you get into this business?"

"Madam, if we are delayed by other parties and suffer their prevarications, you may have the leisure to discover that."

They all talked like that, McCloud noticed. They liked to pretend that what they were doing was the equivalent of any other exacting profession.

Taliq withdrew his hand from Daisy's wrist, patted her shoulder deftly and for a second with the rolled magazine in his other hand, and turned then to McCloud.

"Mr McCloud," he said. There was a certain reproof in his voice but it sounded beneficent. "You must read this. The Zionist press itself. Did you think it published nothing but praise for the dancers? This item condemns you. Not me, but you."

He thrust the magazine, opened at a given page, into McCloud's hands. A childish nausea rose in McCloud. Taliq could have been a teacher handing back a sloppy essay and demanding that it be exposed with all its gaps to the whole class.

"Go on," Taliq urged him. "Take your time and read it."

In the middle of the print he noticed a colour photograph of the Barramatjara Dance Troupe in mid-choreography. Whitey was centre-stage, a startling figure, his breast marked with diagonals of white and ochre lightning, his midriff streaked with waves of white. His left knee was bent and raised, and his left foot tucked in above the joint of the right leg. In both hands he held bunches of eagle feathers. In this potent photograph, metamorphosis – man to bird – seemed only an instant away.

In the same picture Phil the Christian, armed with a spear, stalked Whitey from the perimeter of the stage, and Paul Mungina crouched, cheeks inflated, in the act of making the *didj* wail. The caption read, "Barramatjara Dance Troupe – Who's paying the piper?"

"I haven't seen this article before," McCloud stated.

"Today's edition, Mr McCloud," said Taliq. "Copies would have just made it to the aircraft. A misfortune for you, though the dancers are praised in the review pages. But read!"

There was also a photograph of Bluey Kannata in one of his film roles – a grinning antediluvian cowboy on a horse. One being. *Gun rider*.

The article began by listing the various indices of the dance troupe's New York success. A reception at Lincoln Center, frenzied accla- mation in the *New York Times*. A seminar at the Juilliard, a welcoming from the city's mayor, and limousines all the way.

McCloud felt the normal inside-reader's pulse of irritation at these last two items. There had been few limousines, simply the rented van about whose parking Gullagara had asked the meter question. And the embattled mayor had not appeared, but had delegated instead his cultural commissar to make a small speech of greeting. McCloud irrationally resolved to remember these falsehoods and bring them up at the right moment. They might be able to be used as a defence, when he knew what it was he was to defend himself against.

But was the success and renown of the Barramatjara Dance Troupe a spontaneous phenomenon? the article asked. Or had it been engineered? An Australian leftist politician whose name McCloud dimly knew had claimed in the Australian parliament in Canberra that the CIA had an interest in the Barramatjara traditional ground in the Australian desert. They had made an "as yet secret proposal" to build a satellite tracking and communications station there, on Barramatjara freehold earth. The politician had wondered whether the great dance tour was merely a means of softening up the elders, some of whom were members of the troupe?

It was, the politician in Canberra argued, an outrage to people of this ancient, gifted race to keep them ignorant of the satellite station plan and at the same time fête them in America.

But it was not only the CIA who were pursuing a secret agenda, the politician had asserted. The second largest diamond driller in the world, a company named Highland Pegasus, had discovered a potential industrial diamond field on the western edge of the Barramatjara land. Although the Barramatjara people had given permission for the drilling, the results were being kept from them, and one of the most influential Barramatjara leaders, a man named Whitey Wappitji, had – at a crucial time – been neutralised by his membership of the touring dance troupe. When Highland Pegasus had announced its find, Mr Wappitji and his lieutenant Tom Gullagara had been as far from Barramatjara country as both the CIA and Highland Pegasus could have wished. Both instrumentalities, said the politician, turning ironic, would have preferred an Arctic tour for the dance troupe, but New York wasn't a bad alternative.

McCloud was familiar with the fact that Highland Pegasus was a sponsor of the tour. Their name appeared discreetly in the list of sponsors on the inner back page of the dance programme. A memorable name, with its overtones of kilts, claymores and flying horses, even though third or fourth in a small-print roster.

McCloud looked up at Taliq, who drew on a cigarette and watched him with an aquiline intent, waiting for a confession of movement in his face.

I am trussed and delivered up guilty, McCloud thought.

Despite the growth of peaceful intentions on earth, the Americans seemed to like the deserts of Australia. They went to them to build white domes from which the passage of satellites across the firmament could be measured. From sky-eyes governed by the decisions of men sitting in bunkers in the centre of the continent, the emissions of rocket firings in China and Central Asia could be read. The mail of a dangerous cosmos.

So he had heard of the CIA and their yen for Australian wildernesses. But when it came to Highland Pegasus, he didn't even know what they did for a living. He had had no idea that they had taken a mining lease on Barramatjara ground. The entire continent of Australia was covered with an invisible grid of mining leases. But, of course, his ignorance might be the point Taliq was pushing. Or perhaps Taliq thought him an accomplice in this plot to do with satellites and mining, an officer of the conspiracy!

McCloud had an impulse to say to Taliq, "All I wanted to do was to come to New York to sell my novel." But he knew at once how blameworthy that would sound. Not only that, he understood – beneath Taliq's gaze – how blameworthy it *was*.

He temporised and went back to the text of the magazine article. When he could no longer pretend to be reading, he raised his eyes again, expecting once more to meet Taliq's avian stare. In fact, though, Taliq's attention had moved back to Daisy Nakamura.

In the aisle, the kneeling Cale held the index and middle fingers of his right hand together and waved them in the air, like a man invoking luck. The luck, that is, of an attraction growing between Daisy and Taliq.

"Is something a problem?" Daisy asked the hijacker.

"You do not understand us, madam?" said Taliq. "It is the same as with the other passengers. We don't seem real to you."

Daisy closed her eyes for a time, before opening them and staring ahead. "Mr Taliq, let me say you seem real enough. You've got two guys kneeling in their Fruit of the Looms in the aisle. That's *real* real in my book."

Cale shook his head, as if he wished Daisy would take a softer line.

"Yes," said Taliq softly. "You pay attention to what we do. But you can't understand why it's done."

Yet he smiled so jovially at her that McCloud felt a curious envy. *She* was not being handed press reports which confirmed her culpability.

Now he turned back to McCloud again.

"Well, Mr McCloud? How is your reading?"

"I know nothing about any of this," said McCloud, handing the magazine back to Taliq. "If I had known, I wouldn't have travelled with the troupe."

"There are little folk dance troupes all over the world. They perform in church halls and attract polite if befuddled applause. Weren't you surprised when this one drew all that fuss, Mr McCloud? All that support? All those limousines?"

"There weren't limousines. That's journalistic excess."

"But such a fuss!" Taliq insisted. "Did the Micmac or the Sioux ever cause such a furore?"

"They're very good," said McCloud of the Barramatjaras. "They're absolutely compelling, for God's sake. And they do the painting as well. And I suppose on top of that they might have novelty value."

"Oh, I see," said Taliq, laughing without feigning it, "the curious savages, what? But I agree with you. They have great novelty. For one thing, they sit on diamond fields untainted by apartheid! That augments their novelty immensely."

It was apparent now: Taliq did believe that Francis McCloud was a stooge, an agent of international deceit.

"Do you know what?" the Palestinian asked him gently. "You will become anxious for punishment. Believe me. I can tell that. You already know about yourself what we have just discovered."

McCloud knew that if, within, he accepted Taliq's shrewd dictum he was finished.

"I am guilty of vanity and stupidity," he cried out, and for once it was not his all too familiar *mea culpa*. "But I would never knowingly dupe them. They're my friends, for God's sake! I sought them out because I was impressed by what they did. I wrote articles about them. I'm aware of the ironies of their situation, yes. But I contributed in a small way to their renown."

*   *   *

71

Within three minutes, though, McCloud had – at Taliq's order – divested himself of his outer clothing, his watch and his shoes, and was kneeling in the aisle behind Cale and within his sour ambience.

When Taliq left the compartment, and the boy Hasni – who had returned from delivering the dancers upstairs – was distracted, Cale muttered over his shoulder. "You know why they're doing this to us?"

"No," said McCloud.

Cale said, "Because it works."

McCloud wondered what the beautiful Nakamura thought of his legs, gone a little flaccid from three sedentary years of novel writing, and of his flesh pallid, he was sure, with fear. But this question was small by comparison with the truth of what Cale had muttered: that it was all working. He felt in his mouth the salt of condemnation. Like a child cornered by older and more mysterious children, he was sure he gave off a sour musk of punishability. He wanted to urinate, and this only seemed to compound his blame.

If the news report was correct, he thought, then the Barramatjara Dance Troupe had been badly used. He too was aware of having meanly used them in passing, as a vehicle to bring his novel to New York. It might have been better if he had been the agent of malice Taliq thought him to be. His villainy would have given him more to resist Taliq with. His mere opportunism seemed despicable, left him without the sort of saving anger which tightens the musculature of the thorough-going miscreant.

He knew the Barramatjara would be lenient on him. The Barramatjara were gone, however. On their final migration. Upstairs.

4

MARSUPIAL RAT

THE ancestors of the Barramatjara came to the Australian desert some ice ages past across the shallow-bedded pools and spits of land which once connected parts of New Guinea and Indonesia to the great southern continent. Once, so long ago that it was not even referred to in their vivid mythic accounts of the Barramatjara beginnings, they had lived along a northern tropical coast. But unrecorded pressure from other immigrants arriving behind them, or else some forgotten voice of the kind which drove the Israelites into Sinai or sent the Anasazi Indians out of their fine cliff-dwellings at Mesa Verde, compelled them a thousand miles southwards into the deserts.

The Barramatjara anyhow, unlike historians, did not believe they originated anywhere but in the Barramatjara desert country. They believed indeed that they had always occupied that place, with its unexpected charms and bounties. Their ancestors had handmade it for them, sometimes through robust folly, sometimes through dazzling style and wisdom. For the Barramatjara ancestors displayed all the human qualities.

The people re-enacted the earth-compounding journeys of their ancestors through dance and ceremonial and ochre sand paintings. Their dance and their paintings were liturgy and a kind of physics, a remaking of the eternal earth the ancestors had given them.

But perhaps five years past, as the programme notes of the dance troupe announced, a white teacher came to the Barramatjara settlement called Baruda and persuaded some of the men to combine the painting and the dance into a remarkable one-day entertainment for city people.

The dancer/depictors began by touring the universities. They became a rage. Soon they were performing in theatres in Adelaide, Melbourne, in natural amphitheatres in Sydney. There, one lotus-eating summer's evening, Pauline and McCloud and the two children, equipped with picnic basket, iced orange juice and chardonnay, saw the Barramatjara Dance Troupe perform.

The ancestors had combined human and animal characteristics, sometimes at the one time, sometimes serially, now man, now totem creature. Whitey and the lads had caught from the ancestors therefore a startling gift for animal mimicry, to a degree which transcended imitation and nudged at the edges of metamorphosis.

McCloud and Pauline had seen the casual corroborees Northern Territory aborigines, brought in from the reservation by bus, performed in Alice Springs and Katherine; the dancing of mere tales, of fables fit for children. In those events a kind of justifiable kidding of the callow, suburban travellers was in progress. Just to drive home the point that nothing of heavy worth was being given away, the dancers asked men and women up on the stage or out into the clearing at the end of the show and provoked them, against the mocking background music of the *didj*, to weave about clumsily, manically, painfully.

There was none of that jokiness about the Barramatjara dancers McCloud first saw in the Sydney dark. You felt rightly or wrongly that you were being admitted to serious and even dangerous transmutations. McCloud's children were spellbound by the hairsbreadth nature of what was happening. Would these men return from being emu or wallaby? And then – five minutes later – would they come back from the rim of incarnation as the cassowary? They were playing all the time at that gate between humankind and the rest of nature, the gate which most people had felt bound to close shut so that the city and the steam train, the automobile and the jet, the computer and the garbage compactor could occur. The dancers sucked and weaved you towards the door of loss and bid fair to drag you through it. They let you off that experience only after you had suffered delicious shock and exaltation.

The evening McCloud first saw the dancers left him in a state very close to literal enchantment. He felt that a door in the face of his own continent had been opened, and that he had glimpsed through it a garden of unsuspected wonders. He talked a magazine editor into letting him travel to Baruda to see the dancers in their homes

74

and to write something about them. They were by now famous throughout the nation – although Bluey had been famous in his own right for the past ten years. Like Bluey, the others had calmly, almost negligently, let themselves now be persuaded to sign on with various film agents.

So when he first met the Barramatjaras it was as someone who had come to enquire about their fame, and write something about it.

McCloud landed at Baruda in a light aircraft one late afternoon. Heeled over in the passenger seat during the approach, he had seen red dust, a thread of empty river with desert oaks and eucalypts growing in it, and hills built of fragments of rock. Stones bounced the sun so sharply into your eyes that you would have sworn – wrongly – that it had recently rained and that every surface was glossy with water.

Bluey Kannata was away at the time, acting in what the other dancers called "some picture". McCloud met though with the others – Whitey Wappitji, Paul Mungina the *didj* player, Philip Puduma and Tom Gullagara – beneath the brush shelter outside the settlement store.

McCloud found Tom Gullagara, with his modest beergut and his huge-buckled cowboy belt, the frankest of the four of them. Tom nodded towards some old men on the fringe of the camp. "Those old fellers keep an eye on us, case we give away something secret. They don't want us painting much, dancing anything too secret. Some of them come all the way from Easter Creek to check up on us, whether we give too much away to visitors."

Then Whitey said, "If you want to get something serious back from people, you've got to give something serious out."

The troupe told him they'd paint him a design on canvas laid out on the sand the next morning. Instead of the old dyes, which were so hard to make, they would use acrylics mixed with water. They would paint one of the sober Whitey Wappitji's designs, one that was *owned* by him.

"It's going to be that marsupial rat dreaming from Mount Dinkat," said Whitey, sitting very upright on his haunches, and speaking with half-closed eyes. "He's my dreaming, that feller. He's no rat. It's bad business to call him a rat. He's *Tutinjinga*. That's his real name. He's come across from Haast's Bluff, an awful long way, and he gets into the lizard-women round there at

Mount Dinkat. You can see the lizard-women still lying down, five miles out there. You can find their eggs out there. Just five miles out on the Hall's Creek road there."

The next morning, after he had spent a fitful night in the empty labour ward of the Baruda clinic, McCloud watched the four of them set to, sitting on rugs around the margin of the canvas set on a flat, granular patch of earth and painting as if for a performance.

Though this design was a dreaming which lean Whitey claimed to own more than the others did, the other three men also seemed to have some relative ownership and to be confident in what they did. The main pattern, as left behind by the hero marsupial rat when he violated the blood laws with the lizard-women, was blocked out with a blackened stick by Whitey. For he was the one who had received it directly from an uncle and also – according to what Cowboy Tom Gullagara would say later – had it confirmed in a dream by this being, Tutinjinga himself.

Whitey started the design at the centre of the spread canvas, which was the size of a small room. He worked his way outwards brushing away any red dust with a switch of gum leaves as he backed from the centre of the pattern.

"This isn't any deep secret version," Tom Gullagara told McCloud. "This is serious. But it's the one a lot of relatives can look at. This is the one for the uninitiated fellers, but when you see it you get to be as good as a relative of ours, Frank. Just the same, this bloke here . . ." (he nodded to the pattern Whitey was making) ". . . he's not dangerous to anyone."

Yet there were designs known to these men which *did* have a dangerous form. That was obvious. All the ancestors were capable of forms which blasted the unprepared. You got that idea of danger from the inherent threat and promise of the Barramatjara dancing.

The Christian Philip, Cowboy Tom, the *didj* trickster Paul, on their rugs around the outskirts of Whitey's canvas, began to apply paint – red, yellow, blue, black, but never emerald, since emerald never seemed to occur in the Barramatjara country – to this ritual depiction of the holy desert as made at Mount Dinkat by Whitey's old father and intimate ancestor, marsupial rat.

They leaned inwards, advancing at last over the dried outer designs to complete the inner particulars of the tale. Sometimes one of them stopped to roll thin cigarettes or spit tobacco juice.

The paint dried quickly in the heat. They worked the brushes with a nonchalant style.

The designs to do with the marsupial rat ritual at Mount Dinkat, a plug of stone visible away to the north and the venue for tricky Tutinjinga's seduction of the lizard-women, were a sort of pictorial code which you would need to be a Barramatjara to read. The conventions seemed to be that water and spirit places were circular, with concentric rings, like Dante's Inferno. In the open ground between circles, each of the troupe would place his own patterns of white dots. The spirits of the earth were at least as numerous as these dots.

The circles and lines and dots were not literal accountings of marsupial rat's great Mount Dinkat rut. But so sweetly did the designs connect that everything the Barramatjara painted had a satisfying assonance to it. They could have given lessons to Klee or a host of the Modernists. They were the only people who had been Modernist for fifty thousand years.

McCloud sat for a time near Philip Puduma, who did not chew or smoke. Philip was the oldest, perhaps forty-five years. He had taken his stockman's hat off and sweat glimmered in his thinning hair and along that long, solemn jawline which typified the Barramatjara. He wore a crucifix around his neck.

A question which in some lights seemed crass occurred to McCloud. At length, in the interests of journalism, he asked it.

"This marsupial rat? What do you think of him, Philip? What I mean is, he goes up to Mount Dinkat and fornicates . . . ?"

"Oh, this is a good story," murmured Philip lightly. "This one . . . it tells you not to interfere with women of the same blood. There's nothing wrong with this one. This one's like King David and Bathsheba, this feller."

As the morning wore on, McCloud became a little embarrassed by the time they were spending on this demonstration just for him. Occasionally he thanked them. But they did not say, "It's no trouble!" Nor did they behave any differently than if they had been *performing* the painting in front of an audience of thousands.

Throughout the day, a number of older women with capacious sagging breasts, a block of stomach, high-boned hips and delicate desert ankles would come up and joke with the painters in the Barramatjara tongue. A stone's throw away, under the shade of an enormous river gum, a breed of tree so skilled in spreading wide on a pittance of water, younger men and women sat on a rug playing gin rummy and a game called *nine-up*. Their laughter, like the conversations of the older women and the painters, sounded alien to McCloud and had that exciting quality of coming from an ancient throat: the first throat to clench in hilarity in all this great desert! So it seemed to the suburban aesthete McCloud, whose senses were being stretched by what he saw and heard in Baruda.

One young woman, full-lipped, round-headed, threw in her cards and stood up. She passed the dance troupe at their work, averting her eyes. McCloud saw how she shifted a wad of narcotic weed behind her teeth, around her pink mouth. Paul Mungina made a teasing noise with his own mouth, a sound like the *didj* at which he was the master.

"That there, that's Bluey Kannata's missus," he said, breaking out of his normal reticence. "She never been to Sydney or Melbourne or New York like Bluey." He made yet another, more jazzy *didj* noise. Without malice he said with a smile, "Bluey's got other girls there. Them disco girls."

"And keep her only to yourself, as long as you both shall live," the Christian Philip muttered, not necessarily to anyone.

When the painting was finished, they let McCloud take some pictures of it and then drifted away to drink tea. Doing the thing, being empowered to do it, was what mattered to them. They did not seek to preserve it after the fact, and McCloud felt that it would be wrong, a gaffe of some kind, for him to remove it from where the painters had left it. Dogs and children wandered across the painting, and if any of the card players walked by it they skirted it yet took no pains to avoid kicking dust across its surface. McCloud felt a desperation, like that of a man in a short story he had read, who had encountered in the sand of a beach where the tide was coming in a sketch made by Picasso. And who had sought to preserve it against the merciless pull of the moon.

The scholars called it *animism*, the religion, the cosmogony which informed the painting and the dance of the Barramatjara Dance Troupe. The name *animism* was applied also to the world system of Dayaks in Borneo and Comanches in Texas and the Nuba of the Sudan, so it seemed to McCloud to serve not to distinguish the

Barramatjara but to lump them in. However, as McCloud would learn both in Baruda and on tour, it did mean that their apparently empty earth teemed with spirits. A man and woman were not enough on their own to produce a quick child. It was the spirit which quickened the womb.

McCloud himself had been raised intermittently as a Presbyterian. There had been a lot of Presbyterians on the North Shore of Sydney. Most of them, like McCloud's family, found it more a satisfying label than a satisfying faith. It told you who your friends and suitable neighbours were. You and they were not some unkempt and overbreeding crowd of Catholics or some flamboyantly decorative Jew. You and they were solid people. He knew that Pauline's parents, against all the evidence of flamboyant events which struck them in the midst of their lives, saw that same set of guarantees in their Presbyterian background. And spirits did not roam the orderly suburbs or challenge the orderly virtues of Caledonia Australis, where amongst the gum trees people felt no weight of ghosts and sent their children to well-maintained schools named Scots or Knox Grammar.

McCloud had been bored by religion before thirteen, tormented by it for a year or two thereafter, argumentative about it in an acned, smartalec way for a further year or two, and then indifferent. When he became an apostate – about the same time as he drank his first schooner of beer – he believed he was doing it because the doctrines were irrational and beyond the belief of a reasonable fellow.

But irrationality – he saw through his experiences as a friend and associate of the Barramatjara – wasn't a problem any more. It never had been for humans. Irrationality of the right kind – ordered by practice – was bread and meat to the spirit. The problem was finding the irrational system which fitted you; the satisfying faith.

The closest McCloud could come to that now was a sort of ancestor worship, a vague fabulous memory of McCloud immigration. Great-grandparents had left the rigours of what you might call lower-middle-class Clydeside life, and for some reason taken the earth's longest option, all the way to the antipodes, known also as Sydney, Australia.

What was their impulse? Was it a heroic ignorance of the distances involved? Was it something more visionary? Whatever it was, he was sure it must have cast a light over his own undistinguished (except in one regard) suburban childhood; that it must cast a light now. The ancestral migration – of which he knew so little – was the dimension which redeemed his life, just as ancestral motion had made the Barramatjara world. He, he liked to imagine, was in his own sense an animist and a worshipper of forebears.

He had liked – maybe with a little vanity – to imagine that this was why he felt such fellow feeling for the Barramatjara Dance Troupe and their vigour as artists and dancers.

"I took bad to the grog," the quiet Christian Philip Puduma had told McCloud as he dotted the spirits into the emblematic landscape he and the other members of the dance troupe were painting during McCloud's Baruda visit. "Them old Germans tell me my body is a temple, but I didn't believe 'em. I started to buy that awful stuff, rosehip and meths. I went to Alice and knew some real bad women in that riverbank there. It was about ten, twelve years back Jesus himself come up to me in the riverbed in Alice, and that Saviour says to me, 'Philip, why are you letting booze kill my temple?' Yet he wasn't against my ancestors, like old Freiniemer was. He just wanted me not to bugger myself up. That turned me round. I joined that Evangelical church, the one that started up in Hall's Creek, just for us blokes, just for my people. These days I never touch a drop. Not these days. I preach to the young fellers. I brought round lots of wild fellers in the other settlements too. Not me. But the Lord."

This latest Christianity of the Barramatjara, at least of those like Philip who observed it, seemed to have arisen by its own impetus. It was a separate visitation. You got the idea from Philip that it would have happened whether Dom Estevez and the Lutherans had come or not, and whether they had failed or not. Christ won Philip by appearing in person to him and a number of other Barramatjara rakehells in the beds of dry rivers. For Philip, this phenomenon did not derive from any history of imperialism and its religious variations. It was so much a matter of Christ and Phil that it had nothing to do with Estevez and Freiniemer.

And, seated on his rug, Philip dotted in the spirit places with the same energy as the others. As Whitey, who'd paid no more than lip service to the idea of the Saviour. This design version of the marsupial rat's wholehearted seduction of the lizard-women! It was clear that the Christ who came to him in the riverbed countenanced marsupial rat. That though marsupial rat might stand for some mysteries, there were others – including the mystery of grog – for which Christ alone could stand. For Phil, Christ was that miraculous Deity, a Deity who never appeared in the suburbs of the North Shore. An unjealous god.

On that visit to Baruda then, it had been all the dreamings. And Christ walking on waterless rivers. None of the Barramatjara Dance Troupe had mentioned drillers or Highland Pegasus or the CIA.

5

IN THE PIT

THE balding, stocky Razir appeared in the first-class cabin now. The last time McCloud had seen him he had been holding a primed grenade high in his hand so that all in the rear of the plane could see it. He was not flourishing anything like that any more – it must have been rendered safe and returned to one of the pouches on his belt. Now there was earnestness rather than threat on his square face with its traces of boyhood acne. He looked like a tough child undergoing rehabilitation for some passionate but forgivable crime. He carried in his hands three placards made of white cardboard and covered with large and exactly hand-drafted English script. His own work. With a half-smile he displayed them to Hasni who nodded.

"I know what these are," murmured Cale.

McCloud knew too. He was aware he should see them as fatuous, laughable items from some bizarre system of governance, yet he wasn't able to. Razir handled them as matter-of-factly as a plumber handles a wrench, and this too somehow gave them force. The stale slogans and words Razir had inscribed seemed more acute than knives.

Razir checked the message on each of them against the features of the kneeling men. It was clear the slogans meant something to him. They were not mere tokens. The cardboard was heavy duty and well-chosen to bear the weight of hanging around the neck. Holes had been carefully punched, with some exact device, and the neck strings were deftly tied.

These were props in whose effect Taliq, Hasni and Razir believed.

* * *

Razir hung the first placard around the American businessman Stone's neck. The American did not demur, but stood up as he was told and faced aft. In thick display pencil on the cardboard was written, *Zionist Agent*.

Even bearing the placard, McCloud noticed, the American came out predictably well from his semi-nakedness. His legs, though strangely ageless and lacking in hair, were so well-proportioned. If the placard sits on him, McCloud irrationally thought, then all the more definitely will it sit on me.

Cale accepted his sign without any argument, but as he stood he bent over whimsically and read the inscription upside down. "*Zionist Hack?* You got it half right!"

There was a second of tentativeness in the way the nuggety Razir responded; a sort of tension, like that of a young teacher who fears that the wild children will put too much pressure on his goodwill.

"What is a Zionist?" asked Cale, grabbing the minute advantage. "A Zionist is someone who recognises the right of Israel to exist. Therefore Yasir Arafat is a Zionist. But I suppose that's your whole point, isn't it, son?"

Little Razir, the remaining placard – McCloud's – under one arm, paled astoundingly. He shoved the barrel of his Polish automatic under Cale's left ear.

"You will not speak about your sign. We own the sign. You own only the shame."

When Cale had kept silent for ten seconds, Razir rearranged himself, left Cale and came and hung the last placard around McCloud's neck. It said, "*Exploiter of Landless People*".

In spite of its quotient of falsity, it did not seem a laughable burden. There was surely more truth to it – even as read upside down by McCloud himself – than he would have believed an hour ago.

Hasni pushed past McCloud and lifted him from behind by the armpits and turned him about. It wasn't rough handling. It felt solicitous. There was something about it which, combined with Hasni's earlier studious reading of the news magazine, gave McCloud the idea that the boy might be able to be reached.

Surprisingly, Cale had already stood. Without being asked.

It was to be a procession apparently – McCloud, Cale/Bennett, Stone/Steinberg. Three culprits on their march.

But at the curtain between the first class and the bulk of the plane, Hasni rearranged his three prisoners. "You first," he said

83

to the American, as if his crime was the worst. He positioned Cale in the middle.

McCloud's face was already burning. Even doubts about the condition of his underwear burdened him.

Hasni brushed the curtain aside. "Go," he told the American. "Out now, gentlemen."

McCloud flinched from the stares of all the pale faces raised to view him. Progress was at shuffling pace, since the aisles were full of the people from upstairs sitting resignedly cross-legged. The procession had to tread amongst them, avoiding a knee here, an elbow there. And Taliq was there, standing before the cross-legged passengers in the aisle.

"These!" he yelled through an intercom telephone at a nearby door, resonating throughout the cabin above the quiet susurrus of the engines. "These are three guilty men from amongst your fellow-travellers. One is an agent of Mossad. The second is a writer of lies for the newspaper which maligns my people worse than any other. The third has duped and cheated the native peoples of his land, in exactly the same way that my people have been duped and lied to, cheated and deprived of their land. You should curse these men for boarding the same aircraft as you. Your enemies and mine."

At the head of the column, Hasni motioned the three labelled culprits to resume the procession. At first, McCloud kept his eyes down – it was not shame for a supposed crime, for he was not yet totally convinced of his crime. He cringed because that mean redolence normally held in by clothing and security of the person was now released to the cabin at large. Compounded in part of uncertain guilt, which seemed more despicable than exact blame, it infringed on his breathing; and there was fear too, and the shame of the unsuccessful writer and the careless lover, and of the manager who does not enquire too closely into the causes of his employment.

Then he fixed his eyes on Cale's baggy underwear. There was a big creature moving assertively there. Behind the undistinguished fabric, Cale seemed to know and live by his own name (even if there were two of them) and was sure what to believe of his captors.

For some reason this reminded him of the Girl and the Boy, and the duty he had for their sake to meet the gazes of others. Looking straight ahead, McCloud could not avoid registering what passengers he passed on either side and the ones looking up at him questioningly from the floor.

For the first ten paces there was silence. The combined population of this part of the plane was still assessing the three of them, gauging the credibility of their shame.

The procession drew level with a fine-featured boy in an aisle seat. He had shrunken legs, and it was perhaps for him that the wheelchair had been needed earlier, an age ago in New York, the wheelchair of which that barely remembered, benign voice of the captain had spoken.

The boy, the cripple, now cried out in German-accented English, "This is asinine. This is scapegoating. You are making criminals, when all along *you* are the criminals!"

The effect of this brave outburst was at once weakened. For the young man began to weep wildly. His argument could now be written off as mere hysteria. McCloud saw Hasni, in advance of the procession, brush the young man's courageous outburst aside like a vine in a jungle.

At last they were through the tangle of hostages from upstairs, and the aisle was clear. McCloud saw that many of the passengers stared fixedly ahead, not taking account of the three prisoners one way or another. There was something frightening there: these passengers were locked into the question of their individual connections with Taliq and the boys. No other connection, especially not a connection with three labelled men in underwear, was worth looking at.

Then he saw Pauline's face aimed at him from the far side of the plane. Her gaze was level and she frowned slightly as she nodded briefly, a crisp and competent nod which seemed to promise she had strategies in mind. He felt a brief, berserk happiness. In a minute or so, if the procession was to take in both aisles, he would pass close to her area of cleverness, her field of concern.

They had nearly reached the battery of lavatories, the limits of the plane, when McCloud saw a man wearing a baseball jacket and, far from blinkering his gaze, staring at them with what seemed a disappointed spectator's directness.

"Bastard!" he cried, still seated, at the American businessman, and then with increasing intent, he repeated the word to Cale and then McCloud. Judging by his volume, you would have thought he had taken Taliq's grading of the separate culpabilities of the three prisoners as read. In ascending order: the agent, the hack, the exploiter. "Bastard!" he screamed at McCloud.

It would have been comforting to think that the man was yelling to prove himself to Taliq. But it wasn't the case. His eyes did not shift for approval to any of the hijackers. His outcry existed for his own sake. He had read the labels and the faces and found in them a cause for autonomous anger.

After that, a greater silence than ever descended for a moment along the line of the march. Glancing back, McCloud saw the man's wife soothing him, settling him back into the seat with her hands. Over her shoulder, she directed a certain wifely reproof at McCloud. "You've made my husband very angry."

Ahead, even Cale now seemed slumped and overburdened with threats.

They passed along the rear row of seats and began their progress back to the front of the plane.

The Barramatjara Dance Troupe were not here, in this crowded after-section, amongst the passengers from upstairs who huddled in the aisles. McCloud understood that they would not be encountered. They must therefore still be in Taliq's heaven, upstairs by the cockpit. This meant they were exempt from political demonstrations. They were Taliq's brothers and did not need a mass circus like this to bring them to awareness.

As McCloud passed Pauline's seat, she reached out across the wan young woman who held the baby and detained him by the hand. It was a ferocious grip. "Frank," she said. "Frank, I won't let them do anything to you."

It was an impossible statement, but he could see she was convinced of it. She stood, and the wan girl lifted her baby to make room in front of her for the grip Pauline kept of McCloud's arm.

There were nuances in what she said – she understood perfectly his confusion and dread. She did not despise him for his fear. He understood in fact that she cherished him for his average fear, his pedestrian shame. It was exorbitant fear and shame she hated – the kind her father the Dentist had displayed.

He was as saddened and grateful as a child when she let go of him and permitted him to make up ground with the others.

Yet her promise remained with him. It had been full of breath. You could call it primitive, and this gave rise to his fear that she might try to attack them with her fists. He looked back at her. She had quite muscular shoulders – one of those little women who played good hockey and swam with a tight, sinewy ferocity gangling girls lacked. What they used to call in the nineteenth century *a pocket Venus.*

"Don't do anything," he cried. "I'm all right. The boys aren't in danger. I wish I could . . ."

He wished he could write her a letter advising her against any rash move.

He felt a push against his right shoulder-blade and presumed it must be Razir, the placard-maker.

Turning without volition, he saw though that it was a tall, blonde girl, who had stood and must have wanted him to move out of her zone.

"You looking for sympathy or something?" she challenged him. She moved aft towards the toilets, and Razir allowed her passage.

McCloud wanted to say aloud that he was looking for justice. But he decided that was a dangerous proposition.

Now they came to stewards, male and female, strapped in their seats. Some studied him with a tight-lipped secretive regard and concern, men and women waiting for a sane chance to do something yet doubtful it would come. One man, balding and wearing a badge which said *Chief Purser*, rose and said, "Don't do anything foolish. We are keeping our eye out for you."

The tendency to smile in gratitude towards the Chief Purser was undermined by a quick look at some of the other crew, who looked to McCloud as if they regarded the prisoners with that glum reproach and slightly pursed mouth reserved only for passengers who ask for untimely drinks or service late in a night flight. Through his unfortunate behaviour, these crew members seemed to suggest with their eyes, he had deprived them of any rest this entire night. And now a demanding day was breaking beyond the shuttered windows.

It was beyond the stewards that the air of reproof really thickened, reached a head and became normal. A short woman, no more than thirty-five years of age, dressed comfortably for the journey, red-faced as if she had been weeping for some time, rose from an aisle seat and stood in Daniel Stone's path. McCloud could see her two small children sleeping, locked together by the window. "These are my children you put in danger!" she screamed. "You dirty swine!"

She began to beat the tanned arm of the businessman, her punches fading against his shoulders as he drew away from her. She turned to deal with Cale, but her aggression had exhausted her and she was panting. "Sonofabitch!" she told Cale, and to McCloud as he drew by her, she cried, "Jewish sonofabitch! What's it like now? The boot's on the other foot? Eh? The other foot?"

A young man in a button-down shirt had stood to take her place and now spat fair in the journalist's face. It was apparent that Cale was the favoured and obvious target. A string of spittle hung from his nose.

Hasni had turned around and made gentling motions towards the young man. These movements seemed to say, "I approve of your enthusiasm. But there will be plenty of time for punishment." The speed with which this miscreant-hatred had developed amongst a section of the passengers astonished McCloud.

The first row of the compartment had been cleared of travellers. Taliq instructed the three prisoners to step up onto these seats and face the rear of the plane. So they did, McCloud finding it hard to keep his balance on the spongy upholstery. Three culprits on a shaky scaffold, he thought. The melodrama of it should have made the passengers laugh, but there was no sound. Taliq and the boys controlled the tone of this street- or aisle-theatre. They had made everything serious, even the risible placards.

Standing on the seat allotted to him, McCloud could see the look of neutral enquiry and assessment on many blanched faces, a sort of amateur-dramatic scowl of hate on a few, and on others still the same unforced but authentic contempt which had produced assaults on the circuit around the rear of the plane.

Taliq, however, was not there to be influenced by this feigned or real revulsion. He was still at the curtain space by one of the doors, ready to broadcast again.

"Later in the flight," he promised, "when we have communicated adequately with the ground, these criminals will be tried and punished."

This pledge seemed to produce an almost inaudible sigh of edification from the passengers. Surely they can't all want to see us punished? McCloud wondered.

"But first there are things to attend to," Taliq continued. "Your breakfast, the breakfast of the innocents. And we must land some-where. The prisoners will be confined. Thank you, my friends, for your attention."

As, on order, McCloud dismounted from the seat he had been standing on, he placed his finger to his lips for Pauline's sake. He knew Whitey Wappitji and the others would speak for him. They would laugh at the idea that he was some sort of felon.

Back in the first-class section, Yusuf was tearing up the carpet on the cabin floor. Standing by him was a middle-aged man in a uniform with bands of gold braid on its shoulders. He was a little overweight, but his face was humane. McCloud felt a sort of ecstasy at seeing him. This was an apparition. An intimation that a kindly order might be possible.

McCloud fixed his gaze on the soap-white scalp beneath the captain's sparse hair. A suggestion of everyday deliverance seemed to gleam in that fatherly tone of skin.

Yusuf now lifted a metal hatch which had lain embedded in the floor. McCloud began to shiver, not knowing whether it was the idea of being put down with the luggage or locked in some hole, or whether the atmosphere of the plane had altered.

The captain regarded them. There was at least an unfeigned compassion in his eyes.

"Sorry, boys," he said in his Appalachian accent. "It's just that down there you'll be getting a little cold air from the engines." He lowered his voice. "Listen, I flew B–52s in Vietnam in the 1960s. Notice they don't judge me for my so-called crimes? I have to go on flying *their* goddam plane. And it is their goddam plane, make no mistake!" He looked closely at all three of them, one after another. "I've thought of this situation for two decades, and this is the first time it's happened to me. I believe that means I'm better prepared than worse for what will happen. So trust me! Don't pull any fuses down there. It might put the aircraft in peril."

"There it is," said Yusuf, to the American businessman Stone. Yusuf had heard what the captain had to say but tolerated it easily in view of the leverage he and his brothers had over everyone's life. "Climb down, my friends."

He pointed to a ladder which ran down from the lip of this under-floor compartment into a dim, barely lit cavern.

McCloud's mouth dried from the terror of being locked up in narrow places. But the American nodded bravely and briefly and set an example by beginning a lithe and unprotesting descent. Cale, who had to swing round and face McCloud so that he in turn could work his bulk down the ladder, chose to look like a man forced to play some party trick by friends. Glancing back to his clothes roughly folded on his seat, to what he thought of as the skin of his innocence, his immunity, McCloud wanted to retrieve photographs of the two children. He had a hunger to see them. And perhaps their mute and normally charming faces could work a transformation in Taliq's intentions towards him.

On the other hand, the photographs of bourgeois children – McCloud's children *were* bourgeois because of Pauline's salary – would provoke in Taliq only tales of his own tribe's dispossession, of infants terrorised and harried out of their home villages.

There was a text McCloud remembered from the boarding-school chapels of his childhood. "Look and see if there is any suffering like unto my suffering!" That was Taliq's position. So McCloud obeyed Yusuf and the captain and swung himself onto the ladder and descended.

He saw as he came down into it that the compartment seemed to be some sort of giant fusebox. Thick electrical leads ran insulated up and across its metal walls, and there were switches and levers. This was the true and unsuspected core of the plane, this little cave barely more spacious than a phone box. That it was here was itself a revelation to McCloud, who'd never suspected its existence.

The three of them stood close together on the floor of the cavern. It was as cold as the captain had promised. McCloud was grateful for the contact his upper arm had with the warmth of Cale's. Yusuf closed the hatch on them. Two small lights cast a greenish glare over their faces.

"No one suffers claustrophobia?" Cale asked with that manic merriment of his.

"I used to," confessed the well-made businessman called Stone. "I was a screwed-up kid. My poor mother took me to a doctor for it when I was sixteen." He laughed briefly. "Must have been successful."

Stone could have confessed anything – acne, kleptomania – and made it seem part of the wholecloth of his urban perfection.

Now that the hatch above him was closed, McCloud could tell that the time here would be a trial for his bladder. But he resisted saying so. For he felt he needed to preserve all his slim resources of dignity.

"Is there room to sit?" asked the American.

He tried it, keeping his knees up under his chin and holding his placard clear of his body.

Cale did the same, but more lumpily. McCloud noticed that there was now gooseflesh on Cale's arms. The two of them, Cale and Stone, seemed so self-possessed, like veterans at incarceration. Between them, they took up just about the whole floor space.

"Join us," Cale urged McCloud. "While we consider which of these fucking leads and levers to pull."

Stone and Cale laughed a little at this.

"They've shown a lot of trust in us," said McCloud. "They must know we want to live."

Stone explained though that with the duplicate system, hydraulic and manual and electronic, which prevailed in an aircraft, there was no permanent damage which could be done here. "Even if we wanted to," he said.

McCloud lowered himself. He sought the warmth both of their bodies and of their authority. Frosty metal surfaces seemed to scrape his shoulders and back, however. He remained uncomfortably on his haunches.

Cale formally introduced himself to Stone. "Brother McCloud knows the whole story," he said. "I am definitely a Cale, child of other Cales. I use the Bennett passport for travelling in Arab countries."

"And I'm Daniel Stone," said the American. "Though by the record of my birth, Irving Stone. But I hate that Irving. And of course, my people's name is really Steinberg, and my company does business in Israel – on the merits of our product, not on any sentimental *Yiddisher* basis, just let me make that clear. The goddam Israelis had me set up with that second passport. I couldn't ever see any fantastic benefit to it. I still can't. All I sell is computer programming. And software."

This news seemed momentarily to fascinate Cale. "Programming? Really?"

"That's right. Psychological profiling software."

"Easy for you to say," breathed Cale. Then he winked at McCloud.

"Sure," said Stone. "It's a program called Psychopar. Nearly all governments use it as a tool. Not that we don't have competitors. I'm the programmer, and my partner Hirsch is the psychologist."

"And how does this program of yours work?"

"Well," said Stone. "Say a government wants to find out certain things about this guy Taliq? For example, his percentage likelihood to take hostage lives. They feed the data in and Psychopar gives them the indices, a sort of profile they can work on with something like mathematical certainty . . ."

"*Mathematical* certainty?" Cale asked in doubt. He sounded

solemn now, as if the idea his destiny would be settled by indices distressed him.

"It's a good system. Hirsch and I keep upgrading. And it's only a tool anyhow, not a weapon. It's not as if we made rocket guidance systems or something! But of course there's no way *that* gets me out of this hole. As soon as the takeover happened upstairs, I said to myself, *Daniel, my boy, you just might be a target.*" He pinched the bridge of his nose. "But I didn't expect them to find out about the Steinberg passport. These gentlemen . . . they obviously have some sophisticated backup."

From the quantity of Mr Daniel Stone's confessions it was apparent that he was a frank man, comfortable with his own history. Stone possessed, McCloud thought, an admirable American lack of pretension: the equivalent of the Cockney or the self-made Australian. All Stone's harmless enough vanity was in his clothing and his firm, well-tended body.

McCloud could in fact imagine him growing up in some cold-water tenement of the kind consecrated by the works of Bellow or Doctorow. He would have been the sharp practical brother, much more certain of the world and of women than the dreamy narrator was.

Cale was rubbing his shoulders. "Sophisticated backup," he groaned. "I'll say they have. I wanted naturally enough to – shall we say? – mask the fact I write for a newspaper which gives those sorts of chaps a caning. Slice it any way you care to, *those* boys are totally ominous. Did you hear the man?" And he adopted Taliq's accent. "*We will have a summary trial and execution but first we must have breakfast!* I mean, that's absolutely off-the-planet. *Totally* deranged. If you want to hijack a plane, you hijack a plane and be nasty to everyone. You don't try to be Father Christmas for the port side and Jack the Ripper for the starboard."

He paused as if to allow McCloud and Stone smiling time. "But of course all the literature says they're like this. Their ambitions are of Messianic proportions. They want to be at the same time the saviours and the executioners of their hostages."

Dan Stone made a squeaking noise with his tongue.

"So you've written about terrorism?" asked McCloud.

"Oh, yes," Cale told him. "They've got me to rights on this one. I've even attended the occasional upmarket seminar run by West German and French security . . . the very people our friends upstairs abominate. *Guilty as charged, Your Worship!* And you, Mr McCloud? What do they have on you?"

McCloud hesitated. The other two had both confessed to the possibility of being seen, in certain lights, as guilty. There had been consciousness in *their* acts – Cale had harboured intent in writing about Palestinian factions, and Stone also had in making a better cybernetic device to measure such enemies-of-state as Taliq was. But *he*, McCloud, had not known there was any hostile content in bringing the dance troupe to America. He had had no intent. Though he did not want Cale and Stone surmising that he *had*, there was a subtle shame in that. It meant that he was not a big boy like them; not a player in the larger game.

"Come on," said Cale, winking at Stone. "You can tell us. We're your brothers in misfortune."

This banal accusation that he was one with them struck McCloud as inaccurate and something to be fought. It was perhaps harmless to exaggerate your crimes or play with guilt when there was no risk of dying to prove the point. With Taliq in command, though, McCloud saw he did not have to seek condemnation in his own demoralised spirit. His temperamental tendency to blame himself as a means of forgiving himself needed to be combated now.

So he began to tell them how he had been unlucky with an article published only that day. He laid stress on the point that if it hadn't been published *that* day he wouldn't be here. He would be one of the unlabelled innocents upstairs, still ignorant of the connection between Highland Pegasus and the Barramatjara land, still believing that the CIA were quite happy with the real estate they already owned in remote Australia.

"But you had to expect something like this," Cale argued. "You were getting loads of press, and it was wonderful. Roses, roses all the way. And when that happens for a few weeks, one sweet article after another, a rush suddenly sets in to find a negative story, the worm in the apple. I mean, it's somewhat bad timing that the coloured-person-in-woodpile story hit the newsstands today, but it was bound to appear sometime soon. Because that's the nature of the press."

McCloud felt grateful to Cale for making him feel less ill-starred.

But Cale – like the press he stood for – could not help himself taking with one hand what he'd given with the other. "And what if the article had appeared while you were still wowing them at Lincoln Center?" he asked. "I mean to say, Brother McCloud, wouldn't there have been the risk of what we might call *industrial action?*"

"If I'd seen the article first, I would have brought it to the troupe's attention." It sounded a pompous claim. But it was the truth, and should be permitted to stand. "They would have then discussed it amongst themselves. They're not political innocents, but they might have sought my opinion out of politeness. Then they would have voted on whether they wanted to go on with the tour. It would have been a powerful gesture indeed if they'd cancelled their Frankfurt performances. It would have had powerful reverberations."

"For you too, mate," Cale observed.

"No. My loyalty's to them. I'm not in this for my career!"

"Oh," said Cale. "Independent wealth?"

"Independent ambitions," McCloud explained. "I'm trying to become a novelist."

"Oh, mate," murmured Cale. "That's not a career. That's the last card in the bloody pack!" He shivered. "Christ, I could do with a cigarette now! Do you mean to say, you wouldn't have told them the show must go on?"

"No. I wouldn't. For a start, it wouldn't have worked."

"But you might have tried hard," Cale persisted, still like the journalist he was and not from any animus. "For all we know, you might have been offered some inducements up front. By the interested parties, I mean."

"I hadn't been," said McCloud. "And if I had, it wouldn't have worked with the dancers."

"But Taliq thinks they've already got to you, son. The parties of corruption!"

"Then he's bloodywell wrong." Again he had a sense that his life might depend upon his believing that with an absolute belief. Believing it himself. For he knew there was no scepticism, not even Cale's or Taliq's, as great as his own.

Cale had become thoughtful. "Do you know, our best hopes are in that little Nip tart in the green dress? That's the level of sensitivity of these chaps. At least two of them have done their balls over Miss Japan."

"She's not Japanese," McCloud said. "She's an American citizen in fact."

"Oh, that makes all the difference. But seriously, if Miss Japan would only come good for them, this business might end happily. She could become the intercessor, a not unlikely role for her."

"Or else," said Stone, "they'd turn her head around. The way they've done to that man who started spitting at you, Mr Cale. And she'd become mean as hell then. Maybe it's not a bad thing if she stays aloof for a while."

"I suppose you'd need a computer programmed with Psychopar before you could tell?" Cale asked, making a jokey mouth at McCloud.

"A computer programmed with Psychopar would certainly be a help," said Stone.

"In any case," said McCloud, "it's up to her. And she doesn't seem to want to. Her message is that she's got her standards."

"That's why she wears a dress like that," said Cale.

Stone seemed to ally himself, against the background of massed electrical fuses, with Cale. "She's certainly got bar-girl manners. Reminded me of old times in Saigon. Nice body. And it might work if she put out for some of them and not for the rest. Split them apart maybe. Make them resentful of each other."

McCloud was unwilling to let go of the question. Obscurely, he felt that his honour was intertwined with Daisy Nakamura's. "If our salvation depends on Mrs Nakamura fucking Taliq," he told them, "then we're really in a mess."

Cale and Stone exchanged looks, agreed to agree tacitly with each other and move on.

There was silence, but one full of thought. At last Cale said, "These Abos of yours? Do you think the boys upstairs will manage to condition them?"

"Condition them?"

"Turn them against us. Make them radicals."

"No. I mean, they know how to talk to politicians and confuse them a bit. But they're not political ideologues. They don't use slogans at all. Besides, they're very loyal to their friends."

"Ah," said Cale. "But they may by now have seen the article and changed their mind about friendship."

"I can't see that happening," McCloud insisted, but he began to be fearful.

Cale anyhow treated the answer with the same scepticism he'd shown at the idea that Daisy Nakamura might not be willing to accommodate hijackers *en masse*. "Let's take off these damn signs," he suggested.

They removed their placards and began to stack them at the aft end of the compartment, behind McCloud's back.

McCloud said, "Why don't we sit on the bloody things?"

"A capital idea," said Cale.

They stood and lined the hard steel floor with their sentences. Cale settled himself on the laid-out cardboard. So did Stone. McCloud would still not come to terms with this steel hole, however, and he stayed on his haunches, his flesh itching with the cold.

Lightly, Cale said, "You realise this is to be a show trial and that at least one of us is meant to be shot. Our crimes are not the point. The shamefulness of the West is the bloody point."

They played with this idea: the West's shame and their part in it.

"I bet conditions are more comfortable," murmured McCloud, "up where Taliq has the dancers."

He almost said *my* dancers.

6

SINGING THE BOOK

APART from Tom Gullagara's reference in Baruda to bauxite
mining in the north, there had also been more than a mention
of it one afternoon in New York, early in the tour. Memory
of this came bitterly to McCloud as he sat trembling in the cold
air of the electrical compartment, listening to Cale expatiate on
the psychology of terrorists, the subject on which he had written
so plentifully and which he couldn't leave alone.

As McCloud had told Daisy earlier, the Barramatjara Dance Troupe
on tour did not have ordinary rehearsals. They had in a way been
rehearsing for millennia. They had no one to direct them in the use
of each stage they encountered on their tour. There was no one to
say, "You're bunching"; or, "Paul, you should move upstage behind
Bluey at this point." McCloud himself was certainly not competent
to give such advice. Happily, the Barramatjara had a natural skill in
– as an American watching them said – "relating to their space".
    But they did need technical run-throughs, and to familiarise
themselves for an hour or so with the stage.

It was during one of these lighting and stage rehearsals, when the
dance troupe was learning something of the newly presented space
they were to perform in at the Lincoln Center the following night,
that the matter of mining came up.
    A New York director, who had been hired especially for the day
to take the dance troupe through their cues, stood at the front of
the stage yelling instructions and, through a radio, asking for
guidance from the lighting director high in his booth at the back
of the theatre.

The dance troupe were dispersed around the stage in their street clothes. Tomorrow at noon, they were intended to start painting the publicly accessible representation of the Two Brothers at Wirgudja, which as Cowboy Tom had suggested in Baruda would make the whole audience *relatives*. The troupe would, before tomorrow night, produce the design around which the dance would be performed.

Now, as the lights changed, the director advised them on the various "bridging" positions necessary for making the transition from one dance segment to another.

Whereas in the dances themselves, in their balletic and dramatic content, the Barramatjaras were their own directors and choreographers.

The technical rehearsal was two-thirds over when McCloud became aware that Bluey Kannata had begun to weep on stage.

He was very quiet about it at first, not making any sobbing noises. But then he became louder and the director went to him and asked him, with a peculiarly theatrical Manhattan concern, what was worrying him.

Philip Puduma had also moved to Bluey and stood by frowning, discerning – with his double lens of Christian- and Barramatjarahood – the demons at work on Bluey.

The others kept their positions, looking obliquely at their colleague, discreetly embarrassed by him. The noise of Bluey's distress grew louder. It surprised McCloud, the way the others stood off, as if Bluey were acting in ways which excluded them from brotherly concern. McCloud himself began to move up towards the stage. But Bluey turned and fled.

McCloud hurried backstage after him, through a door at the side of the theatre. He was guided now by the noise of Bluey's great hawking sobs. He followed the sound up a passageway to a door marked *Props Room*. The place had a table and chairs, a cutting table, some coat-hangers vacant except for one splendid purple robe of the *Belle Epoque*, a few bald polystyrene wig stands, and a bowler hat. Bluey wasn't seated on any of the chairs. He was hunched, contorted by sobs, beneath the cutting table. Philip Puduma, who must have moved with great purpose to get there first, stood over the table.

Like a man helpless on the edge of this conflagration of grief, Philip turned to McCloud. "Reckons someone cursed his uncle. If you ask me, that curse is inside Bluey if you ask me."

He raised his eyebrows and spoke in a *don't-look-to-me-for-enlightenment* sort of way.

Obediently, not wanting to intrude in Barramatjara business, McCloud sat in one of the chairs. But at last he couldn't stop himself asking, "What uncle?"

"His uncle in Baruda," said Philip, again trying to put an end to the questions. "Bluey had a stupid dream someone cursed his uncle." Philip returned his gaze severely to his cousin Bluey. "It's all the Jim Beam, and all them funny cigarettes," he murmured. "That's why he's got those bad dreams."

The Barramatjara had a weakness for Jim Beam, rather than for Scotch. It might be all the country-and-western music they listened to, in which Jim Beam's name was often invoked. If an unarguable cowboy like Tom Gullagara drank spirits, it was always Jim Beam.

Bluey was growing exhausted with grief and had fallen sideways against the wall. Yes, McCloud thought, definitely an actor, even in a society of actors such as the Barramatjara. More likely in any society to dramatise his grief than would a solid citizen like his cousin Philip. There was some dementia, a St Elmo's fire of bluer excess, dancing about the surface of Bluey's fit.

The other three dancers had appeared in the corridor. Bluey looked up from under the cutting table, fixed his bleared eye upon Whitey, and then covered his face and slumped backwards against the wall. He seemed to know there was something which separated him from them; something in his demonstration which they felt bound to distance themselves from.

Whitey none the less came into the room briefly to stand with authority beside McCloud. McCloud stood up.

"That one," said Whitey Wappitji, looking McCloud in the eye. "That one there, he's not well. That feller's not well at all."

"What does *not well* mean?" McCloud asked.

"No one curses his uncle. His uncle doesn't have a curse and just isn't dead. There's something inside that feller that's the problem."

McCloud realised Wappitji was authorising him. Saying, *There's nothing I can do. You can move in with your normal suburban gestures of condolence.*

McCloud knelt by the cutting table. "Let me take you for some coffee," he urged Bluey.

The Barramatjara film star had begun to shiver.

"Come on, Bluey," said Philip Puduma. "Jesus loves you, mate. You're okay."

The trite words conveyed nothing of Phil's riverbed epiphany, when Christ appeared in a waterless river and seared Phil clean of alcohol.

"Bluey," McCloud insisted. "We'll go over to O'Neal's."

Though O'Neal's had a bar, McCloud would ensure the overwrought Bluey Kannata would drink only coffee.

When Bluey did not seem comforted, McCloud had further thoughts. "We can call your uncle then," he said.

Baruda was not connected yet with everywhere else on earth by satellite. It kept itself difficultly separate. It was not part of the universe of interconnecting plaints and whispers. But it was possible, through irksome means, through special and time-consuming measures, to speak to the place from anywhere on earth by radio telephone.

This promise seemed to have an influence upon Bluey. He looked at McCloud for the first time. "We can get through from here?" he asked.

"Yes," said McCloud, though he knew it could take two-thirds of the night. He bent to Bluey. "Was it a dream?" asked McCloud.

"Clear as day," whispered Bluey in awe.

"And your uncle . . . wasn't well?"

Tears spilled down Bluey's face again, but smoothly, without affecting his voice. Bluey whispered, "He was sung. They sung his book."

"But listen. How can you know for certain?"

Bluey closed his eyes. He drew his knees up under his chin and huddled.

"Can't you tell me anything?" McCloud asked the others, Wappitji, Mungina, and Cowboy Tom Gullagara by the door.

They said nothing. They turned their unscannable faces to various quarters of the room. Whitey said, "This one isn't a real dream. That's honest, Frank. It's a whisky dream."

"What about you, Philip?" McCloud asked the Christian.

Philip got up shaking his head, affronted. "I can't handle what Bluey sees. What he thinks he sees. I can't handle that. It's stuff I left behind, Frank."

He thought a second. It was written on his face that he didn't believe in the authenticity of Bluey's dreams, and yet that it had its power. Unable to say any of that though, he hurried out into

the corridor. A man pursued, if you like. For the moment, Jesus –
the shield, the lamb, the deep water – wasn't with him.

Whitey was still staring at McCloud, as if to say, *You're the
manager. This is your problem.* They were very severe, the Barramatjara, in their demarcations of duty. It was no use arguing with
them about it.

McCloud suggested therefore that they all get on with the
rehearsal. He would, he announced, take Bluey out for some coffee
and a talk. He was grateful when the others failed to point out,
though he knew they understood it, that the rehearsal did not make
a lot of sense without Bluey Kannata, that his lack of a technical
briefing might invalidate their own movements about the stage.

Outside, in the great piazza between theatres, the air was brisk
and fountains splashed with a steely glimmer they caught from the
seasonal sky and its honed clouds. It was a subtle, treacherously
cold day such as the Barramatjara, in all their millennia in the
western desert, had never before seen.

Shuddering in a paramilitary jacket, Bluey groaned, "Let's go to
The Ginger Man, McCloud."

For a man who believed in curses, he had a good working
knowledge of where the bars were. That was his tragedy and his
success.

"Neither of us can be trusted there, Bluey. I want to talk to you
clearly."

At this refusal, the shuddering increased again – it was as acute as
it had been under the cutting table inside. "My uncle's died of that
curse, Frank," he called out. "Don't you ask me his name!"

"Of course I won't," said McCloud. He understood that command; that you could not utter the names of the dead. To do so
was to invite them to remain in the place they had died in, or else
to infest the place where their death was known – to everyone's
hellish confusion.

Poor Bluey was malleable anyhow. He let McCloud push him
across the street, in through the doors of O'Neal's, away from the
bar and to a corner booth. The shuddering continued. His face
was entirely slick – there was sweat on the brow and tears irrigated
the rest.

McCloud ordered them coffee, during which Bluey studied the
menu through the distorting lens of his fear.

"Listen, McCloud," said Bluey when the urbane young waiter was gone. "Don't nag me about the stuff I smoke."

Some years past, Bluey had been sent down from Baruda to learn the electrical trade at a technical college. He was on his way back, to attend to his mysteries and to service the Baruda diesel generators, when one of the rising young Australian film directors had noticed him in an airline queue and asked him had he ever acted. He read for the part, sang a song or two, charmed everyone in the production office. Within two weeks the young director was introducing him to film writers and other journalists at a press conference. Everyone was captivated.

On the set of the film, some white actor had passed Bluey a brotherly joint. Hash which languidly strums the brain! The hologenic and innocent model of booze! The Navajo had their peyote buttons and the Barramatjara movie star should have a similar catalyst of visions. Such was the fashion of thought in those days. The gesture was a gesture of friendship by a member of Actors' Equity who had read Carlos Castenada and his tales of narcotic illumination. No one considered the influence the joint might have on Bluey's particular Barramatjara catalogue of dreams.

The film became a critical success and a winner of festival awards, amongst them the Gold Palm at Cannes. The world asked, "Where did he learn to act?" Bluey achieved a white kind of fame. He smiled his broad and crooked smile in rooms blue with cannabis smoke. He saw the topless, decadent girls of La Croisette prancing beneath the billboards of the Cannes Film Festival. Far beyond the usual reach of marsupial rat and the Two Brothers, he made contacts.

But he did not look like a man with a wide circle of friends today, not in O'Neal's, under pressure from a different dream than Whitey's. You could tell when the memory of the dream of his uncle's death recurred to him, for he would begin weeping again in the middle of mouthfuls of coffee, spilling tears and coffee wildly down his chin and even onto his shirt.

"You listen to me, Frank," he pleaded. "I can tell a booze dream from a grass dream, and a grass dream from a fair dinkum dream. What I saw then, on the stage . . . it was a fair dinkum dream."

"We'll see," McCloud promised. "We'll get through on the radio telephone and we'll see exactly what it was."

"I don't need any radio telephone to know," said Bluey, crumpling his hands in front of his eyes. "I saw it all happen."

In the end, just as a mercy, McCloud ordered him some cognac, which arrived in a large brandy balloon with a lit candle so that Bluey could enhance the texture over the flame. If he had chosen to.

"You know, those geologist blokes have been out west of Baruda. My uncle's country, that one. Mount Gilbert it's called. It's my uncle's. And they went and did some drilling. You know, they take these core samples. And they drilled, those blokes. And they reckon there's diamonds out there. Out there towards Mount Gilbert. My uncle's country. And they reckon there's diamonds."

The dancers sometimes told their stories this way, moving in circles, repeating chief ideas, teasing the fabric out. It appeared a Barramatjara tale *rolled*, as well as had straight momentum.

"So these blokes are very keen on that place of course, on that Mount Gilbert country of my uncle's. And they take their bits of core samples away. And all at once there's one of those classy planes, the ones that carry about a dozen heavies. Executive jet or something like that. It comes into Baruda. One of those classy bloody planes that . . . it touches down. And blokes wearing those Singapore-style tropical suits and silk ties are on it.

"And they want to go into a conference with my uncle and some of the other old blokes. All these old fellers who have something to do with Mount Gilbert, who have to do its ceremonies. These are the old men the classy blokes want to talk to. And they talk to them, but nothing gets settled. There's a talk session goes on for two days. And no one says yes or no, can or can't. Because it's my uncle's country, but he can't just say yes. He can't say, *Keep drilling, blow the shit out of it with gelignite.* He has to check with all his cousins, because it's their country too. That one called Mount Gilbert. Not just my uncle's, but his cousins' as well.

"These blokes in the suits, they're from the Department of Trade and the Department of Aboriginal Affairs too, and the department of this and the department of bloody that. They say to my uncle, *You don't mind helping Australia out, do you, mate? What with its adverse balance of payments and all that shit? You're a patriot, aren't you, old feller?* And you know what, Frank? They're doing the work for those drillers. And they're saying, *There'll be all these mineral royalties, and you can buy schools and trucks. And there could be other things here in the end, on this Barramatjara freehold. There could be foreign governments come in here and pay you a big rent for a little bit of this country. But before that happens, they want to see you Barramatjara blokes are interested in progress!* And they go on talking the poor old feller blind."

Bluey gave another yelping sob, and McCloud rushed in to prevent it developing.

"Keep going," he urged Bluey. "Take a sip of that stuff, just a sip."

"It's terrible for those old blokes," said the Barramatjara film star, the tribe's only sniffer of white powder. "It's pretty terrible for us fellers who're away all the time. But in a different way, you know. The heat's really on blokes like my uncle. On old fellers like that. *Traditional owners.* There was a time traditional owners were traditional owners and took it for granted. But now those words are in the law. *Traditional owners.* The blokes in the Singapore suits have to keep chattering away at them. And not only the old blokes. I mean I got my responsibilities up there in the Baruda country too. I've got a wife up there you know . . ."

"I know. I met her."

"She talked to you?"

"No, she didn't talk. Not particularly."

"She's pretty shy," said Bluey, conceding a grin towards the memory of her shyness. "Not like that rowdy sheila I'm living with in Sydney, not like that. A bloody old-fashioned girl, that one. My Barramatjara missus. My wife's country's way over near Giles Weather Station. I got ceremonies in the Baruda country I gotta go to, I got ceremonies in Giles, I got ceremonies all over the bloody place. But I'm never there. I'm always making bloody pictures. Or going to the opening of malls. Or poncing round in New York or somewhere."

And he went into a staring contemplation of his destiny, before lowering his voice.

"Frank, I go back into all that country, anyhow. *Badunjari.* You know *badunjari*? It's that dream journey you can make. It buggers you, mate. There you are in the fucking Carlton-Ritz, shagged-out, rooted, absolutely buggered, trying to sleep. And then your spirit gets up. Your spirit comes up out of you. *You* might have checked in to the fucking Carlton-Ritz, Frank. But not all of you. And your spirit, you know . . . he travels you to Easter Creek or Giles or Mount Dinkat or Gilbert or any of those places. You see those places in daylight. You sing to their stones, Frank. You're half dead with that *badunjari*. But you can't get out of it. And at eight o'clock in the morning, when they wake you up, there's some press conference you got to go to.

"And those journos and critics, they don't know any of this and you can't say anything. And they think, what a dumb fucking Abo! They don't know, Frank, I could've been singing those stones half the night. That's why I'm not what you'd call a good bloody traveller. But you know what, Frank? Let me tell you! That Jim Beam stops *badunjari*, and I love it like a brother! And that little white snow you snort up your nose! And screwing yourself stupid with a white girl! That's what works. You get a rest from that *badunjari*, Frank. And Christ, I like a rest."

"Oh, dear God," cried McCloud, who had never heard a story of such anguish, such wrenching of the spirit. "What can I say, Bluey? Do you want to go home? To Baruda, I mean?"

Bluey forlornly considered the idea. Then he half-way smiled. "Don't think so, Frank. Too much of a bloody nomad now."

McCloud looked beyond the glass of the restaurant window, at pale faces which seemed not so much burdened with dream journeys as with their lack.

"So my uncle," said Bluey, resuming *that* tale at last, "caves in and agrees to letting them have a mining lease. They can drill his country! What else can he do? He's big on the Queen, my uncle. Like Paul Mungina the *didj* bloke, you know. You can't say a word against the Queen in front of either of them. So the Queen wants him to let the diamond drillers cut loose. That's the way he thinks about it, poor old bugger. And he thinks, I'm over sixty, and I can't stand the talk and the pressure, and my cousins will sing me for it, but that's okay. I had my life, he thinks. And so he says *okay*. He says, *You can drill!*"

By *sing me* here, McCloud understood, Bluey did not mean the sort of singing of the stones which occupied him during sleep. He meant a curse.

"Poor old feller knows he can't hang on to his country anyhow," said Bluey. "Even though they give it to him freehold. They don't mean it. They don't mean, *We won't come round and talk about the Queen and exports and being a patriot*. Because they will come round. They come round all the time in Singapore suits. They get down out of classy bloody planes and talk bullshit about balance of payments and exports. And my uncle stares at them and tries to sort out how much of what they're saying comes from the Queen."

*   *   *

In the electronics pit on the hijacked aircraft, McCloud would remember with distress that he hadn't even asked Bluey the name of the drilling company, the corporation behind the enterprise. It was likely Bluey didn't know it anyhow, that it was some small drilling company which had since sold the rights to the megalith named in the magazine article. And it would be no use explaining to Taliq that Bluey's tale had sounded generic, to him, that the names almost hadn't mattered, that the story was an encapsulation of the Barramatjara tragedy, and all the rest of the earth's tribal tragedies.

Useless to say to Taliq, "I have no interest in mining news."

Useless to say, "I own no diamond drilling stocks."

Anyhow, in O'Neal's, McCloud hadn't asked for the company's name.

Hadn't he been a compassionate troupe manager though? And hadn't he swallowed down his own bewilderment at what the literary agent had by that stage already told him, and given himself over entirely, companionably, to treating Bluey's bewilderment?

But that counted for nothing in Taliq's court. It did convince McCloud himself, as he shivered and exchanged conversation with Stone and the Englishman Cale, that he must always ask for names. That it was a guilty world, and names must be enquired after. That you needed to live in the whole world, the world of the miners as well as the world of the agents. If I get out of here, McCloud promised himself forlornly, I'll make sure I enquire after names, and match them against the souvenir programmes of dance companies.

In O'Neal's that day, the cognac had levelled out Bluey's woe but somehow given it more authority.

"I was up there on that stage," reported Bluey, "and my uncle came in front of me, and his face was painted white and he had that confused look, the look of dead people. And I said to him, *Yes, you're dead, old man. You got to go back to your country.* His face had that bloody awful look. He didn't believe me or he didn't want to go, but he knew I was on to something all right. I knew something he didn't. For the first time in my bloody life, I had one up on him. And he wanted to do me a harm. Because he didn't know where he was. Poor old bugger. He didn't know whether to stay or start out, he didn't know whether to look for his own blood or put a curse on mine."

More weeping. A trench-coated young man at the bar was watching them. When men wept in places like this, it was generally a lovers' quarrel. McCloud, angry for Bluey's bewilderment, stared the young man down. *To hell with you, you catamite!* was what he wanted to yell. He was offended that Bluey's sorrows had such an authenticity, grew from a profound threat, and that this boy thought that what he was seeing was nothing but a shift in affection! Bluey did not even notice the young man. He raised his chin. "When I saw my uncle there, on the stage, I asked him, *Uncle, how'd they sing you?* And he said to me, *They sung my book.* And I remember he had this book – it was a book by Louis L'Amour, and the poor old bugger loved it. *Under the Sweetwater Rim,* that was its name. Louis L'Amour the cowboy writer. That was his one book. He read it fifteen years ago, and he's been reading it ever bloody since, starting it again as soon as he finishes it. Everyone knew about *Under the Sweetwater Rim* and my uncle. He was always trying to make other blokes read it. He thought it was the greatest thing since sliced bread, you know. And now listen, Frank! The last bloke he gave it to – the last bloke I saw handling it when I went home, you know . . . after you were up there . . . when my last picture finished . . . the last bloke I seen with it . . . well, I know him. I know who it was. Jesus, mate, this cognac's good! Could you shout me another one?"

McCloud suspected that Bluey's enthusiasm for a second drink was merely a ruse to distract him from asking for names.

"Not a chance, Bluey," said McCloud. "We still have to walk you through your cues."

"I don't think so, Frank. Not today." Again he frightened McCloud by conveying his utter conviction of bereavement. "You heard about the featherfoot blokes, Frank?"

"Featherfoot?" asked McCloud. "I've heard something about them."

"They're your sort of stuff, Frank," Bluey observed. "Real exotic. White buggers like to say, I know So-and-so, and he's a featherfoot. Yeah, real glamorous unless you run up against them. They've got these feather moccasins. They don't have to wear them or anything, not in the flesh. They wear 'em in spirit, you know. And they meet a man who's done wrong, and they daze him with a song he can't even hear. Then they wake him and send him home, and all at once, two days later he falls down for good. Or else they creep up and sing a man's book. You can tell the featherfoot because his little toe's broken. It points up. The old men break it when they choose him, when he's just a kid." Bluey lowered his voice to a resonant, teary whisper. "My cousin Whitey's got that little toe, for instance. So he can move and no one sees him. And he can sing too and no bugger hears. You check on Whitey's foot. Don't say I told you, Frank. But my cousin Whitey went and sung that book. I wish I didn't know it, but I know it."

McCloud himself began to tremble. Yet it was easy to believe in Whitey, the calm, pontifical curser, singing a doom into the print of *Under the Sweetwater Rim*. Such was the Barramatjara dispensation! Behind the charming patterns of paint and dance lay the fiercer disciplines. Powerful men and women exercised them. Whitey was exactly the sort of powerful man who might utter a judgment which would chase you through every corner of the night, would viper its way at you up through the print of your familiar book or slide down your throat with the tea from your accustomed cup.

McCloud's nostalgia for Barramatjara life hadn't included up to now any sense of the claustrophobia of tribal judgment. From that second on it would.

There was also the aspect – which hadn't escaped McCloud – that Bluey, being convinced about who had *sung* his uncle, would be bound by blood to inflict a reciprocal punishment on Whitey, his fellow performer in the Barramatjara Dance Troupe.

This was a terrifying and inconvenient duty for a film star like Bluey to live under. It was also an arrangement which would evade and baffle the management skills of McCloud himself. Curses could whizz back and forth across the stage. Blood might be shed. Someone might be pushed off the edge of a subway station platform. McCloud was suddenly as anxious as Bluey Kannata himself was about the uncle who liked Louis L'Amour.

"I'll speak to the hotel management at once," said McCloud. "But we won't wait until it's morning in Baruda. If it's necessary to put you at your ease, we'll wake them in the middle of the night."

Giving up all idea of subjecting Bluey to a technical rehearsal that day, he took him into a cab and returned with him some fifteen blocks to the hotel. The competent Pauline was not there, was away visiting some cousin of her mother's in Connecticut. When McCloud asked him about arranging a line for Bluey to reach Baruda, it seemed to astound the manager that there was anywhere on earth which could not be reached at will by telephone. He was unfamiliar with the idea of the radio telephone by which Baruda had touch with the world. The telephone company supervisors McCloud spoke with seemed equally unfamiliar, but connected him at last to some specialist in one of the company's remoter offices who believed the contact could be made.

It would mean however a journey to lower Manhattan and a wait of some hours in a communications room.

And so, while the other members of the troupe were still rehearsing and as an early dusk sharpened the wind off the river, McCloud and Bluey travelled downtown by subway and found the address in an old building which once – as late as the 1930s – had been a great telephone exchange. On the fifth floor, they sat three hours in front of a radio telephone apparatus, sharing a pint of vodka Bluey had insisted on to ease his certainty and acuteness of loss.

By the third hour, Bluey – so far from Baruda and with only the promise of a tenuous link – divulged sundry other items of Barramatjara intelligence. But never once mentioned Highland Pegasus, the diamond fanciers for whose sake, within three weeks, McCloud would be punished in the electronics pit of a hijacked aircraft.

7

LANDING IN THE MORNING

AT some time the three dazed and pallid men in the electronics pit were jolted out of freezing half-slumber by alterations of noise, by greater vibration, and by an access of warmer air.

"I do believe we're coming down," Cale announced to the other two. For even in this he was first with an interpretation. "Someone's letting us back to earth! Someone is consenting to refuel us!"

They continued to thud down amidst the earth's lumpy rising warmth. "The Mediterranean," said McCloud.

"I would call that likely," said Cale.

"Algeria maybe," athletic Daniel Stone guessed through his perfect teeth.

"Perhaps," said Cale. "Interesting to speculate." And of course he began to. To Cale, you were forced to conclude, the world was a seminar. "We don't know whether we have imposed ourselves on this airport we're approaching – at least I hope we're approaching an airport – or whether they're welcoming us." He pulled a face. "Jesus, I hope they let us out for a piss. I don't want to short-circuit any of this stuff."

"Or smudge our cards," said Stone drily.

McCloud felt his own bladder growing like a stone, brewing like a cloud, within him. He could not countenance the humiliation or the stench which might occur down here.

"Okay, Cale," said Stone, "you keep telling us you're the expert. Tell us what you think is happening on the ground."

"Oh, Jesus," said Cale, trying to pretend he would rather not be put to the mental effort. He crossed his arms reflectively, the hands tucked into each opposing armpit. "Forgive me, Mr Stone.

I don't have a watch, I don't have vision. And I still don't know what Taliq and his lads mean."

For some reason, this amused and cheered McCloud. "But you told us upstairs you *knew* what they meant," he said.

"Oh, of course. That. Well, as I say you can bet they're part of some radical fragment, and they're out to prove their prestige through their acts. But if they were a fragment they would not be welcome, you see, in Algeria or Oran or Tunis, where the more orthodox and moderate Palestinian groups can be found . . . the ones who don't sanction acts of terror.

"However, if this aircraft were ready to fall out of the sky from lack of fuel, then it might grudgingly be permitted to touch down at one of a dozen places." Cale closed one eye. "On the other hand, *this* could be Tripoli, Gaddafi's Tripoli, which very likely approves of what Taliq is doing. See, my friends, we're driven to think in circles."

"The sad truth is," lamented Daniel Stone, "we have here an expert on terrorism – Cale – and a manufacturer of software to measure up their pathology – myself. But we know no more than the folk strapped in their seats upstairs."

Cale winked at McCloud then. "Well, it's not quite as dismal as that. Though we have no eyes and we have no pants, within those limits surely – as I've said already – we can guess a certain amount about what you might call the *profiles* of the boys upstairs. These matters are well-established, as you know as well as I, my dear Mr Stone. I was simply opening up the subject, no more, when we were speaking briefly upstairs earlier, with the other passengers.

"Wouldn't you agree, for instance, it's very likely that each of Taliq's bright, brave, berserk young men has had his education paid for by whatever organisation Taliq represents? Or else by money from some secret police somewhere which has Taliq's group under contract? Because terror is a business, as we both know. *Arab Youth Popular Socialist Front* and such names are so much nomenclature and horseshit. A name is made up specifically for *this* act. The taking of our plane.

"So – as I intimated already – some government . . . or its secret police . . . sees the talents of the organisation Taliq belongs to as *bankable*. Iraq or Syria might put up money – I mean big sums, free of taxes – to enable some act of this nature. Just like selling a house – some on exchange of contracts, some on completion."

"Selling a *house*?" murmured McCloud in disbelief.

"Yes. Say Syria want to discredit the moderate Arabs! They

don't want Palestinians and Israelis talking gently to each other!
A good, solid hijack, and the world barks like mad dogs again,
and the normal hatreds everyone's so happy with settle down in
place once more. A job like that's worth millions in anyone's
money!"

The longer Cale spoke, the more his body spread in this cramped
cell, forcing McCloud's cold haunches together. Just the same, the
Englishman's utterances *did* sound quite sensible and magisterial
to McCloud.

"And Taliq?" Cale went on in a creaking voice. "The pattern of
every hijack we know about tells us he isn't exactly the leader
of the organisation itself . . . he's more what you'd call middle
management. Ambitious, I'd guess. And he doesn't really want to
die . . . he wants to live on and flourish."

"Right," agreed Stone. "Success here will help him *get* the
leadership."

"Exactly. Of course the problem is he's also quite willing to
perish if necessary, more willing on balance than us. He's willing
to blow us up, him and his lads with us. He's a soldier. But he also
knows that if he lives his act will attract more recruits to his flag,
more footsoldiers for the next time some government wants foul
play done. In return for which, as I say, the rewards are so great
you can send those kids upstairs – Hasni, Yusuf and the rest – to
Harvard or Oxford." With a conclusive swipe of the back of his
hand across his nose, Cale came to his peroration. "So how do
I think of those young men with their Polish automatics? They
are paying off their educational loans. That's how I think of
them."

As the plane encountered lower air still, the American Stone,
unanchored in his corner, was jolted forward towards McCloud.
It seemed however not to be purely a matter of turbulence. He
appeared to be in a state of forceful dissent from what Cale was
arguing.

"You can't compare them to honest kids like you're doing," said
Stone. "*Paying off their educational loans!* That's just not a feasible
proposition. With these guys, you don't begin by stating similarity
with normal people. They're essentially different from a kid say
like my stepson."

He blinked at what must have been the inevitable enquiry in
McCloud's and Cale's faces.

"Sure. I have a stepson. I married late. A widow. But the fact is, you just can't compare those bastards upstairs with my boy. They're pathological to the core, and that's it!"

"If you'll forgive me, Stone," said Cale, who of course didn't care whether he was forgiven or not, "I think the difference is only one of degree, not of kind."

"No way," said Stone, shaking his head. "Different in kind, those sons-of-bitches. A different species!"

McCloud tried to imagine his own son the Boy as a potential activist and arm of revolution. Could events make him Hasni?

Meanwhile Cale was raising his eyebrows. "My dear old chap, does your computer program, this Psychopar or whatever . . . does it begin by saying your stepson and the boys upstairs are actually *different animals?*"

"Look, Mr Cale," said Stone, "I might be a simple engineer and therefore easy to dismiss. But my partner Hirsch has often said to me that the usefulness of our program comes from the fact it works from substantive differences, based on verifiable data. In talking about terrorists, Cale, it cuts through all that nature-versus-nurture bullshit. It doesn't pretend that hijackers or bomb-throwers are normal boys suffering from a little too much motivation say, or a lack of vitamin C. If it did, what it told governments and police forces would be useless! No, it begins with crucial departures. It delivers the key because it works in *essential* differences. Like the ones between those sons-of-bitches upstairs and my stepson."

McCloud watched Cale consider the wisdom of such a method and seem to dismiss it. How wonderful that stripped, labelled and imprisoned, he and Stone had space for such passion.

"Oh, God!" declared Cale now. "All I want to do is – I'm trying to project from normal people the sorts of people Taliq's boys are. They're tribal patriots, they remember history as any young man should, they're *compelled* by history in fact, and they want more of an education than they'll get on the West Bank. A combination of motives. I recommend you listen to these kids, Stone. Their own words will tell you."

"Not so far they haven't," said Stone.

With a meaty hand, the English journalist made a concession. "Oh, sure. They *are* different from your lad in some respects. At least in the sense they've probably already been through some initiation he wouldn't even think of. Even though he – like the rest of us males – has probably done crazy enough things in the holy name of initiation into whatever group he wants to be part of. Jesus Christ, I still think most boys are the same. Half-way between a rebel and a rapist. Now those boys upstairs may have placed an explosive device in a night-club in West Berlin, or thrown a bomb into a swimming-pool in Athens – you perhaps remember the Glyphada Hotel there, a delegation of handicapped Britons bobbing around in the pool. Two killed, nine wounded." But at that, suddenly and as if in self-reproof for overstepping limits of taste, Cale shook his head. "Most likely however, nothing dramatic like that. Probably a raid on a savings and loan in New Jersey, or on a post office in Manchester. Funds for the cause, you see, and a rite of passage. And there's excitement and brotherhood in all that!"

Stone gazed up at the blue and yellow, emerald and crimson switches and fuses which must mean something to an engineer but whose code was inscrutable. "But there you go. You're still trying to give them some damn nobility. They don't know what in the hell they're doing. I mean you saw them – threatening that girl in the green dress and ogling her at the one time. All they want is anarchy. My stepson's light years from that, and so is any other balanced kid."

McCloud was tired now of this half-naked discourse. He tended anyhow to think of truth as a blend rather than an essence. He wanted to be let out soon to urinate, and this need overrode the intellectual vanities which dominated the fusebox.

"I reckon," he ventured, "both your models would be of use at various times."

Neither of them were happy, of course, to hear it.

"Okay," Stone conceded at last. "Say they were in any way like my boy . . . What does that tell you, Cale? Where would it get you?"

"Some way," Cale boasted. "It means they're subject to doubt, these boys, just like your lad. They're forced to harangue themselves internally. *This is right, this is right, this is right!* Just like the average young haranguing themselves. And like the average young, they carry their weapons not only to intimidate us, but to intimidate themselves. To show themselves the size of what they're doing. And given its size, its rightness."

"So we work on that?" asked Stone. "That's what you're saying. The way we'd work on a normal kid's uncertainty?"

*   *   *

In that second, as he looked at the sedulous Stone with some envy, McCloud felt his all-too-common bemusement of spirit set in again and unman hope and comprehension and courses of action. Stone was admirable. He was a fighter. His body was a fighter's body. Until last night he'd thought perhaps the fight was against inflation and cholesterol, but he had now switched his restrained defiance and his watchfulness to this new threat, the threat of Taliq's boys.

Whereas McCloud, confused in marriage and in creation, divided in care for both Pauline and the Barramatjaras, was still in the process of framing his resistance to what had befallen him. His limbs threatened to fall apart – so it seemed to him – while Stone's tightened.

He tensed his brain, looking for the focusing idea to take hold of, still utterly unsure what it might be.

"At some stage," Cale told Stone conclusively and with a confidential smile, "we will each be alone with one of them. Even at the risk that he might shoot us between the eyes to prove how right he is, we must work on his doubts."

"Okay. Say for a second they *did* respond to string-pulling the way ordinary kids do. What about Taliq?"

"Taliq's lost," said Cale, and in saying it, even though flaccid and cirrhotic, took on again an authority adequate, when combined with the interior torment of the bladder, to impair McCloud's breath. Air was restored to him, however, by the impact – felt even and perhaps particularly here in the electronics bay – of their aircraft's suspension taking the impact of landing.

On the night Bluey called from New York to enquire into his uncle's health, the microphone at which he was placed sat alone and mute in the dead centre of a metal table, looking like an exhibit in some museum of telephony. And mutely, waiting for it to speak and confirm his dream, Bluey Kannata regarded it. Across the room, the technician beyond the glass strolled from panel to panel, flicking switches, bored, it seemed, with serving that shrinking portion of the earth which the satellite and the laser beam did not instantly make a linkage with or provoke news from. His yawns were very nearly an insult to Bluey's aching focus on the radio-telephone mike.

To distract Bluey's gaze, which threatened to become riveted for good into the mesh of the mike cover, McCloud went out now and then for sandwiches and cups of coffee. Early evening in New York coincided with a morning hour in Baruda when the Barramatjara people would have breakfasted and begun turning their gaze from the morning sun. By then the table in lower Manhattan was covered with detritus – wrappers smeared with mayonnaise from America's whole-hearted sandwiches, cups with lees of coffee, Coke cans crushed to pass the time. Yet still the mike did not speak. Bluey seemed to believe with increasing fixity that the silence and delay confirmed his dream.

It had been a hard room for McCloud and Bluey to find in a building just as hard, surrounded by the shuffling homeless with their polystyrene begging cups. Yet towards seven o'clock admirable Pauline found it. She had stopped briefly at the hotel to pick up news and directions from the dance troupe. She came in still flushed from a day of riding on horseback with her mother's cousin amongst western Connecticut's burnished autumn trees.

It had been only ten minutes before she arrived to reinforce him, that McCloud had given in to Bluey's request for a *real* drink. For Bluey had kept turning his head a second from the mike, still keeping one eye fixed on it, and saying levelly, without his normal roguishness, "A man could do a drink!" It was a serious request, McCloud was sure, from a man at an extreme of anxiety.

So when Pauline came in, there had stood the half-pint of vodka wrapped in its paper bag, sitting upright and uncapped amongst the tumbled coffee cups.

He feared she might think it had been lightly bought and drunk.

For the moment, though, she bent to kiss Bluey on the cheek. His eyes flickered away from the microphone for one frantic instant.

"Gidday, Pauline love," Bluey told her with forced jolliness. "No word yet. Waiting for news from Baruda, you know."

Pauline said, "It will come. It will make you happy too."

"Bloody doubt it, love."

She looked at McCloud. Her green eyes had that wonderful fresh glitter she'd picked up in the countryside. She came closer and spoke to him in a whisper. "Is the booze a good idea?"

"In the circumstances," McCloud murmured, "perhaps. This is *serious business*."

*   *   *

That was a phrase the Barramatjara used to describe the major workings of the earth; benefits and maledictions, blossomings and deaths.

Pauline held McCloud's gaze calmly and with a margin of reproof. He had, during the writing of his book, flirted with alcoholism. A certain risk to the brain *and* reins, it had seemed justified then by the scope of the work he believed he was writing.

"Well," she said, giving up ground with a smile. "I suppose you got the smallest bottle you could."

Her father the Dentist had been an abstainer, of course; his excesses had transcended alcohol. But her grandfather, a dentist also, had been famous in parts of Sydney for damage he'd done with drills and needles while inexact from whisky, for the wrong teeth he pulled, for the ultimate trouble he had got into with the Dental Association. That shame had hung remotely over her childhood home, soon to be overshadowed by further shames and a new generation of trouble from the Dental Association. It had of course all given her a weakness for the company of topers and – at the same time – a fear of their likely excesses. McCloud satisfied both those impulses.

Well then into the New York night and the Baruda morning, the technician in the control room hammered on the glass. Simultaneously a voice, barbed with static, tore from the microphone. It jolted Bluey's head back.

"Baruda main council office here," it said. "Over."

Familiar with the radio telephone, Bluey flicked the switch on the base of his microphone. "Bluey Kannata here, all the way over there in New York. That you, Norman? Over."

"Bluey! How're you going in that scary place, you bloody scoundrel? Over."

"It's a bloody madhouse, Norman. But don't worry about that. Tell me straight, man. That uncle of mine? My mother's brother? How can I say his name, mate? I dreamed he got sung, Normie. This afternoon he was right on the stage here, bloody Lincoln Center stage in New York, Normie. His name . . . it can't be said, can it, mate? Isn't that so? Poor old feller's all finished, isn't he, Normie? Over."

And Bluey crucially flicked the switch again.

McCloud massaged his own sweaty palms. What sort of frightful mourning and hiding-away would Bluey embark on in this alien city? What overdoses of this and that might he try to take, catching and assuaging in himself the infection of his uncle's death?

"Norman here again, mate. Saw the old feller just an hour back outside the store. Eyesight didn't look too good. Apart from that he's there, on his rug. Going to play cards. Waiting for Dulcie Yaminata and Billy Dimiti to turn up with the pack. Over."

A yelp of hope came from Bluey; it was one of those rich and alien sounds of the kind the Barramatjara were able to utter and enchant strangers with all night.

"Mate, mate. Could you get him here, mate? Hour's a bloody long time. A man could go sixty times over in an hour. Right? Over."

"Don't go away, Bluey. I'll see what I can do. Just hang on to the line, son. Over."

Bluey flicked the switch, instantaneously strangling the static deep in the line. "I'm not going anywhere, mate. You bring that old man, eh? Over."

Pauline and McCloud stared at each other. Can an old man on his way to play nine-up die of a curse within an hour? Had some wise woman, a featherfoot ally, turned up with the cards and dealt him his last breath?

Bluey had set the radio-telephone mike to *Reception*, and after two minutes an aged squawk took him by surprise.

"Bluey Kannata? You're well, son? Over."

Bluey surprised McCloud by being gruff. "What about yourself, Uncle Jimmy? Over."

"I got these problems with my eye, son. Can't see the bloody cards, you know. The others try to dud me, Bluey. Why you calling me on the radio-phone? You back home? Over."

A mighty giggle, musical yet assonant, a laugh whose tone McCloud once again imagined might have been capable of vivifying stones, shook out of Bluey. "But you're alive, you old man, eh? You're full of beans and playing that nine-up? And that old woman of yours, Auntie Nancy? How is that Aunt Nancy? Over."

"Too late to trade her in on one of them young sheilas. She ain't got the same problem I got and she can read the newspaper. Prime Minister come up here, she bowls up to the bugger and says, *Hey, Bob*. She knows how to push a bloke round, that woman Nancy. Over."

"She'll be still bossing politicians round when you're gone, old man!" cried Bluey, still laughing in whoops. "She's going to be cheating at gin rummy years yet, uncle. Over."

There was an answering laughter from the uncle. It span around the room in New York. "Over, over," stammered the old man with the giggles.

"I'm real glad you're well, old man! Over."

Bluey had chosen to make his joy sound average now. Not average enough to mislead the uncle though.

"Bluey, son? Why'd you call on the radio telephone? You had some dream about me? Over."

"No. What bloody dream, uncle? I had some business there with Norman. I wanted to ask him about my missus. Had some worries about her. Wondered was she okay, you know. Over."

"You ought to come and see that missus, Bluey. And the nippers. Over."

Bluey put his hand over his eyes. He didn't want to pursue this.

"I will, uncle. Bit hard from here. Over."

"Want to talk to her now, Bluey? You know a woman'll only start looking at other blokes. It's the way things go, Blue. Want to talk to her? Over."

"Can't right now, uncle. They want me to get off the line here. Radio telephone, it's a real rigmarole here, uncle. They're not set up like us. Over."

He had the time now to wink at McCloud, as if Frank too was a man beset with wives.

"Listen. Don't you drink too much liquor, Bluey. You're a devil for that stuff. That stuff's a killer, son. Over."

"One last thing, uncle. Those blokes in the Singapore suits, them miners. They been back? Over."

"Haven't seen them, Bluey. Haven't been no drillers. Might have blown over, son. Over."

"Hope so, uncle, hope so. You keep well then. Love to Auntie Nancy. Over and out."

All the way back uptown in the cab, there were gales of laughter from Bluey. "That old bugger," he would say in a voice which implied he was pinching his uncle's ear. "He still cheating at that gin rummy and nine-up, eh?"

And he would hoot with laughter and beat the cab's window frame until the Haitian driver asked him to stop.

McCloud had noticed that he had not addressed his uncle with the familiarity of that standard Australian endearment *bugger* during their radio-phone conversation. Respect had its ceremonies even in the debased English of the cattle camp and the reservation.

McCloud – with his arm slung around Pauline's shoulders – longed to tell her about his own relief. Whitey had been proven not to be a fatal influence. Bluey was fit again for rehearsal. And in a calm moment McCloud might have the chance to remind him that he should not give all dreams and phantasms equal ground.

Back at the hotel, the other dancers were waiting for them, gathered together in Whitey Wappitji's room, which had a little kitchen attached to it, and drinking coffee and beer. Bluey rushed into the place ahead of McCloud and Pauline. This was unusual; generally he would make very courtly gestures to send them through a door first. An old-fashioned boy, Bluey, apart from the abuse of modern and fashionable substances! But tonight he had to get inside quickly to celebrate and chortle and slap shoulders and discover for himself that Whitey's room was habitable to him. For Whitey, the feather-foot, the man of the reputedly broken toe, had not ambushed or cursed the old man.

Whitey had already pulled the metal ring out of a Coors and placed it in Bluey's hand as the actor reached him. And Bluey held it celebratorily, a vessel empty of spells and full of merest froth. Embracing Whitey, he yelled, "This bugger's my mate, this old Whitey here!"

McCloud felt Pauline's hand grasp his – her friendship, her rejoicing in the tribal room. To honour her, McCloud did no more than take a sip from Bluey's can – Bluey was in a mood of course to which drinking from a common bowl was appropriate.

There remained the medical question – why had Bluey seen his uncle, whitened to death, on the stage at the Lincoln Center?

Even Wappitji, the troupe's centre of authority, raised that matter obliquely. "You got to watch them funny cigarettes, Bluey. Fair dinkum you have. They make you cry for the wrong things."

For a second, Bluey was sobered by Whitey's diagnosis. He blinked and looked away. But then he yelled and reconsidered the black aperture which led into the liquor in his can. "Come on, you blokes. We're a long way from home, us fellers. And all brothers. Let's have a party, eh?"

Whitey considered him soberly. Whitey who had had the authentic dream and was on his civilising mission, like Cortez looking for the core, for the immutable soul of Montezuma. Whitey who was making light in the darkness.

*　　*　　*

Landing in the Morning

Later in the night, their bladders full, rather than use the bathroom water-closet one at a time, they went to the communal urinals down the hall. The dancers and McCloud groaned, released themselves from their pants and began pissing. The room was full all at once of a strange, subtle and not unmusical whistling of which McCloud was not part. *Whistlecock*, the first Europeans into the desert had called this phenomenon. In the sundry grades of Barramatjara initiation, a young man was not only circumcised but sub-incised, the underside of his penis cut open to the urethra. This was how it had been done by the Malu and the Two Brothers. The earth needed the blood from this incision. And when a man pissed you heard the full music of his manhood.

Which McCloud could not match.

The casual attender of the troupe's performance the following night had no way of seeing the neatness of the connection between the finale and what had befallen Bluey in the past two days.

During the afternoon, a considerable crowd who held tickets for the night performance came to one of the seminar rooms at the Lincoln Center to drink wine and watch the dancers paint a canvas called the Emu Dreaming at Mount Wilson. Great circles of red and black dotted with white were connected across a landscape of white, blue, yellow, orange and brown dots by sinuous and – in a few eccentric cases – straight lines. The whole thing looked like a continent seen in clear light from far space.

This making of the dance painting never worked as well indoors, McCloud thought, as it had outdoors in Australia with peculiarly Australian light. But it came up brilliantly at night with help from the lighting technician.

Emu Dreaming at Mount Wilson was a story like Prometheus, except of course that Prometheus was a Johnny-come-lately compared to that millennia-earlier fire-thief the emu ancestor, danced when evening came by Bluey. Wappitji danced the wedge-tailed eagle, casually replete with grace and authority and mana.

McCloud loved this dance for its simplicity and force. Emu, his eye glittering with avian ambition, tries to deprive the Two Brothers of eagle feathers which were their usual and beloved ornamentation. He frightens the brothers away from the eagle nest atop Mount Wilson by telling them of a serpent who occupies the peak. When the eagle itself, divinely enraged, discovers emu's attempt to corner the speed and potency inherent in eagle feathers, he renders the emu flightless.

*   *   *

Bluey was that night and as always superb as the long-legged, long-necked emu whose greed has produced a straitened world. Now he and the Two Brothers, in an eagle-less earth, have only ashes to mark themselves with. Even this limited form of power emu tries to corner by stealing fire from the Two Brothers.

The Two Brothers (Phil the Christian and Cowboy Tom), with Wappitji the eagle wheeling far to the north ordaining the result, pursue the fugitive emu and his small ball of fire, spear him, and take from his body a bone with which they pierce the septum of their noses. Emu perishes in the bewilderment common to those who try too hard to find the ritual keys to the earth. The eagle rewards the Two Brothers by giving them feathered feet for the pursuit of wrongdoers.

That night as every night, the audience were meant to approve the punishments brought down on emu, but in Bluey's performance there was always such a yearning to span all forms of mastery that during the sequence people could frequently be heard weeping.

8

IN THE PIT II

Mc CLOUD, who often found it hard to wait for a sandwich to be made, or for his call to be put through to some administrator, assumed an unusual patience in that great fusebox where he sat cross-legged with Cale and Daniel Stone. If he had known he must wait twenty minutes here, he would have invested himself into the cramp of his legs, into his fierce desire to urinate, into the prickly sweat which broke from him now that the plane sat hotly in the morning sun. The *Mediterranean* morning sun, as they all agreed it must be.

But since he did not know how long all this would take, what span of confinement Taliq had in mind, he let his pains grow remote from him, external, a kind of luggage.

"What about Larnaka?" said Daniel Stone suddenly. "That's an airport hijackers seem to use."

"This isn't Larnaka," Cale told him. Cale was perfunctory and dismissive. "Even with a tail wind, we haven't been flying long enough." Cale turned awkwardly towards McCloud. "You ever been to North Africa before?"

"No. I'd imagine though you have." Why else the question?

"Oh yes, son! I was an officer in Britain's now much correctly booed-at attack on the Suez Canal. Thirty-one years ago. If I'd been shot then, I would have died happy but knowing fuck-all. Now I know fuck absolutely everything. I can look this chap Taliq in the eye. I even profess to know what drives a fellow like him. Perhaps it's time I was shot. I know too fucking much."

McCloud said, "I'm not so sure I do. The dancers are still educating me."

"Come on. You don't really mean that, sonny Jim. It's okay to manage them – it's as good a way as any to make a living. But when it comes to the indigenes, aborigines, natives, first-comers and so on I subscribe to what D. H. Lawrence says, you know. When he was down there at that ranch in New Mexico. Well, he went to see the Pueblos dance and said it was all twilight stuff. He said those Europeans who want to idealise this stuff are renegades. What do you think of that?"

"I think he was a man of his day," said McCloud, not wanting to waste time being angry.

"And you're not a man of yours? Just because we've had a few scares – Three Mile Island and Chernobyl and so on – does that make primitives desirable, wiser, niftier? Christ! I mean, it's charming and all. But as I said to you earlier, let's not call it art."

McCloud was tempted to tell him about the elders who had come to Whitey in a dream and urged him to release the embargoed dances and the painting which skirted the very edge of the danger, but he resisted it. Cale was the sort of rock against which all such dreams shattered.

"Lawrence used to beat his wife as well, Mr Cale," McCloud said instead. "Not secretly either. He boasted about it. Do you think that's a good idea of his too?"

"Jesus Christ!" cried Cale, hooting. "An Aussie intellectual. A fucking living contradiction in terms! An oxymoron in underpants!"

But there was a sort of acknowledgement in Cale's laughter, and even a pleading that allowances be made.

McCloud chose to smile warily, someone bringing up a tender subject. "You were so much in need of a drink last night. You don't seem to need one now."

"Oh," said Cale lightly, "I'm the worst sort of pisspot. I'm an alcoholic by choice, not by need. Nicotine – now there's a genuine addiction. Whereas I drink only from boredom and I love to talk people – stewards, pub-owners – into bending the letter of the liquor laws. They're nectar, those drinks. Nips of whisky which violate some silly sod's law. I particularly enjoy booze in nations where having a snort is subject to penalties of flogging and gaol. But in other circumstances, if the stuff's not there, I don't climb up the fusebox."

Creaking internally in small ways, the plane remained on the earth.

They heard a reverberation from beyond the pit, as if someone was striking the outer skin of the aircraft with a wrench. They listened to it, faces raised. Like a sailor deep in some quarter of a hostile sea, McCloud felt a smothering alarm.

The noise ceased. Even Cale and Stone did not try to discuss what it meant. The possibilities were too numerous or terrible. Was it plane maintenance? Was it sabotage on behalf of the passengers, or sabotage on behalf of Taliq? Were armed men joining the plane to reinforce Taliq or – for some reason equally as frightening to the three men in the electronics bay – to take his life? Had all the passengers been let go; and had these three been forgotten or retained for special purposes?

Twenty seconds or more passed and their breath grew normal again. You could see Cale actually gather himself for further conversation.

But as a result of a sudden illumination whose origin he couldn't guess at, but which grew from his philosophic accommodation to the cries of his body, McCloud spoke first. "Taliq . . . he won't bring us out of here yet. Surely, he'll be busy dealing with authorities on the ground?"

Stone was engaged at the time in slow flexings of his neck, maybe doing exercises he remembered his masseur recommending. "He'll ask for something no one's likely to deliver," he said, as if that much was obvious. "Cale's right about one aspect. What we're seeing is probably an attempt to prevent *rapprochement*. Okay. So the exploit works of its own nature. But they might as well tack on a shopping list. Something specific they want. The release of political prisoners . . ."

"Indeed," said Cale. "Indeed." He conveyed to McCloud that he was gratified by the rate at which Stone was catching on. "And there's another possibility with Taliq's little enterprise you no doubt wouldn't countenance, Mr Stone."

Stone stopped doing his exercises. "How can you know that? I'll countenance any damned thing. Don't for God's sake tell me what's within my powers to contemplate. You don't know that." He raised his hand. "Oh, forgive me! We understand you know everything. It's just that the fact doesn't seem to have done us much good. So just tell me what you have in mind. I'm willing as the next man to run it under the light."

Cale adjusted his underwear. "Okay, sonny, here it comes! There are voices in Israel who don't want reconciliation either. Israel has accumulated its record of shame too, and I regret that. Because the boys upstairs will no doubt bore us with the details over coming hours or even days."

"Oh, Jesus!" Stone cried. Angry now and not as concerned with tidy gesture, he cast his eyes wildly upwards. "You mean that the wicked Zionists themselves buy a raid from the Arabs? So they'll have a reason for keeping things as they are? That's what you're saying?"

"It seems to have happened in the past," said Cale. "And you and I acknowledge that. An innocent like Mr McCloud here – it's news to him. But it's not news to me as a journalist. Nor to you as a – what is it? – computer contractor?"

"Jesus Christ! I *am* a computer contractor! I have my Master's from MIT and my doctorate from Caltech on the wall of my den! They were bought with student loans and at some price of time and effort. And I resent your whole supercilious Limey drift, Cale. There's one thing I agree with those Arabs upstairs about! You and your fucking Empire made this grief for all of us! Scratch any human misery of this century and you guys are behind it!"

"Oh, yes?" asked Cale. "But, my boy, I didn't drive the poor sodding Palestinians out of the orange groves of Haifa! My government didn't make those nifty emergency laws to cover the Gaza Strip landgrab. Heaps of paternalistic folly – oh yes, that's us all over, and I confess to it! We *permitted* the conditions for your success over the Arabs. We didn't actually drive the spike into the poor bastards' hearts!"

"That same tired old Limey mind-trick!" said Stone. "*Our intentions were* too *good! The mean natives took advantage of us* . . ." He appealed to McCloud. "Only one thing more pitiable than the argument is that all the sons-of-bitches actually *believe* it!"

As a witness to Stone's outcry, McCloud thought there was the same bored mischief still working in Cale as had earlier caused him to try so hard to lever a drink out of the steward; as – for that matter – in his literate quoting of D. H. Lawrence. Had Lawrence ever written those words, or had Cale composed them himself? That question was obviously the sort of trouble Cale *liked* to raise in the mind.

Now, not having got quite the display of chagrin out of McCloud which he needed to soothe his ennui or terror, and with the *Zionist Hack* placard still waiting beneath him on the floor, he was enjoying more success by transforming himself amongst the electrical fuses into a Jew-baiter than he'd got earlier as a derider of native culture.

"Come on, Cale," McCloud appealed out of what he thought was fairness. "Mr Stone is an American citizen. He didn't drive the Palestinians out either."

"Fair crack of the whip, eh, cobber?" asked Cale, imitating the idiom in which the Barramatjara spoke. "Who put the weapons in the Israelis' hands? Good American *Bar Mitzvah* boys like Stone here."

"Don't be so fucking offensive," Stone told him.

"Are you saying you haven't had a hand?"

"Naturally I cherish the concept of that state."

"Ah, yes. *Cherish* . . ."

Stone sat forward, asserting his right to his proper space in the pit in the face of Cale's imperial spread of flesh. "Mr McCloud has it right. You fucking conservatives are the worst anti-Semites! Except you hate and fear the Arabs worse than you hate and fear us. And besides that, we're better business. Or we were until Arab oil entered the picture."

"Kindly don't call me an anti-Semite, man," said Cale, pointing his finger with apparent passion at Stone. About the real intensity of the movement though it was hard to guess. "I pushed Arabs around for you when I was a young officer. I wrote glowing reports about your fucking *kibbutzim* and your *moshavim*. And I'm a Zionist – it says so on my label."

"Okay," Stone called, settling the air with his hands. "But you commit the worst crime in your goddam head. You think we've got Satanic cleverness! You believe we're cleverer than anyone else! You look at me and you think I'm full of fucking snake-like cunning. Brighter than the Japanese and twice as alien! Admit it!"

There was a sudden and – McCloud thought – theatrical calm, as if Cale was orchestrating it.

Cale of course chose when to break it. "Those Palestinians upstairs didn't arrest us without a basis," he announced. "Poor bloody McCloud is the innocent. For him the rap is – as they say – *bum*. But they knew that you and I had had an effect on *them*, old son. On whatever miseries they believe they bear on earth. You and I have made things happen contrary to their interests. So, like me, you probably *are* a cunning bastard. I'm willing to believe that. That doesn't take a leap of faith."

Stone began to laugh. "Cunning, Mr Cale? My father came to New York in 1948. He opened a handbag repair shop in Spring

Street in lower Manhattan. His clients were Jews as proud as himself, and the poorer Poles and Italians. Gentrification and high rent drove the poor old sonofabitch out in the early seventies. They needed his shop for the bar of a rib joint! During his life he went every day, morning and night, to the orthodox synagogue down on East Broadway, even though cataracts had just about blinded him by the age of sixty. This is cunning? This is Satanic?

"Sure, he lectured my brother and me to excel academically and not goof off like the Italians. This – again I ask the question – is cunning? And I suppose you think it's a cliché that he was crippled by the age of sixty-five – fall-out from SS beatings he took in Birkenau. It was cunning of him, I'm sure you'll agree, not to seek any compensation from the West German government, though New York was full of lawyers who could have arranged it for him! *They won't put a price on my suffering,* he used to say.

"But see, the problem with New York is you can't sit still without either freezing or frying. You can't lie down with crippled joints. The Rome of the modern world, and its climate is unliveable! Its climate gives you pneumonia. Of which in time, and far too early, he died. And this cunning Jew, this super-conspirator, this agent of the anti-Christ and of Mossad – in your view of things his life crawled with cunning. His life was substantially different from your father's, Cale, or from McCloud's father's. Because *he* was the evil force behind everything that went wrong on earth!"

In this narrow space, amidst the leads in their coloured plastic sleeves, amidst the colour-coded fuses and levers, Cale threw his arms around dangerously and seemed well pleased with what he'd got from Stone. "Oh, the irony! Interspersed only with the piquant and flagrant paranoia. All because I merely *suggest* that it might be certain rabid elements in Mossad who were paying Taliq and his boys for this little excursion! And not so much Taliq and the boys. Paying the people behind Taliq. That's all I wanted to infer. A mere thread of possibility . . ."

"So I may be shot," Stone kept on. "I – a Jew – may be shot. A Jew! And even that is the fault of the Jews?"

Stone was so seriously affronted that McCloud could see the small population of this hole might fall away into fragments: even as the dance troupe might have done if Bluey's sighting of the dead had been an authentic vision. The idea frightened him primitively. It was as if anger might burn up all the oxygen in the electronics bay.

"Gentlemen," he said. "For sweet Christ's sake! If you know so much about Taliq and the others, you ought to know they want us fighting like this."

"The piety of the boy!" said Cale. "Listen, let me tell you something. The world is complicated. And nothing is more complicated than malice. And those who won't see that, sonny Jim, are dead!"

Bladder ache seemed less significant now to McCloud than a weariness which came down on him. The three of them, he and his fellow condemned, seemed to him to be fatally deprived of any grandeur. The secrets were all known by Cale and were all banal. The earth was a complicated but cheap equation, and if McCloud was condemned by Taliq, *that* was cheap too, the result of a finite outlay of funds by the secret police of some government. The sadness of his lack of deeper worth, of Cale's, of Stone's, caused him all at once to slump.

"Move up there, old chap," Cale reproached him.

There was without warning a surge of engines. New air washed into the pit, tempered by the engines.

"We're going to take off again," Stone remarked drily. "It must be the Jews' fault."

9

THE UPSTAIRS DISPENSATION

THE plane had levelled itself in the sky and the air in the pit
grew polar again. McCloud noticed now how grey and
unfashionable even the handsome Mr Stone looked. That
might be what they are doing. They are curing us here. As soon as
we look despicably grey and less than human, they'll bring us out
and exhibit us for trial.

When the hatch above was opened, McCloud was at first aware
of it more by sound than by any other factor. He looked up. Hasni,
the one who had begun the journey beside Pauline, stared down
with such gentle enquiry that McCloud hoped for a moment the
boy was bringing some sort of reprieve.

"You have taken your placards off," he said leniently. "Put your
placards back on."

McCloud was quick to obey and thought the other two were
also. They didn't want that hatch shut again. There was shuffling
and sorting in the pit. "Mine's *Zionist Hack*, I think," said Cale,
pretending to be exercised by his search for the right placard and
smiling crookedly. He none the less donned it like something he
was accustomed to.

"Stand up," Hasni said just as uninsistently.

Their labels reassumed, they all stood, wincing with cramp.

In the first-class cabin, when McCloud at last climbed up from the
electronics pit, daylight had turned the window shades beige.
Stubble was beginning to appear on the faces of the few businessmen left there. Some of them slept. None of them were attending
to their briefcases anymore. Wrapped in their blankets, they looked

like an aristocracy who were certain their rights were about to be cancelled.

He noticed too as, half-blinded with the pain of it, he moved from leg to leg, that Daisy Nakamura's seat was empty.

"Have they shot anyone?" McCloud whispered to one of the businessmen.

The man shook his head marginally. He didn't want Hasni to spot him either affirming or denying.

"Where did we land?"

The businessman's eyes flickered. He didn't know. Or perhaps for some reason, because of the mark of condemnation McCloud wore, he wasn't telling.

Hasni shepherded them to the base of the spiral staircase and let them use a toilet one at a time. Because of an obscure sense of honour, McCloud insisted on going last. Since Hasni would not let the door be shut, McCloud heard the other two voiding themselves. He closed his eyes, trying to suppress his own bladder by mental suasion. When his time came, he felt an unutterable sense of thanks. But since Stone and Cale – on emerging from the water-closet – showed no gratitude for this brief mercy, neither did he.

At Hasni's order, they hobbled up the stairwell. McCloud was aware that stiffness made him look ridiculous, a hateful dodderer. His limbs, Taliq might argue, as crippled as his moral sense. The plane, by contrast, felt smooth and cold as a knife in this highest quarter of a Mediterranean day.

At the top of the stairs, in the front seats, one of the Palestinian boys, Musa, slept embracing his automatic rifle, his radio twittering on his hip. (It reminded McCloud straight away of the threatened *plastique* in the luggage hold.) Musa's armless cricketing sweater hung voluminously on him, as if he'd borrowed it from some West Indian pace bowler at whatever British university or polytechnic he attended. McCloud could see the gooseflesh on his bare lower arms.

Further along, alone and reflectively sipping orange juice, Bluey sat by a window. He had a window shade half-open and was staring forth. At first McCloud felt a spasm of fear for this illicit behaviour of Bluey's, but then understood it must be allowed. The inhabitants of this upper deck, eligible because of the sufferings of their race, were allowed to squint out at the day. Not all of them it seemed. But Bluey at least.

At the back, by the galley, the other four members of the dance troupe sat and stood about, listening to Taliq who was speaking softly, a cigarette held in his smashed right hand, his eyes half-closed rather in the manner of Whitey Wappitji. Two steps closer, and McCloud saw Daisy Nakamura was there also, minute in a large seat, a little shrunken in her green dress, a blue blanket shawled around her shoulders.

"Leave them there, Hasni," Taliq called musically. "Make them kneel."

The idea turned McCloud desperate. "For God's sake, we can't bloodywell kneel. We're half-crippled already with cramp. Do you want to try men who can't even stand?"

Taliq was amused and gestured with the cigarette he was smoking and weaved his handsome head about. "Stand then," he lightly ordered. "But be still. I haven't finished speaking yet to my friends."

He extended his hand to indicate the dance troupe and Daisy Nakamura, none of whom looked in the direction of McCloud and the other two guilty persons.

This gesture of Taliq's, this including wave of a damaged hand was that of an apparently emotional man, and its warmth somehow alarmed McCloud.

He tried to attract the attention of Bluey Kannata, hoping that Bluey's eyes, bruised with fear of curses, would turn brimming with reassurance towards him. But Bluey kept staring out the window. *But I sat with you half the night at a transmitter*, McCloud wanted to yell.

Out there, beyond the Perspex, in the sky Bluey frowned at, it seemed to McCloud there were no points of reference; nothing but a great plain of bright cumulus.

"We're thirsty too," called Daniel Stone suddenly.

"The Jew is thirsty," said Taliq. "*Cut me, do I not bleed?* Pour something into each of them, Hasni."

What a curious sound that command had!

McCloud had not been aware of the extent of his own thirst. He had been fixed on cramp and cold and the dull ache of his bladder; that feeling he'd had on bad afternoons in the classrooms of his childhood: that unreleased fluids were turning to stone inside him. But now the American had alerted him to thirst he found that yes, he was parched.

Hasni went to the drinks-trolley behind Taliq and took three small cans of cola from it. He opened the first. The stuff sizzled in its contact with the plane's cold air. Still the dance troupe and Daisy averted their eyes. Was it that they took no pleasure in any of this? Or was it that they were no longer interested?

Hasni brought the can and placed it to McCloud's mouth. Given a choice, McCloud would have liked to assert his brotherhood with Stone again and to have said, "Him first." But the metal was hard up against his teeth – Hasni would not let him enjoy the dignity of holding the thing – and he had no choice but to drink. And drinking, he became desperate to find every drop Hasni was pouring, to prevent any of it from wasting itself down his chin and into the stubble of his chest.

When his can was empty, he could not prevent himself watching Stone drink. Self-possessed Stone, McCloud was somehow pleased to see, was similarly avid to take in the moisture. His lips too worked prehensilely against the rim of the can.

But when it came to Cale's turn to be offered drink, he told Hasni, "Let me hold it, son."

Hasni could tell somehow that this was a crucial demand. That if it was agreed to, things between Cale and himself would be changed for good.

Hasni held the can in the air but distant from Cale. "Do you want to drink?" he asked airily, like a schoolboy with a weak teacher at his mercy.

"Go and fuck yourself!" said Cale.

McCloud was torn between admiration at this defiance and a supine bewilderment at the man's lack of thankfulness. Hasni stood still and began to pour the cola over Cale's head. The demeaning beverage marked out all Cale's weaknesses, the rolls of plumpness at the back of the neck, the steeply etched lines which divided his cheeks from the region beneath his nose, the depression – almost a pool – at the base of his thorax.

"Yes," said Cale when Hasni had finished. "And when you are in prison, son, people will do the same kind of thing to you. For what occurs to you, the same shall be done!" He wiped his face with one long sweep of his right hand and shook the droplets off his fingers. "You little prick!"

"Go below, Hasni," called Taliq. He sounded happy, and there was an oddity to that. It was simply that happiness seemed irrelevant to this flight, an agenda item for which there was no place. "There is only one of us down there now," Taliq said then, so composed in

this company of Daisy and the dancers that he could freely speak
of points of weakness.

Only one of us. But a whole planeload, McCloud wanted to say
in the wake of Cale's brave abstinence from moisture, united in
nothing but their fear.

"You may wait there, gentlemen," Taliq advised the three of them,
before turning back to what seemed to be his master class.

Locking his knees, McCloud slipped into sleep. A confused,
standing coma filled with a rich, vaporous stream of visions. These
possessed the same quality of light as that which came in through
the window where Bluey Kannata sat. His late father occupied
one stanza – if you could call it anything as extended as a stanza.
Mr McCloud was there for a pulse, and then for another. He
was smoking Tom Gullagara-style cigarettes he made himself
and sitting at a kitchen table, but in this sort of sleep McCloud
was not so much enjoying as suffering, there was very little
furniture. There were mainly faces and voices, including those
of Pauline's small-boned mother, and of her father the Dentist and
goldseeker; and then a lot of serious but elusive argument which
slipped with simian conviction around the wrecked uprights of
logic.

The Boy and the Girl wanted to be taken somewhere, but
Taliq was in the kitchen, laughing and against it. McCloud
began to tongue-lash Taliq. A furious eloquence he could not
afford to display on the plane spilled from him now in his childhood kitchen.

The argument moved on then to the face and name of Peter
Drury, Pauline's friend, the urbane man, the theatrical entre-
preneur. In dreams, the news had for the past year been coming to
McCloud – with a potency of loss which the daytime McCloud
submerged – that Drury and Pauline were habitual lovers. He
would wake with the conviction that it was so, and find out then
that that particular dream fact was without basis, had not yet
broken the surface in the real world.

The argument about Drury the impresario and Pauline and the
children's demands and the sundry parents slid through his grasp
then but tantalised him. It all had to do with his novel, for which
he had plundered the histories of both families, Pauline and his.
Most fearsomely of all, even more incisive than the question of
Pauline and Drury, it had to do with the story of Mrs Clark and
his father.

The Upstairs Dispensation

But then, as was customary in dreams, Pauline and Mrs Clark might become the one woman. Even their faces were not distinct.

A high-school teacher, Mrs Clark had taught McCloud English and History when he was fourteen. In the objective world, the one in which she was not merged with Pauline, she had been a tall, ripe woman, a Presbyterian who took her faith seriously. She wore blouses designed for probity but which somehow drew the engorged imaginations of McCloud and his classmates to the riches contained.

In a sunny land, the boys' passion for her was heightened by her pallor, and by her occasional dizziness. Whenever her dizziness came she would totter sideways all at once, her hand on the blackboard, her orderly writing slewing away in a skid mark of chalk. Or else it would happen in the butcher's, a second before she put her hand out for the wrapped steak, or else at bus stops, perhaps when the sight of the bus made the waiting passengers stir themselves. She would gather herself for a particular act, and one leg would go from under her.

McCloud's mother had noticed this failing and speculated on it at the dinner table. For the English and History teacher Mrs Clark, the soberest woman you could imagine, compelled everyone's impassioned interest.

It's either anaemia or pregnancy, Mrs McCloud suggested.

McCloud could see now, in his ten-second coma on the hijacked plane, what he could not see as a child, when all adult statements had seemed magisterial and based on absolute verities rather than on the grindings and slippages which characterised all souls in all seasons. He could see before it happened the day when Mrs Clark stumbled on the teacher's rostrum; when the brown hair which the boys in the class had always believed to be her own fell from her head.

It was an unnerving transformation when it happened. What the boys had thought of as a lush paleness which, in their rawest dreams they saw themselves soothing, had now shown itself to be a waiflike nakedness.

This incident seemed related somehow – in the mind of the young McCloud – to what had happened in the school library a little time before. In his search for images of nudity, one of the class had come upon pictures of Lithuanian women stripped by the SS for their execution. He called the others to see, but no one had thought there was any merit in this find. The faces were crooked with fear, the hip bones angular from bad food. These doomed women possessed a nakedness beyond nakedness. Even the most tumescent of McCloud's friends were unsettled by the picture. A few experimental jokes hung sourly in the air of the library, and then someone turned the page for good.

That was the kind of hideous undress by which Mrs Clark now confused the desires of twenty-seven antipodean boys. Down on her knees and with unfocused eyes, she felt around her feet for the wig. She was like someone looking for a dropped handbag in the dark. Shaking her head slightly, her eyes still uncertain, she put the thing back on her head.

Some oaf at the back of the classroom was trying to get a hacking chorus of laughter going, but very few of the most influential classroom barbarians joined in. It was as if they were learning too early for their comfort that fine breasts and a tightly-made backside were no protection. That the desirable were struck with the normal humiliations. Like some tortured medieval monk, they had seen the skull behind the lineaments of desire.

It was worst of all that Mrs Clark hadn't been embarrassed. She had been merely like any old woman who drops her stick on the ground and doesn't have the sight or the musculature to retrieve it.

Inherent to the standing dream of his father and Peter Drury, of Mrs Clark as modified by Pauline, of Pauline knit seamlessly into Mrs Clark, was the memory of the evening editions of the city tabloids and the piercing news of Mrs Clark they carried for a season. Mrs Clark's apparently lucky but frowning husband, a man every boy and half their fathers considered wildly lucky, was arrested. He was charged with slowly poisoning his wife. She had compliantly drunk her tea with enough sugar to mask the taste of the thallium he laced it with. Thallium was a subtle substance he brought home with him from work. It collected in Mrs Clark's liver and pituitary. It gave her dizziness and nausea and caused her hair to fall out. In time, it would have killed her.

Fantasies of rescue bloomed in the class then. The young hero, lust tempered with reverence, doing an odd job around the Clark house and seeing Mr Clark put the poison in the tea. And warning Mrs Clark, nursing her back from her paleness and receiving in the end unutterable tokens of her thanks.

But these imaginings were of course vitiated in part by the memory of her dropping of the wig in class.

*   *   *

Some months later, at Mr Clark's trial, his lawyers hit on the strategy of depicting him as an honest husband tormented by his wife's games and possible adulteries with other men. It was a defence which fooled no one. The idea of Mrs Clark as flirtatious or, better still, licentious, was too fantastic for belief. Certainly, none of the fourteen-year-olds now turning fifteen believed it of this North Shore Madonna. If she'd been such a goer, she would have flirted with one of *them*.

But amongst the names Mr Clark flourished in court was Mr McCloud's.

McCloud was humiliated for his mother's sake, but also for his own. There was exquisite horror in the idea of being known by your peers to desire a woman who herself, according to public report – however unreliable – fancied your father.

All four men named by Clark were subpoenaed, but the appearance of the first one was such a disaster for Clark's case that Mr McCloud was never called. When Clark got life, the sentence was read by everyone as condign punishment not only for his trying to poison his wife, but for maligning four innocent men as well.

And yet the possibility that there might be some truth there became something of a submerged rock against which the ship of dreams always ran, as it ran now, even as McCloud slept on his locked knee joints. Mr Clark's poisoning of the earth's most exquisite teacher, a woman every fourteen-year-old was willing to cherish, and the naming of his father by Mr Clark, were the most astounding events of McCloud's childhood.

Both his parents were dead now. His father who had been vindicated by the judge; his mother who had been reassured. The question was, can you write about such a thing as the Mrs Clark story? And the other question: can you *avoid* writing about such a thing? Can you make up some other filter through which to look at your childhood, knowing it will be inferior to the real thing?

And so, there was his father in the novel. A neat and unexceptional man. And there was the reproachful ghost in the standing dream. Whom McCloud had sold, it seemed now, for $12,000.

Was it any wonder that such a son should justly be cuckolded, and that he should feel such dream jealousy and grief?

The book had revived all the ambiguous questions, since that is the purpose of books. Had some astounding passion flared between Mrs Clark and McCloud senior? And if it hadn't, did the son somehow profoundly wish it had? And what conversations did Mr and Mrs McCloud hold on such subjects, conversations the boy McCloud never heard? The book had provided potential answers for all these questions.

In the argument of the dream, someone, a woman he didn't know, an amalgam of agent and wife and mother-in-law and teacher, was brightly showing the connection between McCloud's father's case as he had used it in the book, and his ignorance of Highland Pegasus and its intentions towards the Barramatjara. At the profoundest level, it was all so troubling. More troubling and more mysterious than any accusation in waking life. Subtler than Taliq's placard.

The amalgamated woman offered him a coat to wear, since he was cold even in his sleep.

"McCloud," he heard the woman say huskily. But it was Whitey Wappitji at his elbow.

Returned to the cabin, McCloud checked on everything – Bluey in the shaft of light from his opened blind; Daisy Nakamura, with her head cocked sideways in the rear seat; Whitey Wappitji at his elbow offering his own tweed jacket back to him. Whitey put the jacket over McCloud's shoulders.

"Thank you, Whitey," said McCloud. "Thank you."

Was Whitey still a missionary? After what he had read in the news magazine? His manner suggested that like that earlier missionary Dom Estevez, he was saddened but still lenient.

"Come and sit down, McCloud. Here."

Whitey directed him into a seat behind the one where Musa was sleeping. McCloud let himself fall sideways, crookedly, his right shoulder landing deep in the first-class plush. Whitey sat beside him. For some reason about which McCloud was curious, but which he knew might not be fully explained to him, Wappitji had the freedom – under Taliq and the Palestinian boys – to give people their coats and direct them to warm seats.

Across the aisle, Stone and Cale also took to a seat, without being given any permission McCloud was aware of. Cale had a glass of water in his hand. Had Whitey provided that?

Cale sipped the water and dipped a paper towel in it, to wipe the cola-stickiness off his face.

"Bluey won't look at me," said McCloud, beginning to cry. He felt childishly he might deserve better from someone for whom he'd kept a vigil in a radio-telephone booth in lower Manhattan, in a mean room amidst a city of delights.

"Let me tell you," said Whitey. "Bluey's all buggered up. You know that, Frank. Jesus, you don't need to be Sherlock to know how he's all set up and ready for some big anger. Well, now he's found it, Frank."

But there was more than that buggering Bluey up, McCloud could see. There were other factors which Whitey Wappitji with normal Barramatjara politeness did not mention. Whitey's gaze flitted across the cabin ceiling, speculating on objects, calculating the mysterious algebra by which his announcements would be governed. Then he undid the tray-table in front of McCloud, let it clatter down. He put his large, bony hand there, presenting it as if it were a gift. He still avoided McCloud's eyes.

"This Highland Pegasus thing, and that CIA stuff – it's serious business. You remember Bluey crying for his uncle. It's all in there. That whole dirty shebang, mate. Highland Pegasus and all the rest. And all them lies people get told when someone's dead keen to get hold of their country."

The lies caused him to sigh. He didn't seem enraged though. Taliq had not managed to unleash Whitey's big anger.

"Bluey's mad at me too," murmured Whitey. It seemed a casual statement but it was a glimpse into the largest Barramatjara question: reveal or conceal; admit or rebuff. Maybe Bluey saw all this strife of hijack as caused by Whitey's policy of *reveal*, of *admit*. Of making the audience relatives and understanders.

"Anyhow, we can't call Bluey a silly bugger, Frank," said Whitey then. "Not out loud, mate. Not in front of this Taliq or the passengers."

This was like a warning. Blood was thick. The initiated man might attract internal Barramatjara discipline, but his brothers would not call him a silly bugger in front of strangers.

"We were never into mining," Whitey went on. "When our cousins up on the coast asked us to move up and work in the bauxite there, we said no. Our old men had dreams of all the country dead from the mining. So we said no. We're known all around Western Australia as the blokes who won't be in mining.

"And that other thing, the satellite stuff . . . there's been dreams about that too, mate. We've got old fellers still round who dream of things long before they turn up in the flesh. There's one old man, an important one, dreams of white globes in Baruda, and the sun coming down and melting them."

139

Whitey lifted his hand from the tray-table. "That's what they say, don't they, Frank? The white protesters say it. That these tracking stations are targets for those nuclear bombs?"

A silence grew. In it Tom Gullagara arrived, nodded to McCloud, and then turned to Cale and stuck a lit, thin, cowpoke cigarette in the Englishman's lips. Cale sucked gratefully, but Tom vanished before he could be thanked.

"You knew about these Highland Pegasus blokes?" Whitey asked suddenly and with resonance. "Did you? And that satellite stuff?" Whitey now held McCloud's elbow through the tweed coat and shook it urgently. "Come on, Frank, you've got to really tell me that. To *tell* me, bugger it, Frank!"

He had swung his body so that McCloud now had no option but to stare into his face, into the smoky eye-whites, into the complex green centres with blackness at the core. All the authority Bluey had earlier suggested Whitey possessed, all *the featherfoot stuff*, the power to induce hypnosis and oblivion and curses, certainly seemed to the frightened McCloud to be compacted there.

McCloud was terrified that Wappitji might not believe him. According to the literature on the subject, elders chose boys with such commanding eyes and raised them in the gift of detecting the wrongsayer, the one whose treachery lay coiled beneath familiar features and banal denials. After what had happened with Bluey in New York, McCloud had stolen looks at Whitey during performances and seen the eccentrically broken right little toe, the way that part of the dancing foot had been twisted up and over the usual plane of the rest.

So there was some truth to what Bluey had said, at least to the extent that something had been forced apart there, in Wappitji's foot, for whatever reason, and then pushed together again in a new way. This small sign of Whitey's authority had become hard for McCloud to ignore during dances, and he wondered if some of the audience noticed it and speculated.

But there was even more than that authority to Whitey's demand. There was frank anxiety in him too. For, again, *he* had suffered the dream which commanded him to release the dances to a wider gaze. And the world's answer was this reported satellite-tracking betrayal and this diamond treachery.

Whitey wanted to know where he stood in the universe, and who were his friends. He was permitted by Taliq to ask these questions, because Taliq was certain McCloud was a betrayer, and had projected that certainty to Whitey during all the hours McCloud had been in the pit.

How could McCloud undermine Taliq's hours of conviction in a few sentences?

Full of fear, he said, "I knew nothing about Highland Pegasus, Whitey. I was wrapped up in my own business. I should have known. But I was ignorant as sin."

He hoped Whitey could tell that behind the trite assurances lay the most serious attempt to utter the truth.

"I was too wrapped up in this book of mine," he began again, "to give a damn about real things, about mining companies and satellite tracking. We don't *all* know everything that's wrong. There's too much wrong for us all to cover all that ground. Look, I'll tell you something I haven't told anyone else."

And he told Whitey how he had been too busy selling his own dreaming, the dreaming of the McClouds and of Pauline's parents too, even to be aware of any chance of allying himself with miners and governments. He confessed how poor the returns looked like being, and how these failed hopes had fuelled his drinking and his lapses as a manager. He let Whitey know even about Drury the impresario, and the authoritative dreams of loss he had suffered about Pauline and the man. He expatiated on how he had not had the courage to take news of his failure to Pauline. He gave all these massive tokens of self away to Whitey so that Whitey would believe him.

And as he spoke he became hopeful. For Taliq had had nothing as large as this to give Whitey. Nothing as intimate. Tales of horror, certainly, but conveyed in a mode alien to Whitey. Surely alien!

For some reason it did not seem right to him to argue with the news magazine story out loud. Internally he *did* argue with it, and might ultimately try to undermine its exactness in front of Taliq. For this politician in Canberra would not be the first of any stripe to have exaggerated for political advantage. But to say so to Whitey was not delicate or even wise, since what the politician had warned of was pretty much the standard level of chicanery for dealings between the wide world and the Barramatjara.

He *did* know however that in Barramatjara terms, as in Taliq's, ignorance was no surefire defence. When he gave his permission for the drilling, Bluey's uncle may have acted from a state of shock akin to ignorance. But that did not mean he was safe from being cursed. Bluey, knowing it, had brewed up out of such an awareness the phantasm of his uncle.

The truth was that McCloud's narrow range of ambitions had made him an excellent servant of governments, of sponsors, of those who wanted Whitey and Cowboy Tom out of Baruda. Whitey might well gather together the fragments of his guilty spirit and breathe into them now a horrible malediction. If he failed to, it would be purest mercy.

Yet this is Whitey, McCloud rushed to remind himself. *Old Whitey. Droll and lean, sober and responsible.*

Whitey's hand on McCloud's elbow now turned to a caress. "Okay, mate." There was a grin. "You're just a dumb fucking whitefeller, eh?" And he smiled, brightly as rescue, and rearranged the coat around McCloud's shoulders. "You keep warm."

Whitey stood. Could Taliq see, from the rear of the cabin, that Whitey was not returning with any certainty about the guilt of Frank McCloud, manager and novelist?

"He can talk, that Taliq," said Whitey. "He can talk a streak."

He might have been speaking about another man in a pub. Not of someone who had *plastique* and lives at his disposal. Was he saying he thought that all Taliq's instruction was palaver?

"My friends?" asked McCloud. "Can't they have blankets?" He would be obscurely ashamed to have the warmth of his jacket when Cale and Stone had nothing.

Whitey surveyed Cale and Daniel Stone. When it came to them though, there was a sudden hardness to him. He turned back to McCloud and said frankly, "Those blokes are very angry. Taliq and the other fellers. They got their good reasons for it too. Those fellers. Bloody good reasons, Frank."

A laugh came hacking out of Cale, who must have overheard from his seat across the aisle. "There you go. Turned. Sambo the dancer and the Arabs. New-found friends!"

McCloud's vision was flecked with a sort of shock. Whitey turned away, but Taliq appeared, decisive and fast, stood beside Cale and – like a stock terrorist in a film – put a blue-grey pistol to his neck. "You should be quiet just now, Mr Bennett or Cale. It isn't your turn to speak yet. It may never be."

"One thing I know," said Cale. "You won't shoot me up here. Not in hero class! You want to save me to present to the masses!"

Cale had argued in the pit that the boys might be challenged and shamed and infected with doubt, but that Taliq couldn't be reached.

Now he seemed – wantonly – to be ignoring his own advice. McCloud was almost edified when Taliq changed his cigarette to his left hand, made a fist of his damaged right, and silenced Cale with a blow against the back of the neck. The blow had the unreality, the unrelatedness, of all such acts. A red bruise began to appear there, and Cale blinked and swallowed and wavered in his seat. Taliq stepped back and gazed reflectively at the dazed, intemperate Englishman.

Whitey took this assault in with an economic gaze and an absence of facial reaction. Worse things happened in the desert. Nodding to Frank, he returned to the others in the rear seats.

I'm doing what they say prisoners do, McCloud acknowledged. I am putting the blame for my peril on Cale, the troublesome prisoner, rather than on the bandits. Others will do the same to me. We will pass on our chagrin to each other.

In fact, he remembered from the earlier procession, they already had.

He had of course become informed on this process not only by the conversation of Stone and Cale but by reading in magazines analyses of what hijacked victims went through. The writers of such articles always referred to the Holocaust too, during which respectable and seemly Jews sometimes blamed outspoken, rebellious, visible and awkward ones for the whole disaster. It was said to be a sort of mysterious transference. But even understanding that it would happen did not save McCloud now from hating Cale.

For Taliq, he was frightened to find, he was tempted to harbour a kind of infantile reverence.

After punishing Cale, Taliq vanished. There was what McCloud identified as an interval. He did not rest. He knew that not everyone was finished with him.

At last it was Daisy Nakamura who turned up, in stockinged feet. She sat – without a word – beside him. Nor did she look at him. Her eyes were focused forward, in the direction of the cockpit.

"Hello," she said. Should I be flattered, McCloud wondered, that it's to me that they're coming to test what they've heard from Taliq? To match all that against my plain face?

McCloud noticed that the fibre of the green cocktail dress was spotted with dropped coffee. Around her shoulders and head she still wore tightly clamped the airline's blue blanket. She resembled a disaster victim, which was of course what she was.

When her eyes moved to him, he expected her to speak. It would have been characteristic of her – she was a busy chatterer. But she'd been rendered philosophic up here. She studied him. It was a thorough inspection, so frowning and intense he got tired of its weight and turned his head away.

"I'm surprised you're allowed to visit me," said McCloud. Yet he was not really being visited. It was as if he were being seen from beyond glass and in dim light.

"It's okay now," she said in her western twang after a long time. "We've got freedom of movement. It's a democracy up here. If you want to put it like that."

"*Now?* You said it's okay now?"

"Mr Taliq there, he believes he's found himself a judge from amongst us. He's keen on judgment, that gentleman Taliq."

"Judge? I don't understand."

She stared at him as if he understood perfectly what she meant. And so he did. He knew Bluey was staring freely out of the window. There was plenty of information in that.

"The rest of us are a serious disappointment to that gentleman. I mean, we're sympathetic, and he hasn't stopped working on us either. He's got more faith than a Mormon, that boy. But now he's got one of us to come his way." She spoke with a sort of finality, letting her hand stray out of her blanket and touch his knee. She gave the kneecap a preventive jostle. It meant he wasn't to ask too much. "I can't be my old self up here," she said. "Such heaps of lecturing. We've been talking all night. With just one little sleep while this great contraption was on the ground."

"On the ground where?"

"That, Mr McCloud, I just don't know." There was a narrow, ironic guffaw from her narrow, full-lipped mouth. "Friend Taliq didn't share *that* piece of information with me. Our intellects were all too taken up with the other stuff. I swear it was intense. Like a whole year of political science in some college."

She raised her eyes. Even so tired and diminished, she was wonderfully companionable.

"Why'd you do it, Mr McCloud?" she asked. "To those dancers there? I read the article see. Required reading up here, you might say. But how it seems is, you bring them to New York and Frankfurt, and while they're gone strangers take their land. Neat trick, Mr McCloud. Neato! That's how it seems."

He stared at her. So he might be off the hook with Whitey. Yet in his exhaustion, in his shrunken, four-mile-high brain, more ready to declare his guilt to her than to anyone! If she would open her blue blanket and take him to her heart, he would plead guilty beyond question, guilty without any shade of ambiguity, any mental reservation, any redeeming circumstance.

So before this tribunal as well, McCloud uttered what was becoming his standard plea.

"Oh Christ, Mrs Nakamura. I don't know! Do you think I've been sworn in as an agent? That they paid me for treachery, for God's sake? They didn't have to, Daisy. They could depend on my lack of genuine interest in what they were up to. Oh, I've had designs on the Barramatjara. I've been part of a plot. I've been to the Barramatjara country to write about sand paintings and dancing. But my interest never went so far as asking whether or not some geologist had found promising core samples there?"

Daisy expelled her breath. Even after three decades in the Wild West and a night of Taliq's instruction, she still had that flowerlike neatness of expression, that lilac redolence, that preciseness of gesture which the West went frantic about in the Japanese. The occidentalising of Daisy Nakamura had extended to her larynx and her habits of expression, but the waters of Japanese-ness were still located profoundly in her.

"I wouldn't shoot you like a dog for ignorance, McCloud. Why, if all of us had to face the *coup de grâce* because of questions we haven't asked, none of us would be left standing." She lowered her voice even further. "I mean, I have to tell you I was hugely ignorant of what these boys, Taliq and the rest, have gone through. And that's on network news every night, hanging there above my head in the bar, while the cowboys are yelling for beer and a channel change to the goddam basketball! I mean, in my opinion these boys have been asked to eat far too much dirt! Too much dirt. These are the Hopis of their part of the world. Simple as that."

Should I ask for her intercession? McCloud wondered. He spent five seconds struggling with the idea he should. It wasn't right though, since she felt as adrift here as he did. But maybe she could ask, for example, whether Pauline could be brought up here. He wanted to be certain of seeing her before the judgment everyone took as a certain event. He wanted even to know about Drury too. Not that he would ask straight out. He wanted to gauge by signs. Then he might have a coherent chance of meeting the ends Taliq had planned for him.

What Mrs Nakamura had meant by *judge* now came irrepressibly to his lips, a question like a bubble in a comic strip.

"He wants one of you to condemn the three of us?" he asked Daisy. "Right in front of the other passengers?"

"Exactly right, Mr McCloud. People's court. It makes sense, doesn't it? Whatever happens to you, we all end up with a share of it. Not just Taliq and the boys. All of us up here."

"And it's Bluey? The one by the window? The dancer?"

She dragged the blanket closer around her and looked away. "Is that his name? I get them mixed up. Their names aren't exactly out of the Flagstaff phonebook."

"Well," McCloud said. "God help me."

Again he felt a physical yearning for the Boy and the Girl, together with a strange prickling in his brain and a painful surging of the musculature of the chest and upper arms. Bluey's furious confusion, what Whitey called Bluey's *big anger*, had brought itself to bear on *him*. Bluey did not want to condemn Cale and Stone. He was indifferent to them. He would fiercely condemn McCloud, however. For McCloud was the deceiver, the sleeping agent of all the film producers who had taken him away from the Barramatjara country and confused him with Hiltons and dope, the factor of all the miners who imperilled uncles, all the statesmen who told deferential lies. Everyone who had said, "We respect your ancient culture," while reserving for the cocktail hour, far from the tribal ground, the observation that none of it could last. McCloud would carry the buck for all of them now.

And Bluey, who knew the size of the buck, was the perfect judge.

McCloud didn't know whether he should try to rise from his seat and argue his innocence with Bluey. He did, however, feel some admiration for Taliq. Ten hours ago it had seemed fantastical of the Palestinian to bring these five genial desert nomads of international renown upstairs to this ideological heaven, this platform of dialectic behind the flight deck. But Taliq had already known of McCloud's blameworthiness then, had been able to sniff it out at an hour when McCloud still vainly considered himself merely an unrewarded novelist with a tendency to drink.

"Listen, honey," said Daisy Nakamura at his side. "I'll do what I can with all this. Oh, Jesus God. I don't need any of it! Here I am, a registered Republican voter, American to the core. Say I was Jewish and told Taliq that! He'd put a placard round my head and decide to shoot me. As it is, he says it just shows how I've been conditioned to lick the oppressor's hand. But Mr McCloud, I've got news for Taliq. I haven't been conditioned to do anything. I am American and America has made me what I am. I'm Republican because they believe in arresting the child-killers and the rapists and punishing them real good. And they aren't deceived by the lies of the other side."

"The other side?" asked McCloud.

"The East," she said. She lowered her voice further. "I say what any American would say. America's been wonderful to me."

"But they didn't tell you, your Republicans, what was happening to Taliq and the others!" McCloud argued.

Her eyes slewed away. "They can't cover everything, can they?" She looked away across the aisle. "The other two," she murmured, gesturing surreptitiously to Cale and Stone. "They're guilty as hell."

"No," McCloud told her. "I don't think they are."

He thought of Stone's father, the handbag repairer. It seemed to be a detail of such humanity that it ought to exempt Stone from being shot.

"They're guilty," Daisy Nakamura assured him, putting her hand for emphasis on his knee again. "Taliq has the evidence on them. It kept coming in by radio while we were parked down below. I mean, they're guilty by Taliq's lights, and he and his boys are working by the rules of war here, and for Christ's sake, Mr McCloud, when it comes to sorting out the sheep from the goats, the rules of war aren't bad, and were not so long ago applied in Budapest. But as for you, I can't see you guilty by anyone's lights or rules or principles."

"But I am," he said. "I am by Bluey's. Absolutely."

Jaundiced with filtered light, Daniel Stone and the bruised Cale were now sleeping. Someone, perhaps Whitey Wappitji after all, had covered them with airline blankets.

Daisy's mouth widened as her conversation became even more secret. "That man at the window," she said. "He got angry soon as he read that stuff in the magazine. He said it bore out everything he'd suspected. He got angry with his friends too. They're good democratic boys and they wanted to hear from you. But he said he knew the world better than they did . . . he'd been in movies and he'd had white women. And this article was right on target. It put everything in place. The whole truckload, he said."

McCloud, however appalled, could feel no animus against Bluey. But he saw a forceful pattern of illogic in what had happened, an illogic which just the same made a profounder sense. The other dancers, who lived on their homeground all the time, had not condemned McCloud without a hearing. But Bluey, who felt love and fear for his homeground yet who rarely lived there anymore, who sometimes made fearful night journeys from the Ritz-Carlton in Cannes to Baruda but was always back by breakfast time, had been willing to condemn him *in absentia*.

Daisy said suddenly, "I know you've got your own problems, Mr McCloud. And I don't know why I'm talking like this to you. Look around this cabin. Who else is there to talk to?" She spoke more lowly still, bowing her head. "Everyone here seems to think I ought to give in to him. Just give in."

"To Taliq?" asked McCloud, flinching. Because he thought it too, and was ashamed of thinking it.

"Taliq. Who else? Jesus, I sure hope there's no one else!"

"And everyone? Everyone wants you to?"

"Absolutely. Why me? What signals are they picking up? How does Taliq pick up signals? And how do you? It isn't like I'm some kind of geisha. But even your black guys, Mr McCloud. The tall one and the one with the cowboy belt have both said it to me. What's the cowboy's name? Tom? Tom. They know the score, those guys. I mean, they put it nicely, but you can understand what they're getting at. So we spend half the night listening to Taliq, and reading about you in magazines, and we meet that tough-looking little guy Razir, and the three boys as well, and they fill us in on what's happened to them, and still we say, *Sorry, we feel real bad about what's gone down, but we still can't do it for you.* We still know there's no way we can stand up there in front of the other passengers like some sort of Chinese people's court.

"And that's okay with Taliq. Because he's the one who's said up front and whether we want it or not that we're his dispossessed brothers and sisters. And he can't fire us, can he? You can't be fired from that particular status just because you're squeamish about executing folk."

She looked startled then and put her hand to her mouth.

"Oh Jesus, sorry Mr McCloud! But since it's been said, you ought to gather your wits. Even though you and I both know it won't come to that. Anyhow, Taliq tells us, *You are still privileged people. Your consciousness needs raising, that's all. And it will happen too! It'll just take a little time* . . . Meanwhile your friends, the dancers . . . they're tough people themselves, and they seem to be realists, and they know Taliq is a tough man in a tough corner.

And they take it as damnwell read that I'll do something to sweeten him! For your sake, McCloud. For your sake! Can you imagine? No matter what the article says about the diamond people and the CIA satellites. They want to save you. But they can't be seen to go against the guy in the window seat there, the one who's gone quiet. So they want me to do everything for them!"

She pulled the blanket tighter yet began shuddering. "Do you know, it scares me? The way Taliq says we have time. We have time to come round to him. As if we'll be on this plane for weeks . . ."

She placed the palm of her left hand over her forehead, then moved it down over her ivory nose, her bud of a mouth. "It's the presumption I hate, Mr McCloud. The presumption about me. As if it's *my* job or something."

He would have liked to be able to tell her to resist. But he could not say it. A seduced Taliq might well be less severe.

"And Taliq?" he croaked. "Has he made . . . any overtures?"

"Come on, Mr McCloud! I can tell. One thing I've felt: I've felt the accumulated heat of cowboys and truckers wafting across the bar. Not that Taliq is a cowboy or a trucker. Wish to God he were!" Her eyes were misted with sudden tears. "See, Taliq's young boys don't know just what they are. I mean, they're good at handling orders and they know how to use their weapons and all that. But they behave like a cross between a gangster and a goddam social-worker."

Earlier, McCloud remembered, Cale had said something like that.

"But Taliq knows exactly what he is. He's a soldier. And soldiers, I suppose, take the women they find in their path."

She sighed at the idea of this ancient and deplorable hubris.

"But that's not the whole story either," she went on, distracted, talking it out to herself. "Because he thinks he's a *special* kind of soldier. According to his lights, he wants to use people properly. He doesn't want to say, *I've got the gun, so come my way.* Just the same, he got me up here for reasons of his own, for fake reasons, and he knows it now even if he didn't before. I'm not oppressed, Mr McCloud, I'm American. And he's bright enough to know it too. I mean, there he is pretending I'm like *your* people, who really have a beef. I don't have a beef, Mr McCloud. It isn't like I'm Navajo or something. I should be downstairs, not here. They want an imperialist to beat up on? I'm an imperialist, McCloud! God bless America! May we all be dumb and happy and may renegade Mormons come over the Utah border and drink their beer at my place!"

What was horrifying was that she was working her way towards asking him not just for sympathy but for advice.

"I mean," she said then, "in some ways Taliq's only a boy. Can't be more than thirty-two or -three, and for a man that's young . . ."

She let the sentence hang, but the figure she uttered took McCloud by surprise. He hadn't thought lately of Taliq as the possessor of a finite age.

"I don't know what to say, Mrs Nakamura," McCloud admitted. "I mean, Taliq tells us he can tear the plane apart in an instant with his load of *plastique*. He also told us there was a primed grenade at the pilot's head, and the pilot's head is ours. I think he's relented a little on the grenade: the pilot is co-operative. But the *plastique* . . ."

There was an unspoken connection between the *plastique* and the task everyone had placed on Daisy. Daisy might be able to save everyone from *plastique* by giving way to Taliq. But what if she went with Taliq and the *plastique* was still detonated? That seemed to McCloud an achingly sad prospect, a wasted sacrifice for Daisy. For some reason, he could scarcely bear the idea without tears.

"Whatever happens," he told her, "there is the possibility we'll all live anyway, and it has to be on terms we can stand."

All this was a revelation to him, to hear himself uttering these ordinary yet genuine sentiments. He hadn't believed until now that he thought in such simple and quotidian terms. The writing of a long novel had given him the illusion that his emotions were serpentine and subtle. He had also come to believe that on the level of behaviour he was a man of compromise, a fellow with a nose for convenience.

The idea of his own plebeian solidarity with Daisy, which he seemed to be observing from a long way off, startled him. It was as if this journey had forced on him the same stolid valour which the Scotland–Australia run had forced on his ancestors.

A glimpse of Cale's mottled, sleeping face across the aisle made him want all the more though that she *would* distract Taliq, would stoop to humanise him with a sumptuous climax, Beirut and Budapest, Arizona reconciled and fused to one benign view of what should be done to this plane and its population.

"See," Daisy Nakamura was saying, arguing with herself still, "his reasons add up, but his conclusions – well, I don't go along with them. Not all the way. They scare me real bad, McCloud. Here's a body – Taliq's body I mean – which really doesn't give a dollar for whether or not it will be ground beef this time tomorrow."

"Oh," said McCloud, "Mr Cale over there thinks Taliq gives a dollar for his life. Mr Cale thinks Taliq's got political ambitions."

"*Political ambitions?*" asked Daisy, obviously thinking of politics Arizona-style. "Are you kidding? I mean, this is a man who says, *Daisy, come on, come upstairs, because you're some sort of political heroine or other. And anyhow I like you and your green cocktail dress.* And in the same breath says, *By the way, I just might press this little button here and pulverise the lot of us, you, me, your green dress, the people in row 54.* I mean, I've had some crazy friends . . ." But she could not continue. Clearly, none of her gentlemen friends had ever taken a grenade to bed with him. "Those black guys of yours . . ." Again there was a grimace. ". . .They don't know what they're asking."

"That's not quite true," McCloud told her. His sense of the sadness of what she was being asked to do now passed. She should understand Whitey and Tom and the reticent *didj* player Paul. "Oh yes, they do," he said. It was vital, he knew, that if she decided to yield she should understand what it meant; that she could alter Taliq, she could give a rebirth to all the passengers. She could be emu-mother, she could be lizard-wife. "They know exactly what they're asking. Listen . . . Whitey, the tall one, his world more or less started when someone called marsupial rat fucked the lizard-women. The whole human world was made by a particular seduction. That's what he believes."

Daisy Nakamura dismissed this. "Mythology." As if she'd heard the word muttered in the wake of Indians in her bar in Budapest.

"Not to him it isn't, Daisy."

"Sounds like the goddam Navajo again," she murmured.

McCloud took her hand, the one which had been clutching the blanket tightly around her throat. The palm was so warm, and the fingers translucent, it seemed, so that you believed you saw the ivory bones within. "If you *do* speak with Taliq," he said, knowing that he was asking too much, "could you see if we could get Pauline my wife up here? She's had a strange life too, and I need to talk to her in case things happen."

He had messages for the Girl and the Boy. He should not go into the dark without talking to them. The reason he should not was that they would always count it an injustice if he did. The image and lesson of Pauline's father the mad Dentist was in his mind.

With a minute gesture of the hand, she conceded that she would try. "I just want to visit my sister. I don't want any adventures. I've had all the adventures I want."

The young terrorist Hasni appeared above her, wearing all the appurtenances of the hijacker, the radio, the grenade belt, the automatic rifle. And the further appurtenance of his gentle, Arab scholarship face.

"May I have this seat, Mrs Nakamura?" he asked.

As if to some inner alarm clock, some sign peculiar to their faction, the young man called Musa had also risen now from the seats where he had been sleeping. He looked aft with enormous Bedouin eyes, eyes which made the concept that he had been dispossessed all too credible.

By now Daisy had vanished. So the dialogue would be different now.

"It is my rest period," said Hasni, settling beside McCloud. "But your wife sends her greetings and hopes you are well. I told her your health is out of my hands now, I am afraid."

"Is it?" asked McCloud.

"I did not deceive the native peoples as you did," Hasni reproved him.

"How do you know that article is accurate. You don't trust the Zionist imperialist press as a whole. So why trust it in this case?"

Hasni took thought over this. "Because one of your dancers has verified it. He told us you deceived them."

"But I didn't deceive them."

"One of them is sure you did. And the others are tormented by doubt, Mr McCloud. They are gentle people. They still show the subservience we've all been bullied into feeling. All those who are exiles in their own land."

It was futile to argue, especially since there was truth there and, in any case, messages were still to be exchanged with Pauline. But what could be said through this straight-laced boy-terrorist?

"Would you give her a note from me?"

Hasni frowned and pushed his lips forward.

"A sealed note, Hasni. For Christ's sake it may be our last exchange."

"You're not serious," murmured Hasni.

"What could I put in a private note that could hurt you?"

"This happened in training," said Hasni with a confessional smile. "People think I'm the weak one at first and find out slowly I'm the strong one."

Training. So had they rehearsed this hijack? Somewhere in a cave maybe. Were Syrian or Iraqi recruits the subjects of the experiment? And had *they* chosen Hasni as the apparent weak link?

McCloud said, "I don't think you're weak. I think you're stronger than Taliq. Stronger and more innocent."

"What? Is that your psychological skill at work? Anyhow, I don't know what you mean."

"I mean that you've seen Taliq extend favours to the Japanese-American woman. Can't you extend favours to me?"

Hasni seemed distracted for a moment. He inspected the pouch in the back of the seat in front of him. He fingered the in-flight magazine, the sick bag with the advertisement for twenty-four-hour photographic development, the safety instructions card. He looked to McCloud almost like someone who rummages in a briefcase or handbag out of embarrassment. Once he had decided what he wanted to say, he gave up the rummaging and sat back in the seat, closing his eyes for a moment and adjusting his automatic.

"What's the trouble?" asked McCloud.

"Just that you are so typical," the boy announced.

"I'm sorry," said McCloud. "But I have children. And as well as that, all couples have their mysteries. They want to refer back to them when they're in danger."

"Oh, Mr McCloud, that's not what I mean by *typical*. And if you think I give a damn about your squalid *mysteries* – if that's what you insist on calling them – then you couldn't be more mistaken. You're typical in another sense, a sense which causes me to be ill. All you people, all you nice people with nice wives and what you call nice mysteries. You think that after all that's happened to me I'm still really like you!"

"I don't think you're as exclusive as you think, Hasni," McCloud said, angered.

"Perhaps not. But I'm not like *your* type. Oh, you all have different accents, but the soul is the same. A soul sticky with silly, liberal half-truths. You've read books on most of the human catastrophes. You can give a garbled history of all the century's great uprootings and massacres. And you use this comic-book history as a measuring device to exploit me. And to belittle *my* history, or Musa's, or Yusuf's. *Why should we give a damn about*

*the Palestinians? Why do they posture like that? Haven't they
heard of the Armenians? The Kurds? The Kampucheans? The Jews
for that matter?"*

McCloud studied the boy, the way he put his argument. To be
damned in this weighty, undergraduate style of Hasni's seemed a
curiously bitter destiny; damnation uttered by a serious child.
    "Why should you give a damn what my mental habits are?"
McCloud asked. "You're going to shoot me anyhow, aren't you?"
    McCloud was of course, in the light of Hasni's boyish polemic,
hoping for a denial that this was so.
    Hasni merely said, "I would like to see the light dawn in
someone's eyes. That's all."
    McCloud suspected he should go on pushing the boy, should
inflict a shock if he could. "In that case, watch me when the bullet
goes in. You might see something dawn then."
    "See," Hasni told him, sounding a bit flustered. "You treat
the moment of death in that bourgeois manner. A moment of
enlightenment! The truth is, nothing is learned at that second.
Nothing."

It was hard for McCloud to tell whether – in spite of Hasni's reply
– his audacity had had the right result. Certainly it caused Hasni
to close his eyes and compose himself. Cale had said that hijackers
possessed a sort of vanity, that they yearned for the victim's
approval. This hooding of Hasni's eyes seemed a sign from the boy
that it might be true.
    So, was it best to let Hasni sleep now? Or should there be an
effort to bring about the desired instability, the kind in which
self-doubt *doesn't* cause the pulling of a trigger? For Cale had
already delineated the other one, the instability which caused the
hijacker to go trigger-happy, to produce a dead body as evidence
of the seriousness of his history, the inhuman weight of his commit-
ment.

What Hasni had said about garbled histories struck McCloud in
any case as close to the truth, and distracted him a little from the
obligation of confusing the boy. Acting from his own garbled and
inadequate history of the Barramatjara, he had taken the job of
troupe manager. *Was* there justice in the idea that investigating the
good faith of the sponsors of their tour was a courtesy he had
owed Whitey and the boys?
    It *could* even be argued in this febrile morning light, so high on

this fragment of pirated stratosphere, that anyone who benefited from the world of diamonds, from the valves and pistons and machine coolings, all without enquiring into the price, might also be considered guilty.

And though this was a practically absurd proposition – it meant that all passengers had to be shot, if not the whole Western world, and without a Western passenger and a Western world to use as lever, the hijacker was himself powerless – McCloud felt the shadow of the argument, the draft off it, strongly enough to enquire of Hasni, "Well, then, what is your bloody history? This one I discount? This one which means I can't send a note to my wife? Tell me for Christ's sake! Tell me what it is!"

Hasni looked at McCloud, as if he'd pulled the oldest trick in the book. But then, to McCloud's surprise, the boy began to speak.

"Moshe Dayan," Hasni began with a gravity McCloud thought of as essentially that of a really dangerous man-child, the gravity a Cale – for all his power of analysis – could never approach. ". . . Moshe Dayan once boasted that my grandfather's village had been removed from the geography books. Let me just say that. Did anyone ever do such a thing to you, McCloud?"

"They're threatening to publish my novel for a pittance," McCloud said. "The world is very hard."

"Don't belittle my question, McCloud. Did they take your village and plough it under and erase its name?"

"No," murmured McCloud without malice. "Though of course they did it to my ancestors in Scotland. But that was in the eighteenth century."

"Exactly. And again, your shitty little potted histories!"

"Why does that mean I can't write a letter to my wife?"

"Because you are a criminal, and you try to cast yourself as a victim. That's why! That's reason enough!"

For a time Hasni sat swallowing and then began to speak again. "I thought you wanted to hear my history?" he complained.

"Yes. I'm not as closed to yours as you are to mine, Hasni."

"Oh no? Oh no? Then try this! Take this on board. My grand-father . . . my *grandfather* came from the village of Roshe Pinna in Galilee. Forty years ago he fled to the refugee camp in Quneitra, over in the east. He believed it would be for a month, no more. But the Israelis did not let him return, they blocked his way with armed men, and so they had a pretext for confiscating his land. Every year afterwards, on the Feast of the Ascension, he would walk from Quneitra to the Golan Heights and look across to the point near Lake Tiberias where his home had been. Roshe Pinna. I was raised with the name. I still carry it. I have never visited it. I'll visit it when it belongs to my race again. Do you have such places in your miserable memory, McCloud? I doubt it."

Although there was room for McCloud to ask how a homesick grandfather led necessarily to the hijacking of the New York–Frankfurt flight, he delayed and then said nothing. That was because he saw something awesome in the reverence for place and ancestry this impassioned student harboured.

"Then of course," said Hasni after a long breath, "the Zionists took the Golan Heights. After that even pilgrimage was out of the question. Not only the earth itself, but a distant view of it was forbidden!"

There were tears in the boy's eyes now. He did not glibly flash them as symptoms of compelling and empowering sorrow.

"What about my earth?" asked McCloud gently. "You want to forbid me a view of that."

Hasni waved his hand. "Oh, my grandfather would have agreed with you. He would consider this action we've taken extreme. Because he saw what happened to him as the will of God. He wouldn't have accepted that God's will should be pushed along. That politics is the means by which God's mind is made up for him. And my parents probably think the same as my grandfather, though in their secret hearts they would be pleased that I've taken action at last. But defeated people, you must understand, McCloud!

"They've spent their lives at the Ain Alhilweh camp near Sidon. The Lebanese call it *the zoo*. My parents are in the zoo therefore. My father walks into town every day to sell lottery tickets. Six children were raised in an UNRWA hut in Ain Alhilweh! Three metres by four metres! Oh sure, I've seen worse things even in the South, in Louisiana and Arkansas. There is nothing absolutely unique to my story. And yet what you liberal readers of feature articles forget is that it's awfully unique for me."

"And my story is unique to me too," urged McCloud. "You can call it shitty and despicable. But my situation – you can't deny – is subjectively very serious!"

Hasni shook his head. "Listen! Not as serious as Musa's is for him. He's got *objective* ruins, McCloud. He's a Christian like me. His village was confiscated under one of those emergency laws. Kafr Birim. A defence area, a security zone! His people looked through barbed wire at their own homes but could not enter them.

Even the Israeli Supreme Court took shame and ordered that the people be readmitted, but the Israeli army sowed the town with mines instead. They bombed it on Christmas Day, a timing which has made a strong impact on my friend Musa. Unique to him, but to you just another story from *Time* or *Newsweek*."

It was not lost on McCloud that by using the names of villages no one else on the plane had heard of, Hasni seemed to give injustice a title and a substance. His tale, and these hijacking transactions, were – as McCloud sensed – as much rooted in name and location as was the dance and painting of the Barramatjara. McCloud found himself nodding in spite of himself, registering the names. They were the currency of Hasni's narration. And other names arose. Yusuf's village Deir Hanna, which was confiscated to make the super-town of Karni'el, in which – said Hasni – Palestinians could not live. The sealing of Yusuf's parents' house in Ramallah, the plugging-up of the doors and the blinding of the windows with cinder blocks, the confiscation of the family industrial plant: their sewing machine on which they made wedding suits. All because Yusuf's uncle belonged to the Palestinian group *el-Ard*, the Land.

How at Jalazoun camp near Ramallah, a twenty-two hour a day curfew had been imposed – the Palestinians being allowed to go abroad and do their work and find their food and water and wood, according to Hasni, only two hours a day!

How Razir was beaten as a child with truncheons in Jalazoun and still bore the back injury to prove it, even though it had not stopped him from being a commando for the Iraqis!

How Hasni himself had received a UNRWA scholarship to Bir Zeit University near Ramallah, and found a wreck – building permits refused by the Israelis, courses banned by them, teachers exiled! And how in a raid by security forces he was beaten so badly – he claimed – that certain Palestinian businessmen from Kuwait took pity on him and provided him with a scholarship to an American university!

He did not say which one, since the location was not only *not* an item of currency but would serve as a means of identifying him later, should he escape at the end of this demonstration, this act of making up God's uncertain mind.

And in this there *were* echoes of everything Cale had foretold. Hasni, appropriately disinherited, had been chosen, educated and now activated for this specific cue. Hasni was pleased to return the debt of his education to those Palestinian gentlemen, whoever they were, by means of the arrest of a jet plane. He was in his way – as Cale had also intimated – a boy worthy of a kind of admiration.

Was it possible now, McCloud wondered, to raise with Hasni the Mossad question which had infuriated Stone?

He was trying to frame it in a way which would bring a good result when the boy took up the story again.

"In spite of my kind patrons," he said confidentially, like someone too young giving away too much, "the Arab world as a whole does not want us. Like you, they wish we would go away. Over someone else's border. So we need to go on grabbing their attention too. Even if it's only the attention of their secret services. They like circus acts like this, Mr McCloud, for reasons of their own, and I can't argue. If we didn't do what we could, then we'd be like the Kurds and the Armenians! Stateless people! Ghosts made up of a rumour! Of a bit of grit. Of dust blowing on the wind! Unthinkable, Mr McCloud. Seriously. How can I face that?"

For a moment McCloud was silenced. He was bewildered by the boy's argument: we take this plane and declare you a criminal so that the others, the Iraqis, the Syrians, the Libyans, will know that I am alive and stateless!

And the problem was that Hasni uttered from his marrow that sentiment about grit on the wind, and in the process made naught of McCloud's wish to write a letter to Pauline. Hasni was not some Palestinian poet who happened at present to be teaching creative writing at Georgetown University. The boy was talking – it couldn't be denied – from the pit of his sensibilities, from that exalted and dangerous pocket of the brain where tribalism lies. And he *was* putting his life on the line, and that was supposed to be the apogee of male valour.

If you forgot for a second that he was gratuitously intimidating a planeful of ordinary folk – and it was strangely easy to forget that in the intensity of Taliq's upstairs – then Hasni possessed a certain nobility.

For who am I in my stale underwear and premature flab when put up against him? McCloud asked in effect.

There was a cry behind them. "Tomato juice? Taliq, mate. Have you got any tomato juice?"

It was Bluey, but McCloud would have had to stand up to see him, and in any case did not want either to confront or be ignored by the eyes, the ones – misted with the confusions of culture and rage – which, in the close-ups in the feature movie, *Gallows Crossing*, had won the applause of the international jury at Cannes, taken home the Gold Palm, and then been so recently fountains of grief for the unnamed uncle.

"What's happening?" McCloud asked Hasni.

"The black dancer is thirsty," said Hasni.

Leaning forward, McCloud could see the part of the aisle level with Bluey's seat, though the high comforts of first-class upholstery happily blocked a sight of Bluey's face. Taliq appeared in the aisle. He carried in his right, scarred hand a can of tomato juice, which he shook expertly, as if at some stage of one of his exiles he had been a waiter. In his left he carried a can of cashews and a glass half full of ice. Waiter to the oppressed, he was willing to serve Bluey, who was the success of his night of indoctrination. He put the glass and the can of cashews down on the tray by Bluey's seat. He pulled the tab from the can and poured the red juice over the ice in the glass. It was like a demonstration. It was in the spirit of the Pope washing the feet of old men in Easter ceremonies in the Vatican. *The servant of the servants of God.*

Then he pulled the lid from the cashews. There was a hiss, a release of air, as the lid came loose in one motion. Taliq was reckless with it, so energetic and forceful that the rim rose instantly under the impetus of Taliq's attack, of service towards his disinherited brother Bluey Kannata.

And in the instant, the plane jolted against a column of air. The metal rim bit savagely into the webbing between Taliq's thumb and forefinger. Without urgency, Taliq dropped the lid, grasped the wrist of his right hand with the fingers of his left, and held his bleeding limb upright, considering it with a dazed curiosity.

With no one to prevent him, McCloud stood up. It seemed somehow a horrifying thing to McCloud that Taliq, master of the aircraft, should bleed. Bluey too climbed out of his seat.

"Oh, mate," said Bluey, perhaps with a little of that extreme concern we reserve for the injuries of mere acquaintances.

Or then perhaps the concern wasn't mimed. Perhaps Bluey saw this wound as an undermining of the position he'd taken up, the camp he'd entered.

Whitey Wappitji rushed from the rear of the cabin, a great white bandanna in his hand. In the Barramatjara country handkerchiefs doubled up as dust-excluders, but in this dustless sky Whitey's touring bandanna was immaculate. Whitey began wrapping it around Taliq's hand. Blinking at this activity and concern, Taliq did not yet seem returned to himself. He was for some seconds more like Mrs Clark, who had once searched in a similar state of dazedness for her dropped wig.

You could see memory return to Taliq. He checked on the cabin to see that everything was in place, the unperfected brethren at the rear, the prisoners, Hasni. He seemed to realise that his kinghood might have been diminished, as if in fact the injury had come from a would-be but inept assassin. So he held Whitey's bandanna to his wound, raised his hand higher still, and displayed the whole bundle to the cabin. There was an edge of gaiety in his voice as he called out, "Look, ladies and gentlemen. All intact. And no distress!"

To prove it, he began to wave the hand, encased in its white with a spreading rose of red on it, in the air. "No damage done! No damage at all!"

"You be careful," Bluey told him with a sudden, panicked urgency. "You be bloody careful with that thing there."

Paul Mungina the *didj* player had appeared now and settled Bluey back in his seat. "Your mate's okay, Bluey," he could be heard saying. Was there an edge of sinister meaning to what Paul said: *You chose him, and now he's bleeding, and it's too late for second guesses.*

Turning from this task Paul saw McCloud. Paul's eyes were uneasy. But you could see him decide to be direct. "Frank, all this is pretty confusing. I don't know what to say to you. I don't know who I ought to listen to."

"Sorry, Paul," said McCloud, defeated. It was the best he could do. Whitey, who was busy at the moment, would have to explain things to Paul.

The fracas had aroused Cale and Stone but not excited them. Cale's eyes did not seem to take account of Taliq's small accident, since he had earlier had a small, painful accident of his own. He and Stone regathered their airline blankets about them. As if by rare mutual consent, they chose to see the event as not having much importance. They blinked and gazed and then went back to sleep.

From the flight deck the captain now emerged. He moved with a sort of casual care, a studied saunter. This hulking middle-aged man who had been sad to show them down into the pit. In morning light the residual sandiness of his hair encouraged McCloud in an undefined sort of way. Could the man have sensed Taliq's injury and come to work on his new weakness. The captain, McCloud noticed, had shaven, and his hair had been brushed. By these signs he showed a discreet ambition to outlast Taliq, to take command again in the end.

But he did not look at McCloud or Stone or Cale.

Despite himself, McCloud sat very straight and full-on; rigid where Stone and Cale, unconscious of the opportunity, slumped in their blankets. He hoped the captain would speak to him, welcome him back to the level of all the other passengers, to the plane's fraternity.

The captain didn't. It had to be a deliberate ignoring, McCloud decided. He must know that they had been let out not for their own good but Taliq's. He'd stated his theory of hijack when he opened the hatch: something to do with success through good order. And that he had flown in Vietnam. McCloud worried that he was therefore habituated to the idea that a few should die for the good of the multitude. He was working towards his ideal of good order by giving Taliq's order space to exercise itself and reach its ends.

"Taliq," the captain said as to a familiar. "Someone's calling you, son. On the VHF."

Taliq began to move.

"I hope," murmured the captain, loud enough though for McCloud to hear, "these men will be forgiven. That the loss of their clothes is as far as you'll take it."

"I hope so too," said Taliq, and pushed the captain gently back towards the cockpit.

McCloud felt a filial gratitude to the captain. But Cale didn't.

"He hopes," Cale whispered across the aisle. "He fucking hopes! He should be telling them he'll fry their balls in court if anything happens."

As Taliq moved forward, Bluey rose and followed him confusedly towards the cockpit for a few paces. Giving up then, he turned back and stared at McCloud without seeing him.

"He ought to be bloody careful what he does with that thing," Bluey announced.

"What thing?" asked McCloud.

Bluey hawked and turned his eyes away and returned to his unshuttered window.

McCloud slept again; it can't have been for long. In this brief coma Pauline, always the neat and competent girl, was tidying her schoolbooks on a table, all under the gaze of her small-boned, wronged mother. For the child Pauline he felt the pristine love that had begun things, an unspeakable affection untouched by the daily traffic of their later marriage.

Pauline's father, the Dentist, and afterwards the prospector for precious metals, had turned up at the church for the wedding: Francis McCloud and Pauline Cross. But Pauline's blue-lipped mother, so like Pauline, so handsomely compact, so four-square, so brisk, had spoken to him on the pavement and frightened him away from the marriage feast. These events had of course all now been related in McCloud's book. The grandeur of his, McCloud's intentions towards this material, he had felt, *entitled* him to the use of that raw history, the end-stone of one marriage coinciding, neat as art, with the birthstone of another.

He had even once asked Pauline if he could make free with her family history in his novel, and she'd given a guarded, grudging approval.

"Maybe you could mention it to your mother too," he'd suggested. "But tell her she won't be recognised. I promise she won't be."

"Just don't make us sound foolish," Pauline said, with her economic frown. "It's not very interesting anyhow, but if you want . . ."

But it was. Bloody fascinating, McCloud thought. And having got her edgy approval, he never put it to the test by asking her again.

Pauline's father Dr Cross had in her early childhood run a fashionable dental clinic on Sydney's North Shore. He engineered and repaired the teeth of many knights, military, industrial, conservatively political. He fixed the mouths which spoke in boardrooms, and in those days this gave him cachet. On the North Shore of Sydney there were always ambitions towards fashion. Though these were under siege from the sun and from the sad fact that in Australia nearly all the *riches* were *nouveaux*, they were persistent enough to make Dr Cross what could be called a *society* dentist.

Older people who remembered Dr Cross's father spoke of how gratified they were that the son had not inherited the father's problem with drink.

One day in Pauline's childhood and McCloud's, Dr Cross was filling the teeth of some heavy-engineering knight's second, younger wife when she gave what he would tell the coroner was "a small gurgle or moan", and collapsed in the chair. He did all the right things, even using compressed oxygen to try to resuscitate her. His nurse had already called for doctors and ambulances. They were some twenty minutes arriving, and it was apparent to him long before that the woman could not be revived.

This young woman had grown up in the country, and her fillings had been done by old-school dentists. As he would later tell Pauline in explanation of the new course he would set his life on, he became aware, as he watched the woman's open mouth, of what he'd already known in an off-hand, notional way. Like the teeth of a lot of country girls, hers had suffered considerable decay early in life. Each of her fillings had been marked on her dental chart, certainly. But he had never before paid full attention to the extent of the work which had been done. And most of the holes had been filled with gold. It must have cost her parents a large proportion of their wool cheques to go on repairing their daughter's mouth.

Waiting for the ambulance therefore, he spent a long time gazing into her golden mouth. He accepted the idea that there was something wrong with his gazing, though he acted with reverence and knew that – unlike the alcoholic carelessness of his father – his behaviour would not attract the censure of the Dental Association.

McCloud, who had grown up in one of the less preferred but still affluent reaches of the North Shore, heard of this tragedy by eavesdropped adult rumour, and because the Sunday papers loved the tale of the young woman's death in the dental chair. In what the papers and adults muttered about the case there was the suggestion that Dr Cross had known the woman as more than a patient. A photograph appeared in the tabloids of a New Year's Eve party at some golf club where Dr Cross sat next to the knight's wife. Mrs Cross had been sitting on Dr Cross's right hand side in the original, harmless photograph, but the press had cropped her out for fear she marred the story and the imputation.

Had Dr Cross gassed or poisoned his mistress? That was the question which hung over all the suburban rumours and the circumstantial press reports. The earlier and startling Clark case had set people up, if they needed setting up, to ask such a question.

At the time of the scandal Pauline was twelve and attending a Presbyterian ladies' college on the North Shore. McCloud did not know her then. In fact, when he first saw her she was twenty-four; it was at some party, and she was pointed out to him by someone who remembered the Dr Cross story. Given that a great whisper had altered or perhaps ended his own childhood, he looked at her and wondered how the even juicier rumour which flared for a time in her life had been absorbed into her tidy beauty, her competent, square-shouldered, smallish frame, her air of briskness, reliability and sensual promise.

The coroner had found that the knight's young wife died of a cerebral haemorrhage, and had called the innuendos attaching to Dr Cross unfounded and shameful. (Again, there was a parallel with the Clark trial, which to the young McCloud had been the McCloud case.) The judge uttered the devout hope that Dr Cross's patients would stand by him, for his professional reputation was intact. But there was never a chance that they would.

Dr Cross himself forestalled them. He closed his surgery and sold the practice to the first comer. He took to going to the bush and living, first for weeks at a time and then for months, in a tent on a friend's farm on the old goldfield at Sofala. After the absences became all but permanent, Mrs Cross told him – for his daughter's sake – to keep away from home. Life in a tent had by then made him a different man, an inadvertent and ragged one. He spent his time re-panning old gravel beds and taking to the flanks of hills with a pick. It may have struck Mrs Cross that he was looking for some image of *her* mouth, the mouth of the knight's young wife. In McCloud's novel anyhow, the fictional Mrs Cross would accuse her husband of that.

Reworking the nineteenth-century mullock-heaps and gravel beds, Dr Cross grew old and uncomfortable to be with and became a brief ghost at the wedding of those two orphans of rumour, McCloud and Pauline. He had built a shack amongst old diggings and left-over cyanide treatment tanks used by prospectors who had earned a small living there during the Depression. Here he died of some respiratory illness; though of course to Pauline he had died first when he went to the bush, looking a century too late for all that Sheba bounty of Sofala.

It was the twelve-year-old Pauline, the spruce child in an early stage of her ultimate bereavement, clearing away her homework books, who was a reproach to the novelist McCloud in his brief, random sleep beside Hasni.

When Taliq's voice came crackling – jagged with static – over the intercom, McCloud did not surface entirely, but lay on the underside of the waves where there was light, some sound, and much meaning.

The Upstairs Dispensation

"The Arab Youth Popular Socialist Front action commando is now happy to inform you that there has been some dialogue between ourselves and authorities on the ground. It is possible to make known to you, as earlier we have to the ground, the reward we are doing all this to achieve. The traitors of the Palestinian National Front have been holding three of our heroes and dear brothers, including our general, Mahoud al-Jiddah, as their prisoners in North Africa. The National Front have been so corrupted by the blandishments of America and its allies that they recognise the Zionist state of Israel as if it had a right to exist on the bones of our fathers and mothers, our brothers and sisters. Because Mahoud and our other brothers could not so far forget their principles as to string along with these betrayals, they have been kept imprisoned by the very people who were once their brothers and allies."

More static, and then Taliq cutting it!

"I can tell you that we have asked, indeed demanded, the release to us of Mahoud and our brothers, their delivery from the grasp of these lick-spittle renegades who call themselves Palestinian but who disgrace the name. This does not suit the treacherous faction who hold him. It does not suit their corrupt politics to release him. But their friends the imperialists of Britain and the United States and France and Germany have given us undertakings that they will use their influence to see that Mahoud and our brothers are delivered to us when next we land. If that should happen, all passengers except the three criminal prisoners can look forward to leaving the plane and greeting again their families.

"Our destinies therefore rest with the not-always-reliable intentions of the western bourgeois nations. Let us pray that they have all our interests at their hearts."

"Why do they talk like that?" McCloud asked, a murmur which could not be heard. "Why do they talk that stilted way?"

Maybe Taliq should have got Hasni to make the announcement. For in his vanity, Hasni might have transcended the clichés.

But then it came to McCloud that this planeload of people might depend and rely on the standard pabulum of Taliq's hijacker idiom. He relied on it himself, and though scoffing at it privately, was somehow soothed by it even when it excluded him.

It struck him too that in Taliq's wooden argot, Pauline's release was promised. Conditionally of course. The conditions nearly choked the promise and yet not entirely. Calmly he imagined Pauline the widow, mother of orphaned and – one had to hope –

165

apparently reconciled children. He foresaw the comforters, Peter Drury the impresario amongst them. Divorced and not yet settled with a woman. How good he'd be for the Girl and the Boy. What legitimacy and joy and gifts Pauline could bring him!

From the blind side of his consciousness, McCloud saw far above him Taliq the ideologue emerge from the cockpit carrying a small blue box with a white cross on it. Whitey Wappitji met him. Whitey took the bandanna off Taliq's wounded hand. The congealed fabric, coming away from the injury, made Taliq flinch on one side of his face. The other side, however, retained its sober style, appropriate to the governance of the aircraft.

Bluey had risen from his seat and snatched the bandanna. He returned to his window with it, dropping it with a gesture of deliberateness on the aisle seat beside him. From his own place, McCloud could see it sitting there, more or less in Bluey's care.

Meanwhile, with cotton wool and gauze, Whitey wrapped the wound up expertly. "Real St John's Ambulance stuff," McCloud believed Whitey said.

Taliq began to smile in gratification. The dressing restored his wholeness. Whitey deftly finished the bandaging, fastening it altogether with an elastic clip.

After some words of thanks which McCloud could not hear, Taliq went back to his coterie at the rear of the cabin. McCloud, cold and airless beneath the solidity of his drowse, both saw him and did not see him. How in any case could McCloud observe all this, given that the cushion behind his head blocked his view? Yet with something like clarity he saw Taliq sit, and Daisy Nakamura take his hand by the wrist and consider the bound-up wound, while Taliq himself watched her with sombre desire.

Some time later, though still believing himself to be sleeping, McCloud saw Whitey go forward through the curtain, open the lavatory door and stand in it, facing outwards so that even within the rules of normal eye-lines McCloud could see him. He took out the bandanna impregnated with Taliq's blood. Where had he got it from? Of course, Bluey had fallen asleep by his unshuttered window. Whitey had treacherously stolen the thing.

Whitey considered it, more or less in its own right but also half-turning on occasion to observe its reflection in the mirror above the wash-basin.

He spent what seemed to McCloud a long, long time studying the bandanna, reading Taliq's blood. Only when he had achieved

a level of certainty did he breathe on it and begin to sing or intone
– you could tell it was not usual conversation by the length of time
Whitey's lips were apart, the extent of the vowels. There wasn't
any doubt about it. He was persuading not so much some malignity
but some sort of inevitable event to enter Taliq's veins.

For me? McCloud tried to ask. *For me? To save me from my
own ignorance?*

He was reduced to sobs at this unasked-for benefit from Whitey,
this vote of forgiveness.

At last Whitey was finished, and pocketed the thing and closed the
lavatory door. As he came aft he paused above McCloud.

"Frank," he uttered, piercingly but privately. "He's not a well
man, this Taliq. He's not a well man."

He looked at McCloud significantly. McCloud was sure he was
meant to take courage from this pronouncement. The promise was
that Taliq's intentions would turn cloudy and imprecise.

He was so pleased with this news, with Whitey's infallible
reading of the blood and with the curse of confusion and illness
Whitey had sung into it that he believed he must inform Pauline.
Then she would not need any more to threaten Taliq. For Whitey
had driven the threat against Taliq underground, where it was
more potent.

Whitey threw the bandanna back down on the aisle seat beside
the window one where Bluey slept. So neat, this operation!

McCloud felt himself rise up for a second, but then the weight
of water pulled him down to an angle deep in the sky from which
he saw their aircraft, their threatened planet, lazier than a yacht,
stuck in a transparent firmament.

10

JUDGMENT AND CONVERSATION

AT the bottom of the sky's coldest socket, Hasni shook him
awake.
"There is an hour before we land," Hasni solicitously told
him. The boy's eyes shifted away then to Cale and the American
businessman who were already standing shivering in the aisle.
Their blankets had been stripped from them. Even Stone's flesh
looked porous, cheese-like, on the edge of dissolution. McCloud
dreaded joining them in their nakedness. He hoped he wasn't about
to become again the meat in their debate over the substantial
difference between Stone's stepson and Hasni.

None the less, he was on his feet suddenly and without question.
There was no one else here, on this upper deck, in Taliq's garden
of ideologies. While he slept, the population of the place had been
cleared.

Cale was smiling. "Show-trial time," he muttered. He seemed
totally recovered from the punishment he'd taken earlier from Taliq.

Hasni set himself to straightening their placards, which were dog-
eared now but which had none the less proven sturdy. It made you
think that little bullet-headed Razir probably had a gift for the
placard business, had maybe – for the Iraqis – hung them around
the necks of captured Iranian officers.

Hasni himself quivered now and then, without meaning to, from
the cold. He was dressed for his destination – the balmy shore of
Libya perhaps. He nodded to them and they turned and began to
descend the stairs, Stone first, then Cale. McCloud at the end. He
wondered was there any use trying to read meanings into the
order.

Judgment and Conversation

The front cabin downstairs was utterly empty. An unreasoning fear from the pit reasserted itself. Had the exchange taken place already? Mahoud al-Jiddah and the other brothers for the passengers? And he had slept through it? Had Pauline already been absorbed by her future?

Turning aft, however, they discovered everyone in the middle of the plane, crowded two and three to a seat, wan in the sepia light of the high, shuttered aircraft. At the front of the assemblage, by one escape door, stood the balding veteran called Razir, and young Musa, the one who spoke British Midlands. As if he might have to sit for a test, McCloud's brain fumbled for the memory of the wrongs Hasni said had been done to their separate families.

Hasni halted the three prisoners by the bulkhead which carried the screen where normally films were projected. The pure white side of the screen had been exposed to the population of the plane, and against it Hasni placed the three, wanting them to stand out starkly, isolated in their malfeasance. It was Razir, of course, the one McCloud thought of as *the little veteran*, who orchestrated this, who really knew about light, background, and the displaying of the captured.

Facing the plane's population, McCloud looked for faces – for the blonde woman who had punched him in the back; for the cripple who had wept for them; for the man in the glossy baseball jacket who had screamed at them on their first procession through the plane; for the woman who for her sleeping children's sake had sworn at Cale. And of course for Pauline.

But the crush of people was awful. Nothing distinct could be seen in that mass of crammed, coerced features. Clearer, opposite Hasni, were the Barramatjara Dance Troupe – apart, he noticed, from Bluey. Frail-looking Daisy Nakamura was there, still wearing her blanket, and Taliq smoking reflectively, not with his normal rapacity for the tobacco.

Then where is Yusuf the tailor's son? McCloud asked himself, anxious to make a check on what had become the established order of things. Oh yes, of course, Yusuf – the critic of Singapore stitching – was on the flight deck with the avuncular captain. Ready to blow the cockpit to fragments.

Taliq walked over to where McCloud stood against the screen.

"Hasni tells me," he said confidentially, "you feel badly done

169

by. You paint a picture of an unreliable politician pursuing his own agenda. Is that not so?"

"Yes," said McCloud. "It's so. I'm innocent. And you're believing the enemy press, which you condemn as liars. So why don't I get credit for the fact they lie?"

McCloud was trembling, but happy with the argument he'd put.

"Do you know why I believe the enemy this time?" Taliq asked, dragging a last time on an almost spent cigarette. "Do you know?"

"I'm sure you'll find a reason," said McCloud, allowing himself the aggressive luxury of feeling cheated.

"I'll tell you," said Taliq. "Only one of your dancers condemns you, but none of them defends you."

Taliq looked piercingly into his eyes, and McCloud saw it was the truth, at least in the judicial sense. Useless to say, *But Whitey's defended me with a curse.*

"Have it your way," said McCloud. "Your mental dishonesty will get you in the end."

Taliq half-smiled. "If a peer said that to me, I would worry," he murmured.

He returned to one of the doorways and picked up one of the plane's intercom handsets to speak through, though the passengers were now so crammed together that his unadorned voice would probably have reached all of them.

"Friends," he announced in his way, which should have sounded flatulent but in fact had all the potency, all the sharpness of absolute judgment, "I present to you now the three criminals found guilty by our people's tribunal. It was necessary to choose a judge from amongst the oppressed people on this aircraft. On the evidence presented to him our judge, a plain, sane human being, has – as any plain sane person would – found all three of these men guilty of crimes against humanity.

"So what will be done with them? If the Western powers do not arrange for the release of our brother and respected leader, the hero Mahoud al-Jiddah, and of his two detained brothers, they will be shot one at a time. Again – I trust you see this – we threaten punishment only against the most obviously criminal elements."

"Oh well," Cale suddenly murmured to McCloud. "Oh well, we'll see."

McCloud got a sense that Cale was half-way enjoying himself, waiting avidly for an outcome, something which would entitle him to turn to Stone and say, "See?"

*　　*　　*

Judgment and Conversation

"But our judge? you ask. Who is it?"

McCloud continued to search for Pauline's face. He was aware that some in the mass of people in front of him were no more than vaguely interested in who the judge would be.

"Well, we have a judge. It is a man of a different history from that which my brothers Yusuf, Musa, Razir and Hasni share with me. Different yet shockingly similar. The judge from your midst is a man called Kanduk Kannata, whose land is about to be taken from him by imperialist malice and deceit. Mr Kannata is capable, however – like most victims of tyranny whose tongue has not been ripped out – of speaking for himself. And so I introduce him."

The actor and film star and dancer, fearer of curses and former good companion, appeared from the forward compartment as if from the wings of a stage and took the intercom device which Taliq offered him. Like Taliq, the dance programme called Bluey Kannata by his true name *Kanduk*. Yet at all social occasions Bluey introduced himself by that standard Australian nickname, given to him on some cattle station of his childhood where his father had worked, where white men had seen the reddish streak in the young Kanduk's hair and labelled him with that wry antonym.

Anyhow, Bluey did indeed look blue by the enclosed light of the cabin: looked in fact the majestic purple which characterised the Barramatjara complexion and which McCloud had noticed in the dancers when they were extremely tired.

His voice sounded firm to McCloud, and utterly lacking in the usual apologetic jokiness. There was a frightening resonance too, as if Bluey had repented of all previous claims McCloud might have on him. He clicked the *transmit* button on the intercom a few times, casually, like a man about to make a speech at a bush dance. He looked convincing, McCloud was horrified to see. A man habituated to this sort of speech.

"These men who took over our plane," Bluey began in a screech of static which soon gave way to clarity, "these men and all of us who are in it with them, are at war. This is a serious business here. Either we weed out those who are to blame for damage against people, or we *all* end up in pieces, falling down through the sky. I'm sure you agree with me on that one. That's a message you don't need to be Einstein to catch on to."

The Barramatjara troupe, its other members, were not looking at Bluey, McCloud noticed from the corner of his vision. Philip

Puduma and Tom Gullagara were half-turned away. Paul Mungina the *didj* player was biting his bottom lip and screwing up his right eye. Perhaps he feared Bluey would shame him by saying something radical, by badmouthing the Queen, for whom Paul had such respect.

Whitey, head cocked, examined the ceiling, the pattern of lockers and lights.

McCloud believed he could recognise their embarrassment. They had stood like that at the door of the little costume room at the Lincoln Center, waiting for the spasm and the unfamiliar curse to fade, while Bluey huddled under the cutting table. It was all they could do; be patient until he returned to his skin. They couldn't disown another Barramatjara man, it wasn't allowed for a Barramatjara to deny brotherhood with Bluey. And none of them *were* denying it. They were politely not going the full way with him. As on the day he became frenzied in rehearsal, he was under a visitation. And now his last sentence, the plea for assent – "I'm sure you'll all agree with me on that one" – had somehow, by its weakness, convinced them that he would come back. You could see that. It was legible in the fearsome passivity of their faces.

All at once Bluey Kannata rose, however, above the wateriness of that sentiment, that appeal for approval. Having recognised the lapse himself, and what it could mean, he was strong again. He reset his body, so that the other dancers were no longer in his line of vision. He had come to a decision not to refer back to them, as he did in most normal conditions, acknowledging them at each turn of the day and the dance: the man who had left the Barramatjara country, earned big money and the compliance of white women, neglected his tribal wife and his ceremonies, seeking just the same their unarguing approval. None of that now, his new posture said. For Taliq had given him a means of being free of the Barramatjara system, of being his own judge. And Cale's too, and Stone's and McCloud's.

"So here we have one feller," cried Bluey, "the Englishman there. He writes lies about these people. We've all *seen* these people losing their own country. We come back to our hotel rooms late at night and test the television button, and there it is, every night, happening. Always there. Every night. Before the sport and before the weather. Always. These people. But nothing is done about it, we don't feel we have to do anything. And the reason we don't is that we're lied to. Do you see that Englishman there, do you see that beer-gutted Englishman? He writes the lies, the deadly lies, brothers and sisters, for a rag we know as the London *Daily Telegraph*."

Bluey was not talking any more simply in the argot of the desert cattle station. The Barramatjara spoke in their deliberately simplified cattleman/stockrider idiom whenever they were not speaking Barramatjara. The word *mate* peppered everything they said, along with *you fellers* and *you blokes*. And all politics, all ritual, and the negotiations for the performance fees of the Barramatjara Dance Troupe themselves were – as McCloud had once mentioned to Pauline – covered by the words *pretty serious business*. Such a term had already occurred in Bluey's speech, but it was seasoned with terms Bluey would not normally use. *Deadly, deadly lies* for example. And that awful phrase: *damage against people*.

McCloud had always had a glimmer of a suspicion that the dancers might sometimes speak a more sophisticated English than their usual elliptical, evasive cattle station talk, or at least have it at their disposal. He wondered what inhibited them from using it – maybe a desire not to get out of their depth or give too much away in big cities like Sydney or New York. Maybe a polite care not to surprise the outsiders with too much eloquence, or not to arouse them for that matter. Maybe a fierce willingness to keep their place.

For they might be dancers and New York stars today, but the great first shock of white contact had taken their fathers into the service of white cattlemen, and that was the *remembered* glory of their manhood, and the *remembered* wound. The language of that experience was their chosen argot.

By speaking as he did now, in a language marked in part by cattleman English but also breaking free of it, Bluey may have been outflanking and separating himself from the other men of the dance troupe. By these means he could show them and McCloud the seriousness of the enlightenment which had struck him on the upper deck.

"The man next to the fat man," Bluey continued, "is an American and sells computer systems to the Israelis. There is every reason to believe that he is some sort of agent. Both these men travelled with two passports each. This computer American travelled with two passports. So he's a man who wants to deceive people. But he hasn't deceived us. Do you travel with two passports, ladies and gentlemen?"

It was noticeable that Bluey did not push the rhetorical question. He was as adroit as any prosecutor could hope to be. McCloud dreaded therefore that a special intent would enter Bluey's voice now. For it was time to speak of criminal number three.

McCloud flinched when he heard the altered timbre as Bluey arrived at the question of him.

"This third man . . . this third man. He's the man who has dragged my brothers and me around the world, showing us to audiences as if we were clever apes. The organ-grinder's monkeys. While all along he understood what the plot was. It was to deprive us of our own country, to take from us land which I know with my own eyes, ladies and gentlemen, and have known since I was a baby. Which I know in myself and I know through my ancestor's eyes. Land close to me as this skin."

And Bluey displayed the flesh of his forearm.

"This man's wages are paid by the mining companies and the governments who want us out of the way, who find us an inconvenience. Who want my brothers – Wappitji, Gullagara, Puduma, Mungina – up here, here in the air, on the other side of the world, away from our holy ground. So they can make way for the drilling rigs and the satellite stations. Who think they can say, *We gave you a trip around the world! We let you dance in Frankfurt! Don't be ungrateful with us!*

"And this man . . . this man who smiled at us and called us by our names, he knew all about it. And brought us along softly. And we danced in our innocence and in our friendship. And only today, in a news magazine, we read the truth about him, about us. We read what he was keeping from us . . ."

All Bluey's limbs had begun to shake. Even Taliq looked all at once concerned for him. "This man is the man who should be shot first. If I had my say, I would finish him whether or not those English and the Americans send Taliq's friends to our plane. For this man, and because of his lies, my uncle has to bear curses . . ."

Bluey's voice was aquiver as well now. His arms moved towards the prisoners, shuddering with a ferocious will to do them some damage. He was no longer ineffectual Bluey. He was a vengeance named Kanduk Kannata.

"Look at him!" he screamed. "Look at him, my friends! He is a bundle of softness. And he writes stinking little books. I mean to find out if these people who are taking my country promised him *that* too! That they'd publish his stinking little book. The one he's been writing for years. For years! A lost cause, this endless bloody book of his.

"A week ago . . . a week ago, knowing we were all to lose our land, he set up some little telephone call home to make me feel better. To give me small comfort. When all along he knew what was intended for the Barramatjara folk! This one, this man . . . I would shoot him first! Of the three of them, him first!"

Bluey bared his teeth and gave out a rhythmical scream. He stamped one foot. It was like the beginning of a dance. He pointed one finger at the prisoners and the first sound he uttered fell on them like a bludgeon. He began to advance on them, cursing them as he came. But there was still some disorder in his limbs, which shivered in ways that weren't connected to the dance. This wasn't the normal Bluey Kannata graciousness of movement. Some powerful fever worked in each arm and leg. His forward foot slipped before he had come a yard. He fell against a seat, twisted, and landed on the floor on his back.

One of the women flight attendants, clearly trained to deal with fits in passengers, arrived and put a wet towel between his teeth. A middle-aged German who said he was a doctor knelt over Bluey's convulsing body. He seemed very competent, as if he had the habit of being efficient in chaotic circumstances. A practitioner of emergency medicine perhaps. He looked at Bluey's eyes, took his pulse and calmly held his clenching hand.

"Take him!" yelled Taliq, alarmed both as a new friend, and perhaps in case the fit had put Bluey's judicial authority in doubt. "Take him in there, and let him rest!"

He pointed to the forward part of the plane, and the doctor and the flight attendant-nurse lifted Bluey by the armpits, and Philip Puduma, the oldest dancer, and Paul the *didj* player, took him by the ankles. Does this mean a split? McCloud wondered. Are Phil and the *didj* player part-way in agreement with Bluey?

Whitey Wappitji, who had been ordered in a dream to become a dancer and painter, and his lieutenant Cowboy Tom Gullagara were still impassive, watching Bluey being carried away.

There were now voices from amongst the passengers. "This is ridiculous," one familiarly accented voice said, and McCloud saw that it came from the young German wheelchair-case who had burst into tears when he and Stone and Cale had first been paraded. "Sir, this does not stand up under any system of law!"

175

The voice had the same liquid and desperate emphasis in it as the earlier outburst on their behalf. But it suffered from competition. Someone else was crying, "Shame, shame!" It was impossible to know whose shame they were talking about – Taliq's, Bluey's, McCloud's.

The balding Chief Purser rose and made some observation to Taliq which could not be heard above the hubbub.

And then Pauline could be seen, climbing upright on a seat she shared with another woman, her voice rising in contest with the cries of *Shame* and the cripple's imputation of Taliq's lawlessness.

Pauline was determined to be heard. She called, "Absurd! Absurd! My husband's guiltless."

McCloud lost his breath. It was taken up by admiration for her high Irish-Scots colour, the mark of her divine forthrightness. He wanted to tell her to stop, though he felt exalted that she would not.

"My husband," said Pauline, "writes his books and makes a living managing cultural troupes. To cast him as one of the three guilty people on this plane is . . . is *utterly* absurd." Under pressure of noise, including the hisses of those who did not approve of her, her voice grew shrill. But it sounded to McCloud an appropriate shrillness. She was gesturing and prodding the air with an outstretched arm, her gift of genuine oratory echoing Bluey's terrible eloquence. "That dancer, that Barramatjara man, is a very disturbed man and not to be listened to! Listen, Brother Taliq. You haven't even asked about the accuracy of this story you mention. You haven't even done that! I tell you that if you shoot my husband, you had better be sure to shoot me too, because I'll hound you. I'll testify against you wherever they try you. I'll put you in prison, where men will beat you and sodomise you in a most unenlightened way. I do not recognise your power to appoint any judge, to carry out any sentence at all . . ."

It should have been ludicrous: a small woman unsteady on a seat and uttering threats of a relentless pursuit. Yet it wasn't. It had a most serious authority. No one else had dealt with Taliq as frontally, as thoroughly as this.

Except that now Pauline was forced to yell at increasing volume because other passengers were crying out now, submerging her argument, utterly nullifying the young German cripple's voice and that of the man shouting, "Shame! Shame!"

"Sit down, bitch!" men yelled.

"What's wrong with her?" cried the suddenly visible blonde

woman who had earlier hit McCloud in the back and who was now trying to cast Pauline as a dangerous and heretic voice.

Some of the furore may have been kindly advice to Pauline – McCloud hoped so – but most of it sounded hostile. A solid man in a ski jacket left his place and reached over two other passengers to begin silencing the young German by putting a hand over his mouth. Pauline was being dragged down; hands – maybe kindly, maybe not – grabbed her beneath the knees; blows landed on her hips. Intentions blurred. People raised fists to strike Pauline and other people caught the wielders by the wrist.

McCloud stepped forward but was pushed into place again by Hasni.

"Please," said Taliq indulgently but with force. "Please, ladies and gentlemen."

The mêlée subsided and everyone faced Taliq. There was a sound of sobbing, but McCloud was pleased to find it did not seem to be Pauline's.

"Ladies and gentlemen," said Taliq at last, "I see you have the dissenters well in hand. You can recognise the enemy as clearly as we can. For all else we are in the hands of others. Please return to your seats now in good order with no more outbursts, however well-intentioned. I would simply remind you that we shall land within an hour."

McCloud heard a cry from Pauline as he was pushed and hurled forward again, shivering. Glancing back, he saw her borne aft by two determined people, a man and a woman. Both of them looked as if they might be acting from a regard for her safety, as if they were either rushing her from danger or else were very functional jailers.

"Pauline," he could not prevent himself from screaming. His cry for the nurturing and familiar woman. He realised it was the sort of cry heard on battlefields from terrified men, and that by letting it out he had in a sense defined himself as finished. He looked at Cale, open for advice. But Cale shrugged.

"Save it, son," muttered Cale through lips which in this air higher than Everest's had turned purple. "They won't hurt her," he wheezed. "A good woman! Not too ashamed to go over the top . . ."

Forced forward, McCloud saw Bluey, lain across four seats in the middle of the plane, tended by a doctor and a stewardess, gazed upon by Paul the *didj* man and Phil Puduma. Bluey did not see the prisoners go by on their way upstairs again. His eyes were not closed, but he had no focus.

Kanduk. Torn apart by demons. Of which, McCloud knew well, he himself was considered one; the false voice, speaking the language of unbottomable slyness.

The German doctor called to Taliq. "I have given him some sedatives I had. It was a *grand mal* fit. This young man should be in hospital on medication."

There was contempt in the doctor's voice: he was an unquiet hostage, not easily scared.

Behind the prisoners, Taliq groaned. "It is very likely we can let the poor fellow go. But in the end, it depends on the goodwill of our Western masters."

"That's nonsense," murmured the doctor. "Surely you could let him go anyhow."

But Taliq was not going to let his judge go, his one clear success from the sessions on the upper deck!

Returned to his seat upstairs and in despair about the messages he had not passed on to Pauline, McCloud watched the condemned Cale and Stone, thrown into their seats, slip glibly back into sleep or reflection. They reminded him again of two rival scientists: each believed his theory could be proved right only by the passage of time.

Through his own fevered, spotted vision he observed the four Barramatjara men as they mounted the spiral staircase and passed him. He noticed that Paul Mungina had fetched his *didj* and carried it in a way which gave McCloud an indefinite hope, as if Paul meant to use it as part of some reasonable transaction or feed its sound subtly to others through the intercom.

"Make us some music, Paul," McCloud pleaded, thinking irrationally that it might reach and soothe Pauline.

Mungina looked at him. Other than Bluey he was the youngest of the dancers, and very earnest.

"Okay, Frank," he said. "If that's what you want."

But he seemed confused about it.

Phil Puduma the Christian's eyes were half-closed and his lips moved. He gave you the idea he was voiding into the air something crucial, though you couldn't tell whether what was being jettisoned was something of the Christ of the riverbed or of the marsupial rat at Mount Dinkat.

Tom Gullagara, in his high-fashion version of a stockman's/

cowboy's uniform, a big brass bull still contending with the lariat-swinging brass cattleman in the middle of his enormous belt buckle, looked embarrassed. Beyond all wishfulness, McCloud felt certain it was a kind of shame for Bluey, one which he couldn't have the comfort of uttering.

Whitey's eyes, it turned out, immense and neutral in passing, sought McCloud's.

"That German doctor," he said. "Seems a good man in his field . . ."

"Yes," said McCloud. I have been condemned to death and my wife has been abducted or rescued to the back of the plane. And we discuss the professional manners of a doctor.

"Bluey's beyond himself," Whitey murmured, as if in apology.

Whitey bent to the aisle seat where Bluey had kept the bandanna and lifted and pocketed the thing with one easy, gliding motion which signified possession.

It struck McCloud that Whitey believed nothing would come of the judgment downstairs. This was astounding. Why would Whitey imply it? Unless he was right. Infallibly right.

But he did not stay to be questioned.

The next one to appear at the head of the stairs was Daisy Nakamura. "Hi, honey," she whispered to McCloud. "This has all got right out of hand." She lowered her voice even further. "That brave girl down there who did all the yelling? That's your wife?"

Again McCloud's tears asserted themselves.

"Oh Jesus, baby. I'll see what I can find out."

But she staggered aft as if Taliq, who came next, were her shepherd.

Hasni was the last to rise up the steps. He looked haggard and he and his Polish automatic leaned over the back of the seat in front. "Your wife is not hurt," he murmured. He sounded resentful. His eyes flickered away and then back to McCloud. After his earlier speeches, the lifting up of his grandfather's history above that of any other miserable being, after his references to shitty little marriages, why did these politenesses and compassions continue?

"Thank you for telling me, Hasni."

"Would you like me to take a message to her?" he asked. It was as if a lack of immediate gratitude from McCloud had forced him into this further offer.

Trying to find the right small message, McCloud's head ached.

He seemed to be looking up at the underpinnings, the wires and struts of his family history and attachments, trying to make of them a simple shape.

A tailor called Mr Katz, who had once done invisible mending on one of McCloud's jackets, had looked out on New South Head Road, Rose Bay, and told McCloud, "You want to know the reason I'm here? I'm here because I was the favourite of a certain NCO in Mauthausen. I don't know why I was his favourite – he chose me, I didn't choose him. He had his reasons, I had my reasons. And he is dead forty years, and here I am!"

Would Hasni be McCloud's NCO?

"Tell her," McCloud asked Hasni, "not to make any more outcries for my sake."

Hasni blinked. "Do you have any messages of . . . affection?"

McCloud looked at the young man. He wants all the fathers to be brave, McCloud saw with surprise. All the husbands to be true.

"Of course I have, if you would be kind enough to do that, give her my affection. *Undying* and grateful affection. And tell her to pass on to my children the news that I was thinking of them with love." He coughed. "Just in case your friend Mahoud al-Jiddah doesn't turn up at our next stop."

"Don't joke about Mahoud. He has been to hell frequently. But when I see your wife again I'll tell her what you said."

"Thank you," said McCloud. "I do feel worried about my son and daughter. About what they might go through . . ."

"I will pass it on," said Hasni through non-committal lips.

Hasni did not go at once though. He sat for a while. At last McCloud ventured, "Could I use the toilet now?"

Hasni deputised the husky one, the one called Musa who had got some sleep up here earlier in the morning and had now just arrived again on the upper deck to take McCloud to the cubicle. Musa stood armed at the open door and looked in at McCloud. McCloud took off his placard and placed it against the wall of the compartment. His bowels were creaking and cramped. He attempted to excrete with dignity. He watched Musa's square nose wrinkle.

"What car do you have, Mr McCloud?" Musa asked from the door.

"Not much of a car."

"You were flying in first class. Your car must be a hot model.

Mercedes 420SE? That would be your style. Understated and not too jazzy."

"No," said McCloud. "Mine's a little Japanese thing. A Datsun. Quite serviceable."

"I like the BMW 6 series. They're the peak of the market in my opinion. The American cars, the Lincoln Continental and the Cadillacs – they're right over the top. No restraint. The West can make fun of Arab taste, but not while they buy Lincolns and Cadillacs."

"I've never bought a Cadillac," said McCloud, in weary self-defence.

McCloud began wiping himself. Unless Taliq remembered these things, the paper would run out after one more stop. McCloud had never known and could barely envisage a world without toiletries. Though, in view of his condemned state, he might not have to live in one.

"Japanese cars," said Musa, keeping his eye on all McCloud's operations, "are very good and serviceable. But far too electronic for the Third World."

"Are you a mechanic?" asked McCloud, upright now and beginning to wash his hands.

"I am a student of mechanical engineering."

"Oh?" said McCloud, and asked, "Where?"

"I am not allowed to say. And you know that already. You're being *cute*. You see a time when you're speaking to some fat policeman and saying, *Yessir, one of them said he was a student of Engineering at Such and Such Polytechnic.*" Musa laughed, a very young laugh, not an unpleasant one. "I don't blame you for trying."

The soap was but a sliver. There was only enough of it too for a very short life.

"Do you notice," asked Musa, "that in the Middle East the car bomb is the universal weapon? Generally placed in Mercedes and Peugeots. I could find you twelve-year-old cousins of mine who knew how to install one. What a world, eh?"

The building pressure of their descent woke him by the ears, taking him from another shallow sleep where he moved amidst dreams of school and father, wife, agent, accusation, exoneration, failure, acclaim. There were no delays in this landing. There was no tentativeness, hardly any circling. So direct was the plane's approach that you could believe the promised Mahoud al-Jiddah must be watching its descent, smiling up at his clever brother Taliq who had arranged his freedom.

Glancing sideways, McCloud saw that the window blind at which Bluey had sat was still raised and revealed a sunlit beach, some irrigation, some long aluminium structures which could have represented agri-business anywhere in the world, from the Sudan to western New South Wales. The city they swept over then was flat-roofed – the Mediterranean again, perhaps Africa. The Arab world, anyhow, since there were glimpses of minarets, and some of them were very modern and sharp-edged in their architecture, brilliant in their ceramics, their Moorish filigree exact too, reproduced in pre-stressed concrete.

Somewhere which had oil! McCloud decided. Not a poor country. One which could *afford* its army.

And then, as the plane thudded down onto the earth, and while McCloud still kept an illicit eye out through Bluey's abandoned window, the army in question presented itself. Personnel carriers, tanks and men in deep green lined the runway.

Were they forces friendly to Taliq? Or were they there to exploit his mistakes?

The fringe of troops were still dashing past at a hundred miles an hour, the plane still not quite settled on the earth and still capable of taking flight again, when Musa staggered down the aisle and slammed Bluey's window shut. Restoring blindness to the aircraft, McCloud thought.

A burst of stale air came from the overhead vents, the plane's fetor repeating on itself.

While the plane was still taxiing, Taliq, Hasni and Musa appeared once more. Taliq ordered the three prisoners to stand. Musa adjusted their placards in case there were still people downstairs who had not read them. McCloud looked with uncomplicated hope for some signs of the curse working in Taliq's blood, but there was none, only a quite normal blueness of the overworked operative beneath his eyes.

"What about a smoke?" Cale asked.

Taliq and the boys ignored him.

As the party began its descent, McCloud saw from the stairhead Daisy and the Barramatjaras standing in their places aft, uncertain of their power, of what anyone expected of them. Hasni prevented them from coming forward. For the first time McCloud had ever known the dancers looked reduced in efficacy and wan beneath their coal-blue features. Fear rose like a cloud of acid in his throat. "This is it, boys," murmured Cale on the stairs. "No Mahoud, no Christmas cake!"

Downstairs, as the engines diminished to a whine, you could hear the rasp of Bluey's breath as you passed the place where he slept under the German doctor's care. The three prisoners were led past otherwise empty seats and made to kneel by the main door, the one by which passengers would have left at the end of a normal flight. No order of kneeling was indicated. McCloud found himself in the middle, a position he was not comfortable with since it seemed to make him a compromise victim. He found in himself a strong conviction that compromises were often the political outcome, even of the sort of extreme politics which prevailed aboard the aircraft.

This door was the beginning of the section into which the other passengers had been crowded. The stewards and stewardesses were jammed in their own suburb of seats well down the plane. Some of them looked McCloud in the eye, willing to take action for him if the chance came, but seeming to confess at the same time that they could not foresee what that chance would be.

The entire after sections of the plane otherwise had a feel of a tenement – people intent on their own affairs. Many passengers could – if they chose to look – see the three of them kneeling there, but not all did. McCloud could not find Pauline amongst the watchers and ignorers. Pauline was further aft than he could see, he presumed, under a sort of capture herself. But in safe condition, according to Hasni, who had no reason to lie.

McCloud listened to Taliq, behind him, telling Hasni and Musa in English that he was going to the cockpit. "The next half-hour is the essential half-hour," he admonished them confidentially. "In half an hour we'll know where we stand."

"And where we lie," murmured Cale with his relentless, flippant irony.

After seeing such confusion and lack of mana in the dancers' faces, McCloud felt a shameful itch at the root of his tongue to turn and assure Taliq that he had no interest in bad behaviour, that he would go on kneeling impeccably.

But no sooner had Taliq vanished than Cale again violated the simple responsibility of prisoners to observe good order. He began to speak to the boys in his low, ranting voice. "So you're the ones he's chosen to pull the trigger, eh? What a privilege! He must love you dearly."

Stocky Musa appeared from behind and cupped his free hand under Cale's chin, pushing his head upright.

"So what sort of vehicle do you drive in then, Mr Fat Man?" he asked, seemingly half-amused. His eyes brimmed with his humane passion for vehicles. He was poignant and frightening at the same time.

"My wife owns a Saab," said Cale. "Is that an ideological crime?"

"Saab is good, reliable," said Musa. He drew one hand across his groin. "No sexiness in it. But why should there be? A good car for someone your age, and your wife's years."

Cale still insisted on speaking out of lips forced together by Musa's hand. "My wife is thirty-five years old and a features editor. What would you know about sexiness? Arab fucking lovers? You mutilate your poor sodding women!"

This did sting Musa. He kept heaving his hand against the soft flesh beneath Cale's jawline. "Don't you talk of our women. Their names are profaned by your fat Zionist lips."

But Cale wouldn't shut up. Daniel Stone raised his eyebrows at McCloud, suggesting that perhaps they too, Cale's fellow prisoners, must begin to take responsibility for calming their fellow accused.

"What do you jokers know?" Cale cried. "You grew up jerking each other off in some hothouse of a refugee camp, and then you got your scholarship to wherever, and then you did a little training in some camp in Iraq and learned how to blow things flat. You're monks, you poor little sods. You're stuck in childhood. How do you think you'll look after the commandos shoot you down? Do you think you'll look holy?"

"What commandos?" shouted Musa. "Commandos? We are the commandos!"

McCloud wondered had Musa seen the army – somebody's army – lining the runway.

By this stage, Hasni had appeared too. He took hold of Musa's shoulders and pulled him away, speaking to him softly in Arabic. A nice boy, Hasni; and so perhaps the most dangerous of all. For he was observing the forms. The word for punishment had not been given. For all these hours, McCloud acknowledged, he had been hoping that Hasni would prove susceptible to doubt. It had been there, this hope, since the night before, since McCloud's first sighting of the boy seated beside Pauline and reading *U.S. News and World Report* with a mature dispassion, an air of applying judgement to every sentence, an air too of accepting the editorial bent of the journal. (It could not have been very favourable to his point of view.) But Hasni had seemed to accept editorial drift as a given, an interesting lens, not an affront, an invitation to rage.

He seemed to be dealing with Cale's editorial drift exactly the same way here.

The engines had cut to utter silence now, and McCloud began to notice with interest the growing warmth of his flesh.

Far down the plane a baby cried routinely. McCloud wondered was it the baby whose mother had at the start of the journey been seated beside Pauline. That mother would not have much care for the three men by the door. It was not her job to.

McCloud saw Yusuf permitting an orderly traffic of passengers around and in and out of the toilets. There was an intentness in these passengers, the kind you saw in people getting ready to leave a plane and collect their baggage. The line was a self-regulating line in fact. The whole plane seemed self-regulating now. Perhaps the captain and his crew, embracing their ethos of any form of order being better than none, were themselves now left largely alone.

In any case, Yusuf detached himself and sauntered towards his brothers and their prisoners by the door. He nodded at the bulkhead, in the direction of the outside world.

"You notice they're using machine guns mounted on Toyotas out there?"

"The latest fashion," said Musa. "Everyone's crazy about Toyotas. Ever since the Chadians used them against Libyan tanks at Wadi Dhum."

A groan escaped McCloud. He had had enough vehicle talk. And this spate of it meant that the boys knew an army waited outside and considered it friendly, the basis of a casual chat about hardware.

"And T-55 tanks," murmured Yusuf the tailor's son, nodding again at the bulkhead.

"The Russians have no shame," said Musa. "They palm them off on everyone. But they're dinosaurs. Just not manoeuvrable enough in open country. Built for the streets of Eastern Europe. Good at forward and reverse." He laughed. "A bloody rotten family sedan!"

Yusuf joined in the laughter and turned away again to take up his casual duties aft. From one of the water-closets came forth the man who had punched the German cripple. He wore a look of gratification. He did not seem dismayed by the declining qualities of soap and niceties, he was an adaptor, a glory of the species, a taker-on of protective colour. When it was all over, he might recount how his attack on the wheelchair case had appeased the captors and saved an evil scene. But he would most likely just forget.

And like the baby's cry earlier, this man had an utter lack of connection with McCloud and with Pauline, wherever she might be. He does not see himself as my brother. He cannot even share a joke with me, thought McCloud, the way Musa and Yusuf have just shared a joke about Russian tanks.

Behind him, McCloud smelt Daisy's musk suddenly and briefly, an exciting composition, part staleness, part promise. So, she *had* come downstairs! And were the dancers with her?

"Don't turn round, you boys," she murmured. "I don't like any of this. The dancing guys think nothing at all will happen, that it's all talk. But I'm uneasy as hell. I talked that boy Hasni into letting me come down here. God damn the lot of you!" She said nothing more for a while, but her complicated scent reasserted itself. "I've given Mr Taliq the right message. A man of his experience can take it from there."

McCloud heard Stone sigh, or gag on breath. Cale said, "How can we thank you, madam?" McCloud looked at him, to check whether the features confirmed the neutrality, the apparent cool respect of the statement.

"We did this to you," said McCloud, knowing that what he said was so inexact. It now seemed exorbitant, the thing they expected of her.

Stone was reconciled to it though and now made a businesslike suggestion. "Don't mix with all of them, miss. I know you don't mean to, but I had to say it. Let the young ones get to resent Taliq."

She said nothing to this. It became apparent that she was gone though. Her scent was still there but lacked substance.

"I hope I said the right thing," Stone murmured.

As surely as he had identified Daisy by her scent, McCloud could smell Taliq's return; his individual cigarette reek. He joined Hasni and Musa in their position behind the prisoners. They emanated a musk of awesome casualness somehow appropriate to this hour of the hijack, when everything hung on a word from beyond the plane; and Taliq clearly stood near them. An order must then have been given by gesture, since one of the stewards, the balding man who wore the badge which said *Chief Purser*, moved towards the door of the plane, worked its long lever, and opened it on the day.

As it swung back sighing and admitted the outside air, McCloud was struck by a succulent sky. In its illimitable plenty it hit him like a reproach. It implied he'd lived so poorly, shown such average love, evaded the immensities. It declared him in fact not unfit to live but unfit yet to die.

The balding steward, his face flushed, spoke over the heads of the prisoners to Taliq and the boys beyond. "My colleagues and I have to remind you that we are all witnesses."

"Very well," said Taliq lightly, "that's what you're intended to be."

The steward's bold, polite fraternity stung McCloud's eyes.

"Brave lad," said Cale, though the man was not noticeably young.

But the brave lad was ordered back to his seat.

Warmth from outside was just the same sublime. It made its false promises as it entered and brushed McCloud's cheek.

Behind McCloud, Taliq spoke to Hasni and Musa in an even, unemphatic voice. "They are temporising, they are making logistical excuses, they say Mahoud is not here yet and they blame logistics and transportation failures. It is all the normal lies."

You could in a sense hear the three of them, Taliq and the two boys, reabsorbing and sucking on that datum – the turpitude of the powers, of the Palestinian traducers. "We must convince them about getting Mahoud aboard," Taliq calmly announced. "We must shoot one of these three." It was as shocking as hearing such an idea from a familiar: a doctor, a teacher, an editor, a lover: and it sounded just as unlikely.

McCloud's brain abandoned the threatened remnant in its underwear and nudged the ceiling, now and then – dependent on how it bucked amongst the lights and lockers – observing the breathless and negligible McCloud-flesh below and the posture of servitude and submission it maintained.

McCloud remembered how in the electronics pit both Cale and Stone, experts, had surmised that the reason Taliq had taken the plane was because someone wanted a level of hate restored. But that there would be specific demands as well (the demand for

Mahoud, as it turned out). These specific requests, said Cale and Stone in rare agreement, were a flag of convenience and not the real point.

Yet Taliq now wanted someone shot for the sake of the side issue. Taliq seemed *locked in* and could not relent on this.

It seemed an important question though: how much did Taliq love his brother Mahoud? At the heart of things, how desperately did he desire Mahoud's freedom?

"Which one first then?" Musa could be heard asking in the same voice which had dismissed the T–55 tank.

McCloud believed Taliq would have an exact instruction. He would have memorised a proper order of dispatch, inexplicable to an outsider but cogent to him.

Yet he did not answer Musa. There was a silence. It was exactly as if – like an embarrassed student – Taliq could not remember. The hand wound, pain, sleeplessness, desire, the curse, had borne away the recollection of things anyone could tell Taliq *must* have planned.

The boys waited. McCloud was overcome by an almost pictorial image of doubt invading their blood too, like ink spreading in some simple and immutable element.

Taliq remembered himself then and said at last, "The one in the middle or at either end, it doesn't matter."

But Hasni and Musa were not restored by that.

"But which one of us?" asked Hasni.

"Does it matter?" Taliq sounded brisk now, if not testy. "With all the lies, I fear a number will need to perish. So what does it matter?"

But though it mightn't have mattered to Musa or Hasni five minutes past, now it did.

"All right then," said Taliq, apparently to Hasni. "*You* go first."

Hasni now seemed liberated by this nomination. He appeared from behind them and briefly weighed them with his eyes. There was no element of doubt in Hasni's assessment of the three of them. It didn't seem at all likely now that he might be overcome by hesitancy in the next minute or so. When McCloud had imagined execution, it had carried the blemished face of the old soldier Razir, or even the confident, ladykiller visage of Yusuf the tailor's son. He had never really believed in Hasni as the liquidator.

"This one has a wife on board," McCloud – agog for every nuance of Hasni's words – heard the boy say. The barrel moved from McCloud's face to Stone's to Cale's. Soon it would stop this. It would alight and discharge itself.

Where was Whitey Wappitji now? McCloud, looking down from above upon the three condemned, wanted to know. In the face of Hasni's certainty, where was the benefit of Wappitji's wonderful power to curse? For the boy was studiously asking himself the question: was it more correct to shoot a man with a wife aboard, in spite of the noise the wife would make? Or was it permitted to shoot one of the other two, who had no kindred aboard to wail for them? Was the easy option justified? Was the hard option to be commended?

At least, thought McCloud with a kind of irrelevance he did not believe himself given to, at least none of us are pleading. Stone began to utter *Kaddish*, the prayer for the dead, in Hebrew. It was all unfamiliar to McCloud except the word *Elohim*. The Absolute. The Source and the Darkness.

It made McCloud cry out, a group plea. "We're innocent. The three of us. None of us have hurt you."

This proposition was a revelation to McCloud himself, who had until now believed he was more innocent than the other two.

"Shut up!" said Taliq casually.

"Even if the story in the magazine is true," cried McCloud, "it's not my doing! The other two . . ." he thought of Cale's poignant underwear and of Stone's Hassidic father who would not sue the Germans. "The other two are not guilty also."

"Shut up!" said Taliq. There was a distress and tiredness in his voice now. "This has already been discussed."

And as had been happening lately at the apex of all McCloud's severest perplexities, Cale began to talk.

"Come on, boy," he said to Hasni. "Let's have it then! Make yourself a hero. Stop my education dead, sonny Jim, and pay for yours!"

There was a flutter in Hasni's eyes, a minor wavering. McCloud didn't believe, though, that it grew from Cale's line of provocation.

"Go to it, son!" Cale continued, in some ways a genuine bore even now. "Satisfy the Israelis, you dumb little Hamitic bastard. You think you've got a licence for it? No. You're giving *them* one."

Cale gestured out the door, to the subtle world out there; to the army whose loyalties were a mystery and whose hardware followed the latest Chadian fashion.

"Didn't your political science professor fill you in," asked Cale. "At Tulane or whatever cow college you were at? Come on, you little camel-fucker, do what the Mossad wants. Strike a blow for craziness, son. Come on, come on!"

McCloud's engorged, levitating brain wondered what Cale's harangue of the boy meant? Was it suicide or brotherly love? Was he taking the heat for McCloud and Stone? And why would he? Or was he somehow diverting heat from himself?

Hasni stood back still, merely afflicted by the politeness he'd shown early in the journey. He seemed to be allowing the journalist room to conclude his statement.

Then it became clearer to McCloud: what Cale was working towards. From a lifetime of archness, of journalistic ruses, the Englishman knew that there was a point at which impudence cries out to be punished; and a point beyond that, given a few seconds' hesitation, when punishment cannot clear-headedly be inflicted. Cale, helped by Taliq's earlier uncertainty, seemed now to have led Hasni to that point. McCloud's primal belief in the curse revived. For Hasni seemed now – in strictest terms – spellbound.

"Hasni," Taliq called in warning. "Hasni!"

McCloud closed his eyes on all the intimations of bright day from beyond the plane. But Cale had not shut his eyes or stopped working away on his stratagem.

"Yes, Hasni. *You* do it. Just a question though, sonny. Who are you doing it for? Who put up the money, eh? The Iraqis? The Libyans? Because some of them are just as passionate to see havoc set free as Taliq is. So who is it, lad? All of the above? Or are you going to kill me without inquiry? And can Taliq tell you anyhow? Or doesn't he have a fucking clue either? Better ask, son, better ask. Who's the paymaster? And if Taliq won't tell you, why should you hang yourself for him?"

Opening his eyes again, driven to it by the awful expectancy of the air around him, McCloud rejoiced to see that Hasni had raised his own eyes in appeal. McCloud was convinced then that the person most likely to be shot was Hasni himself. Cale had brought it about by clever talk.

Taliq cried, "Do it! Do it!"

Hasni did not do it. McCloud began to itch with admiration of Cale and gratitude to the word *Elohim*. Everything Cale had ever learned had been applied here, in the waist of the plane, to talk his way out of execution! That was the glory of his line of argument. It not only liberated Cale. It liberated Stone and McCloud as well. It not only disarmed Hasni, but it might well disable Musa, Razir, Yusuf. Leaving only Taliq, whom Whitey Wappitji had cursed and Daisy Nakamura might be willing to confuse and seduce.

But then the car-fancier Musa appeared, stepping from the direction of Taliq's voice. McCloud did not like the look of genial contempt he threw in Hasni's direction. It caused McCloud to shut his eyes again. In darkness, he heard Taliq's voice once more. "For the present purpose, I don't care who does it."

There were two connected and astounding noises, like physical blows not only against the ears but also at the base of the brain. McCloud's eyes were jolted open twice for an instant, but each time he was quick and determined to jam them shut again. At least I have not urinated, he assured himself. For that reason it was allowed now for him to resume his observations.

He did not at the moment know what the noises had been. He knew he had once – very recently – anticipated them and had at that stage, he remembered, known what their significance would be when they came. But now that he had heard them, the memory of that meaning had been erased.

Musa had enlisted the balding steward to help him drag Cale to the door. The steward sobbed but seemed efficient. Cale travelled forward on his bloodied placard, face down, slack-muscled, surely alive yet certainly gone. He left an astounding trail of matter behind him.

McCloud looked at the soles of Cale's large feet. They jolted away up what McCloud took to be Cale's life now converted to a river. It could be seen that he had been shot twice through the neck. And this by Musa. Not by act of God. By Musa.

McCloud was aware of the whimpering of other passengers, as Musa and the steward handled Cale forward over the rim of the door. Here a terrible dead-weight fall began, but merciful people throughout the plane screamed to cover the sound of it.

Stone turned to McCloud. "See?" he said, swallowing. "See?"

Musa returned from the door. He was exactly the same boy who had been contemptuous about the electronics of Japanese cars. He punched the bewildered Hasni's arm. "Next one," he murmured in reassurance.

*　　　*　　　*

191

Stone had been reduced to a purely private anguish. McCloud admired him for being capable of it. He had put his face in his hands.

"Damn you," he said softly. "God damn you."

Hasni kicked him. But it was a fairly gentle and uncertain kick.

McCloud became aware of what he was sure was Pauline's cry from the back of the aircraft, a scream of indefinite grief. Yes, a scream of enquiry. He felt astoundingly honoured by it.

"I'm here," he yelled. "I'm here!"

He heard the sound diminish.

Taliq had taken Hasni away, his arm around the boy's shoulder.

Had the Barramatjara Dance Troupe heard? Where was Daisy Nakamura? How had she absorbed this savagery?

His breath restoring itself, his brain returning from above to the socket behind his eyes, McCloud found it a relief to know now: the boys – whatever flickers there may have been in Hasni's eyes, whatever wavering – meant what they had threatened. From Taliq's nirvana on the upper deck to the battery of toilets at the rear, all the plane understood. Pauline herself would now be living by that certainty. Whitey Wappitji would have no doubts.

Some passengers wept still, and most were stark-eyed.

The stain of Cale's recent life darkened to a memorial on the carpet. Hurled from the plane, he was lovable in retrospect. His anti-bureaucratic demand for whisky before take-off, his gritty rundown on where Taliq's boys might have sprung from, and what the balance of their souls might be, seemed like gifts now. But his strategy – daring them like normal children are dared, facing them out – had failed him.

For a time McCloud and Stone seemed to be left alone, kneeling, looking aft at passengers who largely did not want to recognise them. It surprised him that many faces were uptilted now in shocked sleep. Barely a staring eye met McCloud's. They have written us off, he assured himself analytically and without bitterness. They don't want to catch our disease.

"McCloud," he heard Stone call. Stone seemed very clear-eyed and apparently casual; his arm muscles were flexed though. "Listen ... looks to me I'll be the next. These guys don't really believe *you're* guilty like they believe I'm guilty. And then statistics will be on your side. Hijacks generally only run to two point three seven fatalities. That's in the program . . ."

McCloud of course found himself driven by an obscene sort of politeness. "No, I'm just as likely to be next," he insisted. "My friend actually called out he wanted me to be the first."

"Well," Stone said softly, conceding the needless debate, "he's not exactly conscious. You can't tell anyhow. We don't have a computer and we don't have the right software." He grinned at that – the irony running against himself. "Just this though. Remind my attorney, whose name is Max Freilich, that he's holding special instructions for my wife and stepson – something quite apart from the normal documentation, you understand. Something for her future. Remind Freilich of it. Because he's getting old. He was my parents' lawyer. F–R–E–I–L–I–C–H. Max. In 42nd Street, just near the Century Club. Got that? It's easy. F–R–E–I–L–I–C–H. Do it for me."

There was a hidden resource which would give Mrs Stone a plush widowhood! McCloud had no such thing as that to leave for Pauline. Perhaps the temporary notoriety of his victimhood would make some publisher increase the advance on his book by a few thousand. Enough, as old-fashioned people liked to say, "to take care of the arrangements".

But largely, Pauline would provide. Her father decamping for the gold diggings, her novelist husband – between them they'd convinced her that she'd better; and she had by founding her business. So that was settled.

Time skidded beneath him now. There was no mark of distinction to any of the minutes which shifted away beneath his knees, tearing him down this last little fall to the indefinable bottom.

At Baruda, when four of them had spent all day making a painting for him to photograph, he'd said, "Thanks for taking so much time."

And Cowboy Tom had replied, "We don't take time, mate. Time takes us."

Time was taking McCloud at a harsh pace now.

Musa and Hasni were behind him and no longer in view. Hasni had returned from the little tutorial stroll Taliq had taken him on straight after Cale's murder. McCloud heard Taliq return again now, heard him whispering to the boys in Arabic – a report of transactions he had just been carrying out by radio from the flight deck. From all McCloud could tell, Hasni did not seem to have sacrificed his standing by the hesitation over Cale. He seemed equally informed with Musa, who had done the casual killing.

For Taliq had been there, and gone again, and then returned, and all without an angry word to Hasni. Once he moved down the plane, taking his time, to talk with Razir who – according to Taliq's mysterious timetables – had turned up again in the rear section. It meant Yusuf was back on the flight deck. The choreography of these lads was ceaseless and almost to be admired.

Taliq came back without a glance at McCloud or Stone but with what looked like a bitter plan written on his face.

McCloud, breath gone again, soared above and outside the plane. He achieved all at once an airport-perimeter-eye's view of the bright white, liveried sheath of the aircraft, a black hole opened in its flank, a geometrically concise patch of darkness levelled at the day.

Hasni stepped forward into McCloud's view. The young man seemed revivified, his face a little florid. He believed he was proof against eloquence this time, even if McCloud and Stone should unexpectedly show any. The maw of his Polish weapon traversed an easy axis between Stone's face and McCloud's. McCloud listened for Taliq's order from behind his head. He was taken by surprise instead to hear Taliq's voice emerge from the intercom, from the flight deck upstairs.

"My ladies and gentlemen passengers," Taliq began. "I have further news on possible outcomes."

Not all the passengers, McCloud noticed, woke up or stopped talking for this. Had they lost faith, or did they choose to live normally under Taliq's dominion? If there was a memory of Cale's murder, it had been sucked deeply down and would be retrieved only by a painful effort.

"The men with whom I have been speaking by radio," said Taliq, "the agents of the amusingly named *great* powers, claim they cannot quickly present my brother Mahoud and his two associates. It seems a small request, but they cannot satisfy it. The Palestinian traitors have kept him hidden away as a prisoner in a remote place, and it has been difficult to find him and deliver him. They require that we be refuelled and then fly to another destination, one much closer to Mahoud's place of detention. There they swear – though we doubt the value of their oaths – that our brother will be delivered to us. They ask us that in view of the refuelling, no other criminals should be punished at this time. They claim that they have been influenced greatly by receiving the body of the criminal Cale. I hope as keenly as you do, ladies and gentlemen, that *that* is exactly right."

There was silence from Taliq, but the intercom spat and crackled on. Was he reflecting or had his breath failed?

"And so we shall take to the air again, a short flight. You know the old saying, *Happy Landings*? The happy landings depend on the great powers, who have not shown themselves to be great or good or reliable in any way. But we have our hopes, don't we? I believe that what you could call *moderate* hope is justified . . ."

11

HERESY

THE end of Taliq's communication brought a spatter of fairly casual applause from amongst the body of passengers. Hasni and Musa, nudging them gently with weaponry, got McCloud and Stone up on their unfamiliar, their forgotten legs. On the way back to Taliq's ambiguous place at the peak of the plane, the party yet again went by the sedated Bluey Kannata. McCloud, confused by his own deliverance, studied the actor's face, the point of the cheeks turquoise, the brow knotted studiously, the eyes shut up against all accusation.

Musa pushed McCloud along past this mute face. But the glimpse of Bluey, his brother and his inquisitor, came to McCloud as a sort of revelation, an urgent demand. The revelation had the resonance that the obvious achieves when it stops being the obvious and becomes the only option. Bluey had taken his action and become a judge. Whitey *his*, peculiar to him, and cursed Taliq's bloodstream. Cale had acted too, not simply waiting – under the general threat of *plastique* – for the bullet.

Whereas marriage befell me, my book befell me, the hostage-taking befell me. I must not let anything more befall me. I have been a mere, brute medium on which other forces have acted. I have sung the tunes proposed by other impulses than mine. Now I must become singer of my own songs. Now *I* must become an actor.

This plain conviction came to him with all the accoutrements of enlightenment, a light sweat, an annoyance at being so long in the dark, a transcendental excitement, a fit of delicious fright.

The necessity for doing something became absolute in a second now. He knew he'd be damned if he failed to obey it. If shot dead by Hasni or Musa having failed to act, he would never be liberated from the fragments of the plane. His blood would never rise from the functional carpet. His memory would poison the lives of the Girl and the Boy.

The dancers and Daisy, still hostages to ideas at the rear of Taliq's cabin, all stood, watching Stone and McCloud arrive. They frowned and – McCloud was sure of this – counted and took account of the returning faces. Their stares had enormous solemnity. But McCloud saw Phil the Christian's face begin to flutter and close down on itself at the sight of the two of them, perhaps at the lack of Cale.

Before anyone could speak, Stone and McCloud were seated on opposite sides of an aisle. Stone settled grimly into his place. He looked pale behind his tan. Yet he had his faith: that on the ground governments using his software were fetching up from their computers a design on how to act.

Therefore Stone had his weapon, though it was far from his hands. There was still a blessedness in that.

The young murderer in the cricket sweater – Musa – sat down in front of Stone. He wriggled his shoulders. Cale's death sat lightly on them, or so Musa thought. It did not seem to disqualify him from his status as dormitory mechanic, willing to discuss and work on anyone's jalopy.

Wappitji came up the aisle, or – more exactly – appeared at McCloud's side with the old Barramatjara suddenness. He looked severely at McCloud, as if saying, "You never told me it would get as serious as this!"

Unchallenged, he now sat at McCloud's side. Taliq was still busy further forward, though even if he hadn't been, a certain leniency of contact still prevailed between the chosen and the condemned. Maybe this was based on Taliq's idea of democracy; maybe on a conviction that Daisy and the dance troupe, by speaking to the treacherous McCloud, would be brought to true understanding. Or maybe he thought, *I can blow up the plane in any case, or I can shoot the condemned at any second.*

In any case, Wappitji was here now, beside McCloud.

He took out his bandanna, the one still marked with Taliq's blood. He gave it his attention.

"There's none of that *plastique* down with the luggage," he announced, eyes still lowered to the cloth. "Down there in the hold, there's none. You can tell. That's all a kind of bulldust. There's no *plastique*. Taliq won't blow himself up, Frank. He wants to have a voice left."

That was what Whitey read in the hijacker's gore. Whitey, forced back to this text, forced to a more profound study, by Cale's frightful end.

Whitey said, "If he's holding the *plastique* over you there's nothing in it, Frank. There isn't any of that *plastique*."

McCloud's faith in Whitey's imprecation, tested by Hasni's wavering automatic and by Musa's quick dispatch of the Englishman, revived now. He believed he had been told something utterly crucial.

Whitey stood up then and passed aft without another word.

I will go downstairs then into the rear of the plane, McCloud told himself. Pauline must be told instantly about this startling shift. I will get paper and pass out notes to all the passengers, the ones who can safely be told. *There is no plastique.*

It meant that in the world of this aircraft there could be a limited and not an absolute war. Protest and rebellion could mean the death of the individual flyer but did not mean that the plane must be torn apart. Taliq had chosen to tell his hostages that disobedience would destroy everything, and chosen at the same time not to pack the means for accomplishing what he threatened.

And so as Whitey had announced, Taliq did not want the physical ruin of the plane. He would use conventional means to suppress a revolt. For he had not packed *plastique*! He could shoot people down, yes. But his utter dominion was a lie.

Hasni, it turned out, had been delayed by Taliq, who had pulled the curtain at the front of the cabin to allow himself a private discussion with the boy. When it was over and Hasni emerged, he wore without any apparent pain a bruising over his right eyebrow. There was an unnatural glitter in his eyes as he climbed over McCloud to get to the window seat.

McCloud reassumed his old jacket, the one invisibly mended by Mr Katz, favourite of some forgotten *Oberscharführer* in Poland.

He was delighted with his banal discovery about the sin of passivity. It was never the answer. The enlightened risk was the human way. If you died of it, your death was holy.

And what Whitey had said to McCloud seemed to be unreasonably but potently verified by what happened next. Coming from the direction of the cockpit, of the alcove where he had disciplined Hasni, Taliq himself appeared in the aisle, level with McCloud. He looked ahead pensively for a time before taking three steps, then wheeling, gasping, and putting both hands to the right side of his stomach just beneath his grenade belt. As he fell, Hasni rushed up past McCloud and leaned over his leader.

"What is it?" Hasni was asking. Whitey had also appeared, and then Daisy Nakamura, who knelt and took hold of his shoulders.

Taliq drew his legs up twice and released them. "I have an ulcer," Taliq told Daisy. "Get that German doctor!"

It was the dutiful Hasni who went.

"It's duodenal," Taliq explained through clenched teeth to Daisy and Whitey Wappitji.

He arched with pain once more, but Daisy held him strongly and, after the paroxysm, drew her hand over his brow. It was a sort of daily, curative, maternal stroke. But it made Taliq aware of being held. For two or three seconds more he was happy to lean back against her. Daisy raised her eyebrows at McCloud. "Well," said her expression. "Here we are. And what can I do?"

The doctor who had tended Bluey arrived and knelt by Taliq. A glass of milk in his hand, young Hasni was also in attendance.

The doctor turned to Hasni. "Take the milk away. It's bad for ulcers."

Hasni looked affronted. "My grandfather always had milk."

"Do you have pain-killers?" Taliq asked the doctor. "Nothing narcotic. I know the pharmacopoeia, so don't try to fool me."

"I have only codeine," the German doctor said. "I have no anti-spasmodics left – the one injection I had I used on the black man downstairs. As you must know, sir, if you take codeine, it may cause you to haemorrhage."

"Give it to me," Taliq ordered, as one more convulsion drew his legs up. "I need only a few hours."

"Don't drink the milk," the doctor advised him. "Above all, don't take the codeine."

"Bring it to me!" said Taliq.

The doctor went for the codeine. Taliq waved Hasni and the milk away. He reached up behind him with his scarred and bandaged right hand and grasped Daisy's shoulder. "I will be well," he promised her, as if he feared his throes must have given her especial distress.

*   *   *

The doctor was back with a small bottle of white pills and a sheet of paper, handwriting on it. He pushed the sheet of paper towards Taliq.

"What is this?" asked Taliq.

"It says you take the codeine against my advice and by your own authority. I do not want to be sued."

Taliq grabbed the sheet, crumpled it, tossed it over his shoulder and Daisy's, seized the codeine bottle and took four or five of the pills. He chewed them. He wanted quick efficacy.

Soon he was on his feet again. He half-leaned against Daisy, unwilling to leave her totally until he saw where he stood with the pain.

After a little while though he was strolling independently. He dismissed the doctor. He took further experimental walks up and down the cabin. Having survived them, he readjusted the set of his shoulders. He had resumed command, and wished everybody to believe it was so.

With a smile towards Daisy and Whitey, he turned back to the cockpit and his magisterial purposes.

Confident in his leader still, Hasni had closed his eyes. Everyone seemed somnolent as the engines turned and cold descended from the roof. The bruised young warrior beside McCloud may even have been asleep before the plane had got into the air or levelled off again.

Still convinced of the beatitude of action, McCloud searched the pocket on the back of the chair in front of him. He found the airline's in-flight magazine and a cheap ballpoint pen. It barely wrote, but it wrote. In the clear spaces at the tops of the magazine pages he scribbled, *There is no plastique.* He wrote partly to reinforce and assert himself, for he did foresee the chance of disseminating this, his underground tract, amongst others.

He wrote the message eight times, on eight separate pages, before the pen ran out for good. He tore off the top of each of the eight pages, folded the message up, and dropped all eight little wads down the front of his singlet. He felt the edges of folded pages rankling against his skin; this message of utter heresy for which he would happily perish.

By now he was dizzy and had no breath left. He sat back and considered the boy Hasni, examining the bruised eyebrow, the minor stubble on the neck, his shirt collar, and all his equipment. The same belt which held his radio, with the buttons which could supposedly command the *plastique* in the hold, also held little leather sockets in which small grenades sat. The metal rods of their necks emerged through holes in leather flaps. These flaps were connected to the holders themselves by press studs.

Standard issue from some army.

From one of these grenade pouches, hanging from Hasni's left side, the stud had come unstuck. A small, brassy grenade sat there exposed. Presenting itself, you could say, if you wanted to stretch things. If the audacity could be found to snatch that small bulb out, and if the stud were then pressed down, Hasni would not notice it was gone, at least not by the weight. His tired revolutionary brothers might not notice either.

McCloud knew he could not make efforts of will to take the thing. That would be useless. The daring would need to descend upon him as if from outside.

The question was, though, whether this was the activity he was waiting for? He'd expected something subtle. Something like Cale's ill-destined speech, some device, however, which – if possible – left you alive at the end of the process. For he *was* a kind of artist, and he was best at the less obvious stratagems.

Yet of course that was his failing, the limiting factor of his existence: to neglect the evident and wait for something more exalted to present itself. To remain a passive man because the instruments of action didn't match his self-defined, high sensibility.

At the back of the compartment, as earlier requested, Paul Mungina began playing his *didj*. It was a solemn, throaty rendition of *God Save the Queen*. Paul the royalist could not imagine a white man who would not be reinforced by this weirdest of renditions of the old anthem. From the throats of lizards and serpents it rose, from this dinosaur of an instrument. It all had the feeling of an overture to the final arrival. Pre-destination music in the strict sense, if you liked. It opened up above McCloud's head like a cavern in a dream. Paul trying to sedate the plane, to sedate the revolutionary force of Taliq and the boys, to soothe the energetic despair of the people who had attacked Pauline. Paul trying to gentle all that back down to earth.

Yet the effect on McCloud wasn't sedative at all. He felt twice as alive. He felt astringent, ready for the deed.

But once more, what was the deed to be?

A voice joined the line of the *didj*'s plaint. McCloud was sure that it was Cowboy Tom Gullagara's voice.

The ordained style of a Barramatjara singer lay somewhere far out beyond the normal strain of sounds people heard; far out beyond the lyric tenor say of Irish sentimental ballad or the piercing delivery of Chinese opera. It had more of a twang than either. It worked by longer intervals. It carried in it the pulse of a genuinely murderous sun. It shimmered with bemusing distance. As well as inviting the planeload to shut its eyes, it also lulled them to avert their faces from Cale's confused spirit, and offered to Cale himself a seductive invitation to rise from the essences of his body staining the carpet downstairs and slip to earth along the filament of his own murder.

McCloud became convinced too that the song was meant to add muscle to Whitey's already uttered and sealed curse. It was a surprise to McCloud that Taliq could not *hear* that intention in it. If not in the training camps of Iraq, then surely around the refugee hearths of his childhood Taliq must have learned to read such clearly uttered tribal purposes.

Mungina's *didj* and Cowboy Tom's voice continued to wash into him. It struck him that, for no easily defined reason, they were singing him safe.

"God save our gracious Queen,
Long live our noble Queen.
God save our Queen . . ."

More astounding still they may even have been singing him brave.

Stone was not aware of this shift though. Cale's death had not slowed Stone's rate of reasoning. He leaned across the aisle and muttered. "I've been thinking about all this. It doesn't compute, McCloud. If the people on the ground meant to give this Mahoud back to Taliq and the boys, they would have shown definite signs back there. They wouldn't have told us to take off again and cruise along to some new rendezvous. They could have had Mahoud flown to us in a supersonic fighter, for Christ's sake, if that had been their wish."

McCloud half-smiled. He felt indulgent towards Stone. A doom-sayer from the start. A man who'd needed software to discern his enemy.

"I'm afraid, my friend," said Stone, beginning to sneeze and having to stifle the noise with the rim of his blanket, "that from the larger view, you and I account for very little to our masters."

"But I don't have masters," McCloud said.

"Well," said Stone, "neither – in the strict sense – do I."

* * *

The light beyond the shutters turned glacial blue: the coming of the high, icy night. Handsome Yusuf the tailor's son was suddenly amongst them, slinging cellophaned packets of water biscuits into McCloud's lap and Stone's. Even tearing the package open, McCloud found that he could not take his eyes from Hasni's little grenade of unknown manufacture. He imagined it stuck intimately and organically in the socket of his arm. Its bite would give him a slight, improper pleasure. It would be something Stone lacked. Stone had trained and tanned, played tennis and kept two passports against this moment. He had won his argument with Cale. He had even made arrangements for his widow. He had done everything. He had nothing more to draw on.

So McCloud fished down the front of his singlet, extracted one of the heretical wads of paper and – picking his moment – passed it across the aisle. Stone did not seem pleased to receive it, but at last, under cover of the crinkling and wadding of cellophane, opened the message one-handed and read it.

Stone frowned. *How do you know?* he mouthed.

McCloud deliberately gestured, suggesting that proof existed in some palpable, legible form but could not in the circumstances be produced. He did not feel this was misleading. The evidence *did* exist, but only he, McCloud, understood its force. He felt exalted. The distribution of the message had commenced.

Stone put the paper in his mouth and swallowed it. It did not go down easily. Then he covered his eyes with his hand and considered the advantages and disadvantages of believing what McCloud had written. As McCloud himself had, Stone too had cherished, you could tell, his belief in the *plastique*. There was the comfort of being powerless. As soon as Whitey had uttered the truth, McCloud had shrugged that comfort off without thinking. Stone, a more careful man, did not want to let go too easily of any of the condemned prisoner's standard mental props.

He closed his eyes for a time and then, swallowing once more, stared at McCloud and smiled marginally. The mystery of faith, unleashed in McCloud by Whitey, had now mysteriously crossed the aisle and worked, more modestly and without any supporting data, on Stone.

So, thought McCloud, heady with revolution, a network has been set up. This making of a cell, he saw, was the *action* he had been straining towards. Hasni's grenade meant nothing, was not the option. In its unfastened state, it was supporting evidence of an incompleteness in Taliq's plans. That was all.

*   *   *

McCloud's mouth was full of biscuit when Philip Puduma visited him. The Christian dancer, arrived at his side, dropping to his knees in the aisle the better to confer. He touched McCloud's wrist.

"Frank," he confided solemnly, "I wanted to tell you this, mate. In this mucked-up set-up we got here, you've got to put your trust in the Lord as your Redeemer. I mean, this is serious business, Frank. They shot a man. You can't have any big faith in them old people, those ancestors. I say it though I love them and they're my people, mate. But Jesus is Lord, brother. Them others do what they do. But they couldn't handle that booze for me. And see, they won't handle Taliq for you."

He coughed. He looked forward towards the cockpit and aft again. He wanted to be certain his complicated message would not be interrupted.

"I mean, you know me and Whitey, we respect each other. And Whitey has to do what Whitey does. He's angry with that Taliq and he thinks he's fixed his wheel for him now. But only the Lord can fix wheels, mate."

McCloud remembered how in the dance, according to the Barra-matjara orthodoxy, the dancer became the hero. He was lost to himself, and might remain awesomely lost for ever unless he awoke. Paul Mungina would in fact leave his *didj* at the end of the evening's entertainment and tap the four dancers on the shoulder, returning them to their daily identities.

"That's a bit of bullshit for the tourists," Mungina had explained once.

But there was a truth behind the levity, and an awareness of a threat. That the ancestor could capture the soul.

Maybe now Phil could see a kind of soul-capture in Frank McCloud, and felt bound to warn against it.

Phil whispered. "Don't put your faith in any curses, brother Frank. Don't you swear by any name but Jesus's name. Okay? This is *really* serious business!"

He rose from the kneeling position and his leg creaked. Once he had broken it, McCloud seemed to remember having been told, working with horses on Easter Creek cattle station.

"And listen, another thing. You know Bluey? We've got to get Bluey back to Baruda, working on the diesels. No more of them movies or discos or Jim Beam for Bluey. The truth is not in them, brother. We'll get Bluey home, eh? So . . . Jesus your Redeemer, Frank."

Since Phil was inviting him to take part in Bluey's rehabilitation, Phil thought he, McCloud, would last.

There was a wink from the Christian then, so full of meaning that McCloud felt his ribs expand.

It seemed important however that Phil shouldn't be deceived. "Phil," McCloud pleaded, "listen. The only hope I've had in this whole shitheap is from . . . from *signs* Whitey's given me. I'm ready to meet whatever comes. But don't confuse me now, Phil. For Christ's sake don't!"

Phil sighed, shook his head and looked away. What the Spanish Benedictines and the German Lutherans would make of this! What the drowsing Hasni at his side would think for that matter. A Presbyterian pleading with a Barramatjara elder for the freedom to believe in Wappitji's visions and curses.

"You got the message, Frank, anyhow."

But McCloud was as willing as any heretic to die clinging to the only beliefs which made the universe habitable.

In this case the belief in no *plastique* and in a siege-by-curse of the blood of the chief hijacker. In the effect these two articles of faith had on his will and his intentions.

Credo, thought McCloud. *Credo*. And no recanting.

The theological argument with Phil the Christian was interrupted then by an event which had been long prefigured but took McCloud's breath – by a further clear slippage, that is, of Taliq's power. The chief hijacker edged past Phil and, looking unsteady in the legs, progressed down the aisle towards the cockpit. Beyond the curtain by the lavatory, lacking strength to drag the drape back into place, he knelt all at once. More accurately, he fell onto his kneecaps like someone struck, and on his knees he began to rock his body.

Stone could not see this, but it was visible to McCloud, who believed the image was designed anyhow for him, that he was *authorised* to behold it.

Was the codeine eating the lining of Taliq's stomach, as the German doctor had darkly suggested it might? In any case, its action was interrupted now by Daisy.

Hasni had risen beside McCloud and was ready to go and help. He was pre-empted by Daisy, though. Pushing palely past McCloud in her green dress, free of her blanket, she came rushing up from her seat towards Taliq. The sweet, green garment, McCloud noticed, had declined further. Its mileage had always been a cocktail party of two hours or – at a stretch – a transatlantic novice flight of six. It was not designed to stand up against an all-night, all-day hijack, to carry a woman through a revolutionary education.

Where McCloud and Phil could still see her, she knelt as Taliq had and took his head onto her shoulder. The flesh Taliq leaned against was alabaster, and with his forehead he nuzzled the green fabric of her shoulder. Daisy looked aft across the crown of his dark hair. Her frank eyes met McCloud's. They were not easily convivial – as they would have been behind the bar of the Polka Barn in Budapest, Arizona.

"Yes," McCloud believed they said. "Yes, don't worry. I'll take away what he has left."

Her hand reached up and she dragged the curtain across.

"Not right," said Phil, departing for his seat as if for the moment his task was done. "Her going sweet on Taliq."

But even Phil, McCloud thought, lacked conviction.

McCloud was aware that Hasni had witnessed Daisy's comforting of Taliq. The boy knew at the same time that McCloud had also seen everything. He glanced towards McCloud, but the eyes did not engage. He had not yet consulted with himself about this, had not developed a policy, had not reconciled himself. There was something undisguised and painful to watch, McCloud thought, in the young hijacker's vague pain at this business of Daisy and Taliq, at the struggle first to absorb the scandal into himself and then to decide what attitude to take towards the world.

Hasni decided on a policy though and turned bravely to McCloud. His lips had a scholar's, a seminarian's delicacy as he framed the words.

"Taliq is a hero, a combat soldier," he said. "He's been through things we cannot imagine. He has led battalions on the Euphrates. He's raided Iran's oil wells. Mossad have sent men to Baghdad to kill him. He dodges out of buildings a half-second before the enemy blows them up. He has had to swallow his own fear, day by day. So now he is in pain. Did you expect me to condemn him, Mr McCloud? Just because he's rightly chastised me?"

McCloud wondered what they thought of this Arab kid at Tulane or wherever his hall of residence was located? What did they think of him with his relentless convictions and his old-fashioned words like *chastise*? In America they said *bawled me out, busted my chops*. They wouldn't have heard of *chastise*.

While Taliq and Daisy remained beyond the curtain, the air the plane traversed scarcely nudged the wings. While Daisy distracted him with her mouth, the smooth African night cosseted and – McCloud felt sure about this – betrayed Taliq.

When Daisy reappeared at last she wore a worldly, twice-shy face such as the truckers and drinking Mormons and Navajos of Budapest may never have seen. Otherwise she seemed the old immutable Daisy, the one McCloud felt he had known a lifetime. Holding her right shoulder with her left arm, as if to imply that blows had been traded in there, she readjusted the curtain behind her. Taliq was not with her. His pain arrested for the moment, he must have gone through into the flight deck to speak to the pilot, or to deal with the negotiators on the other end of the radio. He must have seen himself as restored and fortified and made sharper.
Daisy and McCloud knew better. Did Hasni know better too?

Hasni seemed to have lost interest now, though. He dozed again under his bruised brow. McCloud dredged from his singlet one of the seditious wads and handed it to Daisy as she passed. Frowning, she opened it, read it, and her eyes widened – in her case a wonder of anatomy, so broadly written were they on her face in any case.
She frowned down at McCloud. But, he felt sure, it was a frown of belief. He was certain that to her too this was news which changed everything, which guaranteed or at least held out hope for a communal survival of the flight.
His missionary work, he thought in unalloyed delight, was doing better and working more instantly than Taliq's missionary work. Taliq, with the persuasion of his special if stilted oratory and with the backing of muzzles, had powerfully converted Bluey. But in minutes, with a scribbled message in dim blue fished out of his string vest, his sweaty singlet, he had converted the Jew and the Japanese. So broadly based was his mission and the catholicity and breadth of what he uttered!
Daisy handed the message back to him. It was not a rejection. It was that something so dangerous should only be handled by its creator.
He saved it for further use.
Air turbulence reasserted itself. Daisy was jolted on her way back to her seat.

In such a bountiful planet as the Frankfurt flight now seemed to be, there had been options to spare. The option of Hasni's grenade, for example. Except that he had not needed it. And as for Daisy, the workable universe which McCloud saw from his own seat had no need for her any more. McCloud himself was surprised to feel no gratitude. The Jewel of Budapest had done her part, as he would do his. Gratitude would at the end be meaningless, though those who had acted would never cease – of course – to be bound to each other.

Musa, who had shot Cale, rose from his seat in front of McCloud now and went aft, and Hasni got up, stepped across the conspirator McCloud and followed Musa. If you were my terrorist, I would discipline you for that loose stud, McCloud promised. It was the erosion of Taliq's powers of surveillance which made the loosened belt stud go unnoticed. It was a symbol of the woe Taliq was earning.

The changes of light outside the blinds, the deeper blue ascending now from earth, told McCloud that the negotiation he intended to have with Taliq, one not yet listed on Taliq's agenda, the coming crux and crunch and stand-off, would take place in the meat of an African night.

And though the *didj* music had stopped, it still seemed to be there to McCloud, just beyond the angle of hearing like a familiar animal. Still there as the wheels ground down and locked in place; as from the intercom came one groaned, paternal sentence, a sentence of the captain's. "Folks, we're going in. Strap yourself down if they'll let you."

McCloud listened for the yelp of wheels on runway and the panicked scream of airbrakes. When they occurred, his breath fled him. Yet his imagination stayed resolute. He could still achieve a mental picture of what he meant himself to do.

Before the touchdown was fully accomplished, Taliq had moved warily into the cabin from the flight deck. He was beginning – it seemed to McCloud – to doubt whether Daisy had done him well, for he trod like someone facing the risk of ambush. Blue patches of bad blood stood beneath his eyes. He believed, however, McCloud could tell, that he had oxygen and peace enough to accomplish the result, and that then he could sleep.

"Very well," he told Hasni and Musa.

The boys pulled Stone and McCloud upright, adjusting yet again their tattered placards, those stale inscriptions bullet-headed Razir had written an age ago and which the people downstairs must know by heart.

"It's over and settled," McCloud, despite himself, found himself quaintly telling Hasni and Musa. "Taliq and Daisy are the one flesh. Daisy won't ever escape the weight of his husbandry."

"Give it a rest, mate," said Musa in his Midlands accent, not understanding a word.

He was very pleased that the boys ignored him and took his submission for granted. He decided that he had better stop himself from talking like a prophet. That he had better be on his watch against that.

Along with Daisy, the four dancers were also gathering themselves to go downstairs. Why this time and not last time? Was this Taliq's choice – to have the justified present to witness what he hoped were final transactions? Or had they asked to be counted in?

Whitey called ponderously to Taliq, "We think Frank isn't to blame. That doesn't mean the other ought to be shot."

"What?" asked Taliq. "Don't presume on our friendship, Mr Wappitji."

Daisy also, however, wore a frown. "Nothing's going to happen to these two boys," she stated as a fact, nodding towards Stone and McCloud.

"It is not up to me," said Taliq.

Daisy became gloriously enraged. "That's not what you said," she shouted. "That's *not* what you told me."

Taliq shook his head, as if to clear it. "Madam," he said, "please don't misunderstand me. I said I would *try* to save them, and I will. But it is not up to me, and I also said that."

"So, nothing's changed?" asked Daisy, agitated. "You know what? You *want* them dead. You want all of us dead. You love the dead, you sonofabitch. Because their ideas are straightened out!"

It was hard to tell whether Taliq was more enraged than affronted. "Madam, that's not just or fair." He kept putting his hand to his mouth, seemingly to check nausea or fatigue. "The saving of these men is out of my hands. I *put* it in the hands of others." He took a profound breath. "I will not argue," he said. "If you are going to shout and be unruly you can stay here. If you come downstairs you will be silent throughout."

It was like a scene from a classroom, as bathetic and as farcical. Daisy and the Barramatjaras said nothing.

"You are a serious disappointment," said Taliq, waving a finger of his bandaged hand. But the authentic threat had returned to his manner and he did not sound querulous. His oneness with them had its limits. Even in Daisy's case, he was willing to end intimacy with a bullet. "But you will have enlightenment," he promised them. "You will have it."

And so everyone began to leave the upper deck.

Downstairs, where Bluey Kannata, actor and dancer, was still resting, it was dark. As McCloud and Stone and their guards passed through, Bluey rose from the seats where he lay. Kneeling upright as the German doctor grabbed for him, Bluey was not to be denied.

"That one!" cried Bluey, pointing at McCloud. "He knew my face, that bastard! My face was in front of him. He still sold it off to people! That one! That one!"

The doctor and a steward wrestled Bluey back down but, "That one! That bastard!" Bluey kept yelling.

McCloud understood Bluey but felt unrepentant. He used the turmoil to pass one of his tracts, perhaps the one already handled by Daisy, to the doctor.

Glancing back, McCloud saw Whitey Wappitji, Phil Puduma, Daisy Nakamura detach themselves from the rear of the procession from upstairs and stand by Bluey. Whitey and Phil said nothing, but Daisy spoke soothingly, according to the traditional pacifying tasks she had assumed to herself. Phil Puduma fetched drinking water and the doctor produced two white pills and surreptitiously checked the strip of paper in his hands.

The door by which Cale had perished had already been swung back. Hasni, carrying the heroic bruise on his forehead, and Musa the home mechanic pushed McCloud and Stone downwards, making them kneel there, on the rim of the stain. Again the soft air from beyond the plane warmed their exposed arms. This is the last time, McCloud was sure, we'll feel that mere exhalation of the outside, living world.

Stone shifted his limbs in small ways and made occasional sighs. McCloud felt a childlike anticipation of revealing himself, of startling the company, of turning events in his own direction. He knew that Whitey too was expecting something, a phenomenon. He and Whitey were one in expecting an end to Taliq, or at least an acceptable end to themselves.

Emanations of Cale from the bloodied carpet fortified him. Cale who had approved of stirs as a means of managing people. Now – in Cale's absence – McCloud himself was the potential stirrer, the ordained arouser and confuser. Such were the febrile excitements, he understood, which would now keep him on his fixed, unlikely course.

"Is Mahoud here?" the kneeling Stone suddenly asked his captors, Musa and Hasni. They stood in full view of Stone and McCloud. They looked very calm, as if this time there would be no hesitations and no doubts. "Is there any word at all?"

Along with all the other questions of the day, there was this one: Why hadn't Taliq replaced the sensitive Hasni on this execution squad? Had Hasni pleaded for the chance? Or was this like the grenade-belt stud: another symbol of creeping inadvertence in the Taliq camp?

"Is Mahoud here?" Stone reiterated. Clearly, he had given up all theorising about whether Mahoud was the first or side purpose of this exercise of Taliq's. He seemed to believe he was finished if Mahoud did not appear.

But from the door could be seen only blue perimeter lights and some indefinite movement of trucks and men in quasi-military uniforms.

Hasni and Musa made a mouth at each other. Obviously neither of them knew, and Taliq was not there to ask, was away upstairs again with the captain's radio, wavering over it no doubt, corroded with codeine and suspicion.

"Oh, Jesus," Stone said with level despair. "I knew there wouldn't be any Mahoud. They don't release these guys any more. It just isn't policy."

McCloud was struck by the polite regret in Stone's voice, as if he wished Mahoud al-Jiddah and his colleagues nothing but a felicitous escape and a bountiful future.

It made you worry if he had really absorbed the message about no *plastique*.

This time McCloud could *hear* Taliq returning down the stairwell precisely because his tread was so light, unmilitant, irregular. His arrival sounded like that of a man with little strength left, yet when he appeared in front of McCloud and Stone his eyes retained a vigorous glimmer.

He spoke softly to Hasni.

"They are playing with us. Clearly. They are playing. They tell us now that Mahoud will arrive in thirty-five minutes by helicopter!"

Musa and Hasni shook their heads.

"*Thirty-five minutes!* It's a fiction. There have been too many improbabilities. We will need to feed them another one."

Hasni, though ready in principle, seemed to have not quite gathered himself for the task, and McCloud was still collecting himself for his performance, when Stone began to speak in a direct and sensible voice. "If it *could* be the truth, why not wait the thirty-five minutes and see?"

"Oh, Mr Stone," said Taliq. He was not smoking any more. Perhaps he was too ill. "You understand all this as well as anyone. *Tell them thirty-five minutes*, they say on the ground. *Buy time, buy time!* And when the thirty-five minutes is up, buy another slab of time – tell them there are contrary winds, or a rotor has broken." He covered his mouth for a while. Settling his gorge, McCloud hoped, and not succeeding. "If I had one of your computers to play with, it would tell me to do this. Isn't that the case? So be brave, Mr Stone. Man of two passports!"

"But after you've used McCloud and me? What then? No more class and race criminals left!"

Taliq pinched the bridge of his nose and laughed privately and with weary tolerance. "You don't believe that on a packed plane like this there won't be a second wave of criminals? And a third? There are always criminals, Mr Stone."

One look told McCloud that Stone's objections hadn't softened Hasni, who was still out to assert his revolutionary character. He spoke to Taliq through pursed lips, "Not the Jew. It's too easy. The other one first."

"But," argued Stone, who must have heard Hasni, "if you shoot us, where *is* your leverage? See, you *did* declare the rest of the plane innocent, for Christ's sake! And if you change your mind on that, why will they trust you further?"

But Taliq – with a nod – indicated the reason. Hasni's black and awful weapon.

"Hasni," said Taliq simply to the boy.

McCloud did not look at Hasni but at Taliq. He could see the leader waver on his feet. Right on time, pain and nausea were bringing him unstrung.

Under cover of Taliq's duodenal crisis and of the minor debate Stone had begun, McCloud had shifted his kneeling angle. He rose towards Taliq's face. In the peripheral dimness where Bluey Kannata lay, the features of those exempted from sentence, of Daisy and the dance troupe, could be vaguely seen.

He was quickly shoulder to shoulder with Taliq.

He hunted down the front of his singlet for the handful of paper wads and threw them over the nearest seats of passengers.

"Read that!" he cried. "Read that! There's no *plastique* in the hold . . . *None!*"

This must have taken many instants, and neither the resolute Hasni nor the confirmed killer Musa had done anything to prevent it. He felt sure that this was because they were accustomed to the idea of his powerlessness. If he rose up, they may have thought, it must be at Taliq's mandate. Even now – McCloud could see it – they believed that their power would easily be reasserted. They had not yet reached the assessment that everything was altogether changed.

In fact McCloud watched Musa give a quite charming shrug, the shrug of a young man pretending still to be in the game, a shrug which carried with it at the same time an expectation of the bizarre; the gesture of a young man whom history has taught to expect erratic turns.

McCloud wrapped his right arm around Taliq's waist. It yielded. Taking further hold of Taliq, he felt the man stagger within his arms. Taliq, McCloud was astonished to find, had little strength; had postured, radioed and threatened with no more than a minor sinew or two to drive him. And perhaps every movement had been for him a crisis of will, since – rather than move now, in this new and unscannable arrangement – he gave himself up to McCloud for the moment like a child.

"Pauline," McCloud screamed at a height of certitude, "there's no *plastique!*"

Under cover of this liberating cry, McCloud believed he saw his wads of paper being passed from seat to seat, the data about no *plastique*, read by Whitey Wappitji from Taliq's blood, creating speculation, unleashing debate, falling like a unifying net over the cabin. Making everyone relatives, to use a Barramatjara phrase. Not everyone of course – that was fanciful to expect. There would be unbelievers, he knew, and there would be mothers, like the one who had sat beside Pauline at the outset and who would have duties outside belief. But enough relatives. Enough.

Hasni and Musa were still scanning the tangle of movement, McCloud embracing Taliq, holding him as a buffer between the muzzles of their Polish automatics and himself. He was triumphantly convinced that now they thought he was armed and had some weapon stuck against Taliq, and that they held their hands at this early stage for love of Taliq. It just showed you. *Act*, and the world fell into place!

Hasni looked as if he was not only uncertain what the revolution might demand of him in this subtle new set-up, but as if this too might be blamed to his account.

McCloud caressed Taliq more tightly. Taliq now tried to evade his hold but could not. McCloud's musculature had been sung up by the same Barramatjara seer who had sung Taliq's musculature down.

"I'm watching him," McCloud announced. "I'm with him. Both of us will go."

It was an unerring statement, beautifully crafted for its purpose, lacking in any reality. But he believed they *saw* its shining infallibility.

Extracting his radio from its case at his hip, Musa the car enthusiast began without hysteria to communicate the news of this altered circumstance to the unseen others, to Yusuf and Razir, who were elsewhere in the plane.

Smelling Taliq's sweat and the sourness of his pain, McCloud looked down the angle of the hijacker's shoulder and saw Stone regarding him, a wistful doubt in his eyes.

"You're really pushing it, McCloud," murmured Stone. "Do you think you can be madder than they are?"

McCloud was half-amused. "I *am* madder," he claimed with berserk pride. "I am fucking madder."

He was willing to let the closely-embraced Taliq be torn apart with him. As far as McCloud cared, they could all wail with sorrow. Musa and Razir could go crazy with an orphan grief.

Taliq began to move himself tenderly in McCloud's arms and stared him more or less full in the face. Taliq's eyes blazed with a fellow madness. "My brothers," he told McCloud, "are dead. My wife was beaten by Israeli security forces in Ramallah and is on life support in Damascus. The Syrians foot that bill, and I foot this one."

McCloud remembered that in the remote origins of this flight, Taliq had mentioned a savaged grandmother over the intercom. Now he was appealing to a savaged wife. Were they – an awesome idea – both genuine? Was one? Was neither?

"Yes, true stories!" cried Taliq. "Don't think I give a damn about the instant of impact." He raised his voice. "Hasni, Musa, fire at him!"

But neither of the young men were happy with the order. Hasni looked at him from beneath a bruised brow, still perhaps believing McCloud to be armed. He began to weep. "We love you too well, Taliq," he explained. "We forgive you the Japanese woman! We love you too well."

It struck McCloud now with some astonishment that it *was* true – their brotherly love gave him his margin.

"There is no *plastique*," he screamed a last time for the benefit of residual unbelievers. His war-cry, his revolutionary slogan.

People were advancing from the rear of the plane – Razir first, yes, his radio in his hand as if there was indeed an explosive code he could punch into it. Behind him could be seen Pauline and the middle-aged people who had earlier dragged her aft as if for her own safety.

He wondered what had made them advance. Had it been his yelling about no *plastique*? Had it been Mungina's unheard but penetrative *didj* music? Did they know without even knowing it that Taliq had been cursed by magisterial Whitey?

The re-emerged Pauline was intact but bare-footed. She looked wan. She wore her overcoat, and, as the blanket had done for Daisy, it gave her the appearance of a shipwreck victim. Her eyes were wide, appropriate for assessing such a scene. Everyone seemed to stand still, even Razir, as if to allow her her learning period. She filled out so perfectly the limits of her spacious smallness that he began to laugh. She was the daughter of the revolution wrought by Whitey and now half-delivered by himself.

Strangely she smiled and moved her hand, something like a wave, and it showed him that all actions would be as untoward and deranged as his own from now on. What he could tell was that none of them had expected to see this; the seizing of Taliq's body by a class-and-race criminal.

In the added fragment of time this gave McCloud and his uprising, there was a movement of people from amongst the seats to which McCloud had shouted his heresy, where he had thrown out his slivers of paper.

Pauline and the others behind Razir looked for a second as if they were holding back pressure from behind. McCloud saw form in

Pauline's face the scheme not so much to give way to that pushing but to be the brunt of it. He saw her heave against Razir's back. That would not have meant much if a dozen of her fellow rebels had not also pushed.

Razir had all at once fallen to his knees. There was now an awesome crush of people from behind who wanted to trample him. McCloud saw his jaw, his scatter of sad acne scars, go down in the ruck of passengers.

Pauline did not seem anxious to tread on him though. She broke through the mêlée, projecting herself off the shoulders of taller passengers who were themselves pushing forward and grinding downwards. It was just like a print of any revolution in full fervour, and shining in the midst of the enraged, Pauline held her breath for an instant and then returned it in the form of a smile without precedent in the years he'd known her: the wild but compliant smile of one primitive conspirator to another.

This smile, this outletting of breath, recalled him to all his lost ranks, set him up in business, restored him to all the basic functions of his state, to all his frittered-away authorities. It ratified him as husband, sure announcer of directions, arranger of events, adequate manager. There was no vainglory in any of this, in having been made complete by a smile, in going through the sudden heat of this curative glimpse of Pauline. But, being who he was, still wanting this subtle, knowing and worshipful instant to last without limit, he saw too that the smile had somehow been a trigger. For he had a sense of the dancers and Daisy and the German doctor advancing from the other direction, and a wing of passengers, the ones amongst whom he had thrown down the dangerous wads of messages, surging at Hasni and Musa.

There was immediate firing now, awfully loud yet somehow customary. Its size seemed reduced by the crush of people, and it was momentary. There were screams, which he was sure were not his or Pauline's. They stunned him however. He astonished himself by letting go of Taliq. The man had felt so supine in this noise and fury, so slack-muscled, that to McCloud's mind – which seemed to be ruggedly headquartered somewhere between his heart and intestines, in the piratical gizzards – the task of continuing to hold him seemed unnecessary.

As soon as he let go, though, Taliq vanished. In doing it, he must have side-stepped even the dancers.

People began pursuing him up the aisle past the place where Bluey rested in his dazed condition. McCloud was only one amongst the chasers. They came to first class and the stairwell, up which Taliq was dragging his body and disappearing. Someone close behind McCloud was yelling, "Bastard!" in the same way people had earlier yelled it at Cale, Stone, at himself.

On the far side of this pursuit and capture of Taliq, he promised himself, I'll see Pauline. The revolutionary smiler.

Squeezing onto the stairs, competing to be in the impassioned front rank but not quite succeeding, McCloud noticed that – just below him – Tom Gullagara also fought his way upwards towards Taliq's garden of ideologies and control centre. Near Cowboy Tom was the balding steward who had once, in another history, bravely declared himself a witness.

There was urgency in the people ahead of, around and behind McCloud. They knew that Taliq might try now to call in reinforcements from the army which lay at the airport perimeter, and by these means reduce the pursuing mob back to the status of hostages.

From the top of the stairs, McCloud briefly saw Phil the Christian standing by the bottom as people milled past him. There too – a witness like Phil – was Stone, regarding the scene as if he was wondering whether McCloud might be as great a source of peril as Taliq himself. There had been no more shots though and Stone was intact. Stone's widow would not need to call on the lawyer called Freilich. What was his problem then?

Then, smiling, Stone displayed a weapon taken from one of the boys, snatched from Hasni or Musa. He had cornered it, like a professional warrior who did not want it to fall into the wrong hands. McCloud hoped Hasni had not been hurt by this capture. But it was a side-hope. It was not a main issue. Hunting Taliq was the main issue.

Sure of his primacy as revolutionary leader and full of plans for Taliq's recapture, McCloud began forcing his way through the scrum of insurgent passengers at the top of the stairs. He made headway. He had authority now. He thought, with some wonder, that Taliq's mind must have worked all along as his own did now, at the peak of this upheaval. This is the mind of an autocrat, McCloud marvelled. With a mind like this, everything would have added up for Taliq. The sifting out of the criminals and the chosen, the making of a judge, the shooting of Cale!

Just as McCloud reached the upper cabin, word was passed back that the door to the cockpit was locked. Men and a few women were hammering on it. One of the men who wanted to get in was the same one in the baseball jacket who had once attacked the German cripple.

The intercom crackled and the pilot's voice was heard at full volume. McCloud heard it, beneath its po'-boy intonation, as an extension of Taliq's now neutralised voice. Desperately, it commanded silence. But then it resorted to the rustic, common-sensical and seductively paternal tone which was its norm.

"Folks," it said, "I believe that one of our passengers has assaulted Mr Taliq and some of his friends. I speak to you with an explosive device held to my ear. It is held by a Mr Yusuf. If Taliq is harmed, Mr Yusuf will detonate *this* device. He is a determined young man. And so I demand that all passengers return to their seats. There are women and children aboard. We are trying to settle this in an orderly manner . . ."

McCloud and the other rebels, including the man in the baseball jacket, began to look at each other consultatively now and to talk all at once. McCloud noticed that Stone had arrived in the upstairs cabin. He began waving the Polish weapon he had acquired around in the air, as if he were no longer happy just to keep it safe but would think of using it. You could tell he found it beyond belief that the voice on the intercom seemed to recognise the legitimacy of Taliq's dispensation.

"They were about to murder one of us," he screamed above the hubbub – in fact McCloud may have been the only one listening. "Does that hick up the front understand that?"

"Let me tell you," the captain continued, "there are troops surrounding this aircraft, and their orders are to shoot on anyone who leaves. They are here to witness the arrival of Mr Taliq's confrère, and they fear disorder . . ." It was the second time the captain had used that word. ". . . they fear disorder which might attend any exodus from this aircraft. I urge the passenger concerned in this senseless activity to desist, to put the safety catch back on any weapons they may hold and hand them to one of the cabin crew for safe-keeping."

It was at this time of greatest chaos, when some ordinary citizens who had not joined the crazed uprising wept in their seats down-stairs; while others close to the doors were contemplating the terrible jump from the plane to the unidentified pavement below; while still others – McCloud and Tom Gullagara and the steward and the man in the baseball jacket amongst them – pushed towards the cockpit; while weapons taken from Razir or Hasni or Musa were being passed from hand to hand to the front of the plane, many wanting them used but few willing to assert they knew how to use them – it was at that point, when the universe did seem to McCloud to have a malleable shape in spite of the temporary bafflement inherent in the locked cockpit and the captain's voice, that a cataclysm, a massive, unbalancing incident occurred, so unexpected that no one at the time understood its meaning.

Commandos flown in for the crisis, commandos for whom the authorities on the ground had waited, kept on a lead and now decided to unleash, commandos who were the world's response to Taliq's demand for the iconic guerrilla Mahoud, now surged into the plane by ropes and ladders run up to the opened door. They found the downstairs section already secure – Razir and Hasni and Musa battered and disarmed and lying on the carpet. Hacking their way upstairs with fists and gun-butts, bludgeoning for their own good the people they had been sent to rescue, they came to the mass of passengers in Taliq's former headquarters, the cabin at the head of the plane.

They knew they must clear a way to the cockpit.

Then began the brief but enormous rage of firing which stunned the hostages and made the lay besiegers of the cockpit drop to their bellies and hug the floor. McCloud, no longer a leader, his authority shattered by this new, astounding fracas, took to the carpet with him an image of the suddenly opened cockpit door and Yusuf, beige with terror, holding a grenade in hand.

It would be discovered by the commandos that Yusuf had not pulled the retaining rod on the grenade. That through confusion or mercy or over-confidence he had not done what Taliq had promised from the start, had not held to the captain's ear a *primed* device. Whatever his reason for merely holding the thing in its safe condition – it may even have been that he welcomed the commandos as liberators – a time would soon come when McCloud found that news affecting. Had Yusuf taken a care for lives? Was that it?

Taliq also perished in the shambles of the cockpit. The commandos shot him down with a special urgency, since with the bandaged hand he had injured trying to open cashews for Kanduk Kannata, he had been punching the keys of his radio as if sending a coded message.

12

DOWN TO EARTH

WHEN the passengers descended that night, rediscovering the earth across the pavement of an African airstrip, they knew neither the name for where they were nor why they were rescued.

The papers would give great credit to the authorities, who had withheld Mahoud and unleashed the commandos at the right moment. They wondered also, as well-informed Cale had in the electronics bay, whether it was Iraq or Syria or even extreme elements in the Israeli secret service which had put up the money for Taliq's adventure. The trail was hard to trace, and Hasni, Musa and Razir, recovering but grief-stricken under guard, proved to be as largely in the dark as Cale had always maintained they would be.

Rumours about Mahoud would multiply in the press: he had been *turned* in captivity and had come to terms with the moderates. He had already committed suicide or been shot. His helicopter had crashed on the way to Taliq's plane, leaving the authorities no choice but the military one.

The popular media concentrated on personalities. Mrs Cale appeared on television as an elegant widow to explain what a character Cale was and how she would miss his humour. The British tabloids, however, concentrated on her "close friend", a morning television anchorman. The claim was that even as that British bulldog Cale was bravely baiting the terrorists, she and the anchorman had been tenanting the one flat.

Stone became everyone's favourite item in support of the ironies of the hijack. While he knelt under the gun-muzzle of the terrorists, people on the ground had used his own software to devise a plan of action! He appeared on television too, and always ended with a plea for the unconditional release of the Japanese-American Mrs Nakamura, who was still being questioned as a suspected accomplice. His gratitude to Daisy became him, since others were so avid to condemn her.

Reflecting publicly on what had befallen them, most passengers saw the revolt against Taliq as a spontaneous uprising, and McCloud was given little credit for it, except by his fellow-condemned Stone.

His agent would however call him in Frankfurt and report ecstatically that she'd got the imprint's offer up to $20,000. At Pauline's proud insistence, he accepted.

Bluey was hospitalised. The other members of the dance troupe were at first rushed by the media, but after proving almost wilfully monosyllabic were given up as unsatisfactory.

But the account gets ahead of itself.

On that famous African night, McCloud and Pauline, having found each other after the mêlée, were amongst the last of the passengers to disembark. McCloud looked in her face for an after-image of her earlier, remarkable and paramount smile, and not finding it there yet hopeful it might recur, he took off his placard, which had somehow stayed in place, a tribute to Razir's handicraft, through all the turmoil.

When at last then the McClouds made their tremulous descent, by way of steps which had been rolled to the door where Cale had perished, and began testing the earth to see in what sense it might still be habitable for them, Gullagara the cowboy, Mungina with his *didj*, Whitey Wappitji and Philip the Christian were still lingering companionably on the runway.

Two of them, Whitey and Paul Mungina, began the walk across the airstrip with McCloud and Pauline. The other two waited behind, probably for their fellow dancer and initiate, Bluey, to be carried out of the plane. Indeed paramedics in jungle green had already fought their way up the stairs through a tide of descending soldiers and passengers to bring Bluey and other damaged victims of Taliq's enterprise out.

Whitey and the *didj* player said nothing to the McClouds now. They *accompanied*. It was clear they saw that as their function. Only when he would see in so many newspapers a photograph of himself, a man in underwear, Pauline in an overcoat, and Whitey and Paul in what would have passed in New York as *cowboy chic*, would he understand that they were indeed an odd company.

*　　*　　*

Traversing the runway, McCloud began to feel usurped. The commandos had cut him off in mid-strategy. He had been succeeding and could have fulfilled without any help other than that of the passengers the sweet rebellion instigated by Pauline's smile. It was not that in any sense the commandos had stolen glory – he had not thought of presentations and reverent interviews on television. What he regretted was that the flow of conspiracy between himself and Pauline had been aborted.

He became aware his shoulder was being dragged from behind. The captain faced him. The captain's shirt was soiled with blood – Taliq's or Yusuf's – and his genial features seemed engorged with rage. "You nearly screwed it, you sonofabitch!" he roared at McCloud.

He began, the father of them all, to land blows on McCloud's face and shoulders, blows which brought no secretions of anger to the surface of McCloud's own skin, hooks and straight rights which merely made him step back and feel ashamed. Whitey and the *didj* player, and the plane's other two officers, strangers to McCloud, restrained and wrestled with the captain.

"How did you know?" the pinioned captain asked. "How did you know you weren't going to blow us all to fucking pieces?"

"*I* knew," said McCloud. He was blushing. The captain's anger was so grievous. "There wasn't any *plastique*."

Yet that conviction was entirely unrecallable to him now. The certainty had left him.

"Look," continued McCloud. "At the time . . ."

"I'll have you arrested, you stupid asshole!" said the captain as his discomforted officers tried to bear him away towards the terminal. The stretcher on which Bluey lay, carried by two commandos and accompanied by Phil the Christian and Cowboy Tom, drew level with the imbroglio between the captain and McCloud, and then passed on.

The captain kept talking, but McCloud did not find what he said very pressing. McCloud turned to Whitey.

"You saved my bacon," he said. "Didn't you?"

He was further arrested by the way Whitey turned to him.

"It's okay, Frank," said Whitey, his eyes full of all the lenient and disappointed love of the missionary he was.

"Oh God, I'm sorry, Whitey. Look after Bluey, eh?"

"If he can be looked after, Frank."

"One thing's certain," said McCloud. "You're the only ones who can."

*   *   *

Stalked still by the enraged captain, bemused McCloud and Pauline and the two dancers continued their progress. Far ahead, beyond a garden of palms at the terminal door, they saw a mêlée of weeping and arguing passengers. A ring of hostile people had formed around Daisy Nakamura, who had merely wanted to visit her sister in Frankfurt and had inherited something more complicated. The attackers included the man who had an age ago assaulted the brave German cripple.

"She's a tart!" one of them was telling an armed African soldier. "She's the hijackers' moll. She worked with those bastards, and slept with them."

Stone, disarmed and in his shirt and pants, joined this circle and put his arm around Daisy's shoulders, defending her. McCloud also meant to go to her aid, except that he could not shake himself free of the angry captain.

"There were passengers wounded, for God's sake," the captain yelled. "Exactly what I was trying to prevent! And listen! The commander of the troops who came aboard tells me there's a wad of *plastique* in the hold big enough to blow us up five times over! What do you damnwell say to that?"

McCloud stared at Whitey who, unblinking, looked back.

"There was no *plastique*," said McCloud.

He looked at Pauline, and he could see she did not believe him any more, though she conveyed this with the sort of frank yet gentle wariness which normally characterised her dealings. She was no longer the daughter of the revolution. She was again a creature of light and shade and professional standards.

"There was no *plastique*," McCloud asserted again.

"You ask the fucking commandos," said the captain. "You ask them!"

"Leave him alone!" called Pauline then. There were sudden tears on her lashes. "For Christ's sake, leave him alone! He fixed it. He liberated the plane! Listen, you were essential to those bastards. So they didn't harm you. But none of us counted. We had to make different kinds of decisions."

What McCloud found a wonder was that she understood how to him all the captain's palaver seemed to be carping, seemed to be literalism-gone-crazy.

"Well," McCloud challenged the captain on his own behalf, "we're all standing, aren't we?"

Though he knew Cale and Taliq and Yusuf were not, and that Razir and Hasni and Musa were concussed and had broken bones, and that two passengers had been shot, though not fatally.

"You'll do time, you bastard!" yelled the captain. But at last his lieutenants were able to drag him off and begin to soothe him.

McCloud and Pauline strode off again with Whitey and Paul, who had waited for the confrontation to end. The knot which had surrounded Daisy seemed to have vanished, as had Daisy herself.

Whitey, whose curse had finished Taliq, seemed to McCloud to deserve further thanks.

"So," he said uncomfortably, imitating the apparent cowboy casualness of Barramatjara speech, "you even talked Paul into letting me off the hook. Even Paul, eh? You talked him round."

McCloud punched Mungina's arm. It had held the *didj* which played the strangest monarchical anthem ever heard by human ear.

Whitey paused. "Yeah, well, Frank," he said. "You know. You're not really the villain, eh?"

Of course, he meant, *you don't know enough to be a villain.*

They walked more. Now they entered the garden of palms before the terminal building. There was silence from the two dancers but obviously not an end to the topic.

Then Whitey spoke again, "Some of the blokes back at Baruda will want all those mineral royalties. The others won't."

He let an anxious passenger, going through into the light, push him aside.

"So we're all still bloody hostages," he said. He stopped and cocked his head. "Eh, mate?" he asked.